LOSS *of*

CONSORTIUM

A woman is violated.
Her husband is counsel for the accused.

BRIAN L. MCCOY

ISBN: 978-1-60645-199-1

Library of Congress Control Number: 2017957382

FIRST EDITION 2018

Cover Design: Linda Neddo

Printed in the United States of America

10 9 8 7 6 5 4 3 2 1

This book is dedicated to all the lawyers who devote themselves
to the principle of justice on behalf of their own families
and the community at large.

CHAPTER 1

Mr. Slick Lawyer

"All rise," announced the bailiff, "the Superior Court of the State of Washington in and for the County of Pierce is now in session. The Honorable Myron B. Steiner presiding."

The Judge, appearing on cue with black robe flowing, ascended the bench, peered over his spectacles and directed, "Please be seated."

Taking their seats in front of the bench facing the Judge were the two combatants. The Prosecuting Attorney — Franklin Cartright, a man in his mid-forties, about 6 feet tall, athletic, smart, and fearless. A man absolutely committed to the criminal justice system as the preferred means of enforcing law and order in society. A family man, whose ideals are rooted in the belief that justice will prevail and the guilty will be punished. The consummate law enforcement officer of the Court.

Seated at Defense Counsel's table was Lloyd B. McCallum, in his mid-thirties, a little shorter than Cartright, well built, very bright, and smooth. Next to him was seated his client, the Defendant — William Roundtree, who could pass for the kid next door but looked just a little too streetwise

1

to be convincing.

Judge Steiner then cut through the uneasy, muffled rustling in the courtroom with, "Has the jury reached a verdict?"

The Foreman, a middle aged real estate broker stood and answered, "Yes, your Honor, we have."

"Please pass the verdict form to the bailiff," Judge Steiner instructed.

The bailiff stiffly accepted the verdict from the foreman and delivered it to Judge Steiner, who opened it and, after reading it, said, "Will the Defendant please rise. Of the charge of Rape in the first degree, the jury finds you Not Guilty. You're free to go. Court will be at recess."

The prosecuting attorney's facial expression belied his feelings of disgust and defeat.

Willie Roundtree leaned over to his attorney and, looking directly into his face, said simply, "Guess what. I did it." He then cocked his head back and smiled, knowing he'd beat the system. "What do you think about that, Mr. Slick Lawyer?"

Without flinching or showing the slightest expression, McCallum responded with a stainless steel voice, "Just make sure you pay your bill." And with no more thought than that of his day's work, McCallum stood up, grabbed his briefcase, and walked out of the courtroom.

As he strode through the halls of the courthouse toward the parking lot outside, he knew he was good at his job. He emerged from the courthouse, slipped on his Foster Grant shades, loosened his tie, reached in his coat pocket and pulled out the electronic key for his new BMW 850i. He slid into the sleek, black machine, started the engine and cranked up the latest in auto stereo technology.

Leaving the courthouse in the inner city, Judge Steiner, Cartright, and most importantly, Willie Roundtree behind,

McCallum sped toward his yuppie suburban neighborhood, immersed in the sounds of high-tech classic rock-n-roll.

"This is livin'," McCallum thought. In the ten years since he had graduated from law school, Lloyd McCallum had established quite a reputation for himself as an adroit legal technician, with a real flair for courtroom dramatics. In the arena of criminal defense, he was already a master at trial preparation and persuasion. He learned long ago that it doesn't matter what happens out in the real world, all that really matters is what you can prove in court. That becomes reality — virtual reality, if you will. The government has the burden of proving its version of the case while the defense need only to establish a reasonable doubt. Indeed, the government must prove beyond a reasonable doubt every element of the crime — the corpus delicti.

McCallum relished the challenge of forcing the government to do just that. He scrutinizes the case from top to bottom looking for police blunders and ways to exclude evidence with pre-trial motions to suppress. He examines the strengths and weaknesses of potential witnesses. And in a rape case, he can subtly change the entire focus of the trial away from his client to the alleged victim. It takes a skilled advocate to work around the rape shield statute, designed to protect rape victims from undue personal scrutiny. But for McCallum that was all part of the game, a game he enjoyed and for which he was paid extremely well.

Indeed, in the relatively few short years he had been with the firm of LANCASTER, VERNON and EVERETT, he had proven himself a formidable influence and risen to partner in the thirty-attorney firm faster than anyone in recent memory. He did it with brains, ambition, and shear aggressiveness. He loved the rush of going head to head in trial when the stakes were high, and they always were in the newsworthy, emotionally charged cases he took on. And with those cases, came huge fees, sometimes even six figure

3

retainers up front. In the world of big business law firms, that moved him up the ladder to partner faster than anything else.

But now it was time to kick back and relax. McCallum cruised into his driveway and parked his yuppie-mobile in front of his 8,000 square foot split level home with manicured lawn in Briarwood, an exclusive housing development, far away from the crime and violence of the inner city.

"Hello, Mr. McCallum," yelled Norman Macintyre, the McCallum's hired gardener.

"How ya doing, Mac?" replied McCallum.

"You involved in any interesting cases lately?" queried Macintyre.

"All my cases are interesting," declared McCallum.

"You do mostly criminal defense, don't ya, Mr. McCallum?"

"Yeah, it's kind of exhilarating actually. I enjoy getting in there and mixing it up with some straight laced prosecutor who thinks he's got an iron clad case against my client."

"Well, from the looks of things, you must do pretty well at it," observed Macintyre.

"Well, let's just say I win a lot more than I lose," said McCallum wryly.

Then came the classic question that every lawyer gets asked at one time or another, "Mind if I ask you a question, Mr. McCallum?" probed the middle-aged gardener.

"Sure," replied McCallum, "But, if it's legal advice you want, I'll charge ya and deduct it from your pay," joked McCallum.

"No, nothin' like that, but I was wondering, how can you defend somebody you know is guilty?"

"Elementary, my dear Watson," answered McCallum. "First of all, just remember that a person is innocent until proven guilty. In other words, it's the jury's function to decide guilt or innocence. Ours is an adversarial system. The prosecutor presents his case, the defense attorney presents his, and the jury sifts through the evidence and decides whether the accused is guilty. If the attorneys get involved in trying to second-guess the jury, the whole system is subverted and the role of the jury undermined. It's not my job to determine guilt or innocence, but it is my job to present the best defense I can, and then let the jury do its job," explained McCallum.

"But what if you know that your client is guilty?" pressed Macintyre.

"I make a point of not knowing. I don't ask my clients whether or not they're guilty. I guess I believe in the system. I believe that the jury has an almost sacred function in our system and I don't tamper with it," McCallum said almost defensively.

Then old Norman Macintyre cut right to the heart of it and asked, "Sounds good in theory, but have you ever had a client come right out and tell you he's guilty and went ahead and defended him anyway?"

McCallum's mind went back to the events of that afternoon. He could honestly say that he'd never had a client pronounce himself guilty before the fact, but that afternoon he'd had the unnerving experience of a client declaring his guilt after the jury acquitted him.

"Well Mac," McCallum finally said trying hard to insulate himself, "it doesn't really matter anyway. Like I said, it's the jury's job to determine guilt or innocence." Macintyre, still unconvinced, took one final jab, "But what if the jury's wrong? What if you get somebody off that should have gone to jail?"

Somewhat subdued, McCallum simply answered, "Well, no system is infallible," and with that he concluded the conversation and went in the house, his house — the kind of house only lots of money could buy.

As he stepped into the spacious entry way and shut the door behind him, he finally felt secure and able to relax. To the left was a circular stairway to the upstairs bedroom area of the house. To the right was a sunken living room, expensively decorated with thick beige, almost white carpeting. He walked straight ahead down the hallway toward the large kitchen, dinning room and entertainment area of the house. As he neared the kitchen, he could smell the tasty aroma of enchiladas baking in the oven. McCallum loved Mexican food and his wife Valorie knew just how to fix it. Other than the dinner in process, there was no sign of life anywhere in the house. McCallum walked toward the double-wide sliding glass doors that opened out onto the patio in back and there across the yard playing on the big-toy was Valorie and his two children — Gerald, age 9, and Emily, 7. McCallum stood and watched for several minutes savoring the moment. Not yet 36 and he had it made. A beautiful devoted wife and two lovely children who thought he walked on water.

"Daddy! Daddy!" Emily cried as she ran toward him, finally noticing him standing there watching. As she got within reach McCallum bent down, scooped her up and hugged her as they spun around and Emily planted a big juicy kiss on her dad's cheek. As they walked toward the big toy, McCallum gently set his little girl down on the lawn just as Gerald reached him and traded places with his sister in his dad's arms.

"How ya doing, little man?" inquired McCallum in his best fatherly voice.

"Daddy, look at my new tennis shoes mom bought for me today. I can really run fast now, wanna see, wanna see?"

"Sure, but I bet I can beat you to the big toy," as father and son raced off across the yard toward the woman they both loved.

"I beat, I beat," cried Gerald with Emily coming in a close second and dad a rather distant third.

"Hi, Lloyd," said Valorie with that captivating smile of

hers as she stood up from the swing and wrapped her arms around his neck.

"Hi, you," he said in a soft low voice like he hadn't seen her in a week.

"Fixed enchiladas for you," said Valorie.

"Yeah, I smelled them coming through the house. What do you say we go eat 'em."

They turned and strolled back into the house hand in hand while dad got commitments from the children to help set the table after they washed their hands. Dinnertime, especially on Friday night, was special time for the McCallum's. Lloyd made it a point not to work late on Fridays if at all possible since he had to work late so much of the rest of the time due to his heavy trial schedule. But Friday nights were family time, a refuge from all the meanness and combativeness he dealt with almost daily as a kind of professional mercenary. Indeed, it seemed at times to Lloyd as though he led a double life. After dinner and the kids were off to watch their favorite video, Lloyd and Valorie finally had a chance to talk while they cleaned up the kitchen.

"Did you have a good day?" Valorie asked politely.

"Yeah, it was alright, I guess."

"You don't sound convinced. Did you lose one?"

"No, the jury said I won but I had kind of an uneasy feeling about my client afterwards. After being acquitted of first-degree rape, he looked at me and confessed. I don't think I've ever had a client do that before. It was like he got a freebie and he had to brag about it. Then I got home while Norman was still working on the front yard and he started asking me the same old questions about how a lawyer can defend somebody he knows is guilty and all that nonsense. So, I should feel good about the win, but maybe I'm having second thoughts. Something a criminal defense lawyer should never do — second guess the jury, especially when you get a defense verdict!"

"Well," started Valorie consolingly, "if the jury acquitted him, it sounds like you did your job and they did theirs. You can't retry every case after it's over."

"I know, once the verdict's in, game's over, right? To the victor go the spoils."

"Sounds a little crass when you put it that way, but you're a good lawyer, you've said so yourself many times," Valorie said with a slight grin.

"Yeah, our legal system works pretty well, and I know how to work the system," admitted Lloyd. "Besides," he continued, "what else could I do that would be more fun and pay better money?"

Indeed, as a 35 year old partner in LANCASTER, VERNON & EVERETT, Lloyd McCallum made very good money — $20,000 a month salary plus a share of the firm's profits paid quarterly with a lump sum bonus at the end of the year boosting his annual take to as much as $500,000. Valorie thoroughly enjoyed their success as well, she having worked and slaved to put Lloyd through school. But now she didn't have to work and she enjoyed all of the luxuries money could buy as well as the status and influence that goes along with financial success. She enjoyed her work as a volunteer for the P.T.A. and for Hospice, but in the back of her mind she knew she could quit anytime, unlike other women who had to work to help pay the bills. She had also become accustomed to the extra courtesies extended to her as the wife of a successful attorney. When she went to the bank, the school, the doctor's office, people were a little more solicitous and extra polite toward her.

Valorie liked that and had almost come to take what her husband did for a living for granted. Over the years, she had only met one or two of Lloyd's clients by accident when she happened to be at her husband's office. They struck her as being pretty unsavory characters but what did it matter to her if they needed legal services and could pay for it. She enjoyed the benefits and was far removed from all of the slime and grime that her husband dealt with on a regular basis.

Soon it was time to bed the kids down for the night, although they were allowed to stay up later on Fridays.

"Come on you little squirrels, it's bedtime," said Lloyd affectionately.

"Ah dad, do we have to? It's not late."

"Yes it is, tomorrow's a big day, gotta do our Saturday chores around here."

"We don't like chores," said Emily.

"Why can't mom do it?" complained Gerald.

"Wait a minute, what about those new tennis shoes you showed me before dinner, didn't mom get those for you? It's time to reciprocate and show her a little appreciation," said Lloyd intentionally using bigger words than a nine year old could understand to help him develop his vocabulary.

"Okay," Emily finally consented, "but you have to give us a ride upstairs on your back."

"How can I give both of you a ride at the same time?" protested Lloyd.

"Let Gerald get on your back, and then I'll get on him," explained Emily.

"Okay, let's try it." Lloyd got down on one knee, first Gerald then Emily and then up the circular stairway the pack team went, Lloyd clutching the banister all the way.

The two little tots safely tucked in, Lloyd headed for the master bedroom hoping to find Valorie waiting for him. As he entered the spacious, plush room decorated in soft gray and mauve colors he saw her sitting invitingly on the sofa with her eyes fixed upon him. The room smelled of sweet perfume. Valorie looked absolutely beautiful, her long brown hair melting around her shoulders. Her large brown eyes, full lips and perfect teeth presented a striking blend of feminine sensitivity and intelligence. She wore a shear short beige negligee making it difficult for Lloyd to tell in the subdued light where her flawless skin left off and the garment began.

Without taking his eyes off her, Lloyd unbuttoned and removed his shirt, slipped off his shoes and moved across the room toward her. As he neared the sofa, he knelt down before her almost worshipfully, like a subject before his beloved queen. She did not move as his face came closer to hers and he kissed her lips, her cheek, her neck. Valorie then slipped her hand around behind Lloyd's neck and pulled him to her. Mr. and Mrs. McCallum loved to make love to one another. Their relationship was an intimate one, not just sexually but emotionally and intellectually as well. Their kisses and embraces grew more and more intense as their feelings and emotions plunged together like two rivers rushing into one and cascading over a swirling waterfalls.

CHAPTER 2

While Hubby's Away

Saturday morning 8:00 am found Lloyd McCallum already at the office. He usually worked on Saturday, though he tried to avoid Sundays. For the most part, all the partners in the firm at least made an appearance on Saturday, if for no other reason than to spur the younger associates and interns to rack up more billable hours. Unless you're a personal injury lawyer, who works on a "contingency" basis (just a fancy word for working on commission), the more billable hours you put in, the more revenue you generate. And since associates are paid much less per hour than they're billed out for, the extra goes straight into the pockets of the partners. Hence, huge firms with a few partners and lots of associates.

At LANCASTER, VERNON & EVERETT, Lloyd McCallum was among the elite half dozen who controlled the entire firm. His office was strategically located on the upper floor of the firm's two level suite in the corner with a view of Commencement Bay. Very yuppie, just like his house.

As you walk into Lloyd's office, the entire far wall is tinted glass, looking out over the bay. To the right sits a huge desk piled high with files and papers, in-out boxes, a brass lamp, and an expensive leather swivel rocking-chair mounted on wheels behind it. The latest in dictation equipment and computer technology sat on the credenza behind the chair.

Above the credenza was mounted the only evidence of Lloyd McCallum's pre-law days — an engraved full-size replica of a bowie knife given to him by the men of his Special Forces A-Team, with whom he had served in Central America. The Green Beret — the elite of the world, experts in gorilla warfare, trained in everything from hand to hand combat, to clandestine communications, to all kinds of weaponry, to survival techniques, to emergency medical procedures — were and are incredible fighting machines, individually and collectively. The physical riggers and mental demands of the training more than adequately prepared Lloyd for his work as a criminal defense attorney. Strategy, tactics and the shear intensity of combat were, for Lloyd McCallum, easily transferable from one arena to the other.

Lloyd sat musing over the facts of his latest challenge — defending a serial arsonist. His client had a history spanning several years of setting primarily residential fires, not just locally, where he happened to get caught, but apparently all up and down the west coast, or so went the prosecution's theory. About then in walked Mr. Gerald Everett, one of the three partners after whom the firm was named and McCallum's mentor and close friend. Indeed, this was a man McCallum thought so highly of that he named his first-born son after him.

"How are you doing this morning?" said Mr. Everett cheerfully.

"I'm fine Gerald, how are you today?" replied McCallum.

"Did you see the sports page this morning?" asked Everett. "The Seahawks are just rolling over everybody. I don't think there's anybody in the NFL that can stop them this year. They're going to go all the way."

If there was anything Gerald Everett enjoyed besides the law, it was sports, particularly pro football and the local Seattle team had his complete devotion.

"Yeah, they're really looking good," said McCallum. "They definitely got a well rounded team with depth and I think they really want it this year."

"Yeah, that's definitely the key," said Everett. "Got to want it more than anything else."

"I'll tell you what I want more than anything else," declared McCallum. "I want to figure out this case here. You got a minute, Gerald?"

"Sure," said Gerald as he sat down in the chair in front of McCallum's desk.

"This guy is something else," started McCallum.

"You mean our client?" questioned Everett.

"Yeah, he seems to single out small boarding houses for elderly people where the risk of injuring or killing someone is the greatest. He doesn't seem to just burn places, he selectively sets fire to places where the residents will likely have the most difficulty escaping. It's almost like he's trying to punish somebody or something."

"Well," responded Everett, "you know better than anyone that a crime consists of two parts, the act itself, and the state of mind. Maybe this guy is really wacko and an insanity defense is just too obvious for you. Does this guy have any family?"

"I don't know. According to the work up here in the file, he's got a step-father that lives in the bay area."

"Well, maybe you ought to hop on a plane and head down there and talk to the guy, maybe he could give you some insight into our client and you can pull off another Perry Mason or something. By the way, congratulations on your verdict yesterday, I hear our client was acquitted."

"Yeah," said McCallum as he stared out the window.

"That one was a little different, but I have things to do and places to go."

"Why don't you have Sally arrange a flight for you first thing Monday morning? There's all kinds of commuter flights down to the bay area and you can just go down there and do some poking around on this arsonist character. By the way, does he have the funds to cover this?"

"Oh yeah," assured McCallum, "that's another interesting twist in this case. The guy is loaded."

"Alright," continued McCallum, "I'll run down there the first of the week and see what I can find out about our man. Who knows, maybe I'll actually find a reason to defend him beyond the fact that he can pay my fees."

"Awh, if that's all there was to it, you wouldn't be nearly as good at it as you are," smiled Everett.

"Yep, that's me, your friendly neighborhood knight in shining armor." Then pausing, McCallum added, "for hire."

"Yes," rejoined Everett, "send us your down trodden, your persecuted and your accused . . . provided they have money. But we both know there's more to it than that," said Everett reassuringly. "It's our job as defense lawyers to find out what was going on behind the scenes, what the state of mind of the accused was and protect him against the massive power of the government. So you go down there to San Francisco and find out everything you can about our client and we'll sit down together when you get back and brainstorm. In the meantime, I think I'm going to duck out of here before noon today and try and get in a round of golf before our kids' soccer game this afternoon."

"Well, I'll finish wading through this file. Thanks, Gerald."

"Yep, see ya when you get back, Lloyd," said Everett over his shoulder as he walked out of McCallum's office.

Lloyd then pressed his intercom button for Sally, who also often worked Saturdays, and asked her to arrange his flight to California Monday morning.

Sunday night found Lloyd McCallum again immersed in his arsonist file as he sat slouched down on his living room sofa half watching the late night news. This was a bothersome case. It's one thing to burn down buildings, but it's another thing to burn down rest homes where the risk of death is so high. Lloyd had only had a brief opportunity to interview his client, who was articulate and well to do, but seemed to have a submerged kind of unhinged recklessness about him. During his interview of the guy it came out that he had served a couple of tours in Vietnam as a member of a LRRP — Long Range Reconnaissance Patrol who were sometimes off in the jungle by themselves for days or even weeks at a time. While their mission was reconnaissance, sometimes contact with the enemy was unavoidable and some of these guys were renown for their viciousness.

About that time Valorie walked into the room and hesitated to interrupt her husband. Yet, he looked up unable to resist engaging her.

"What's this one about?" she asked.

"I'm not sure you want to know, but since you asked, it's about a guy accused of being a serial arsonist who picks out small boarding houses or rest homes for the elderly and sets fire to them. There have been about five or six such incidents between here and northern California and the police arrested our client, and the prosecutor thinks, in fact is convinced, that our man did the crimes."

"What do you think?" asked Valorie, inviting Lloyd to share his own analysis.

"I don't know," he said, "that's why I'm headed down to the bay area tomorrow to go talk to our guy's step-father, see what I can find out about him and just poke around a little bit. One of the fires occurred down there too, so maybe I can access the investigation they did and come up with something. Funny, but sometimes you find the best defense

B. L. McCoy

right in the police department's own investigation file. I think I can get a friend of mine that owes me a favor to let me take a peek at the file, so I'll just see what I can find."

"What if you find just the opposite?" queried Valorie.

"What do you mean?" asked Lloyd.

"What if you find something that absolutely confirms that your client burned down a rest home or whatever and is responsible for the untimely deaths of several little old ladies?"

"I'm already feeling uneasy about this case," replied Lloyd. "You don't need to make it any worse."

Yet he knew that his wife's question went right to the heart of the matter.

"Besides, you know the drill," continued Lloyd, as he fixed his eyes on his wife. She unflinchingly however, returned the gaze as though to probe his soul, searching for a firm connection with reality. Apparently satisfied, she finally said with a slight smile, "Well, it's bedtime, are you coming?"

That's all it took to motivate Lloyd to stuff the file in his briefcase and drop it by the front door as he trotted up the stairs after Valorie.

The next morning both Lloyd and Valorie were up early as Lloyd hurried around to make it to the airport on time. Before rushing out the door, however, he made sure he stopped by his son's and daughter's bedrooms to kiss them goodbye and reassure them that he would be back home in a couple days. Lloyd didn't have to be gone on these kinds of trips very often, maybe a couple times a month was all, but it was still a little stressful for everybody. Valorie assured Lloyd that she had plenty to do to keep her busy for the next couple of days and wouldn't miss him a bit, though they both knew they'd miss each other plenty.

The flight down was a typical crowded commuter flight arriving at San Francisco International at 10:35 am. Lloyd picked up his rental car and headed for the address he had for his client's stepfather. Back at the hotel that night, Lloyd was restless. He finally found his client's stepfather's home, but the guy seemed totally detached and unconcerned about the charges against his stepson, whom he had apparently raised since about the age of six. Lloyd wondered how a man could live in the same house with a child and assume the role of father without any apparent emotional investment whatsoever. What the guy told Lloyd about his client's mother was even more disturbing, however. Apparently, the family used a wood burning stove for heat in the wintertime when they lived up near Lake Tahoe, and when the boy misbehaved, his mother punished him by tossing one of his toys into the fire in the stove. Lloyd wondered to himself how he got involved in things like this.

"No wonder the guy is wacko," he thought.

After dinner by himself in the hotel restaurant, Lloyd retired to his room for a movie and a phone call home. As he punched in his phone number, his mind immediately went home as he pictured the nice house with those he held dear comfortably secure inside. In his mind's eye, he could see the beautifully furnished interior and his children tucked in bed for the night. Valorie, he imagined was lying in bed enjoying a few quiet moments reading the latest issue of Women's magazine. The phone only rang once and Valorie picked up.

"Hello," she said.

There was a slight pause on Lloyd's end as he savored the sound of his wife's voice.

"Hi, how ya doin'?" he asked.

"Oh, just lying here reading my favorite magazine. How'd your day go?" inquired Valorie.

"Oh, the trip down was your typical commuter flight — a little crowded, but otherwise fine. I found my client's stepfather and got a little information out of him, but other than revealing a somewhat freaky background, I didn't learn much of any substance. I'll try again tomorrow. How about you? How was your day?"

"Oh fine, the usual — a little shopping, picked the kids up after school and just kind of milled around at the mall and had dinner at McDonald's, so at least I got out of having to fix dinner at home tonight."

Lloyd and Valorie enjoyed these chats, especially when they were miles apart. Somehow, it enabled them to be together, even when they weren't. Finally, they wound down and bid each other good night, reaffirming their love for one another, Lloyd in San Francisco and Valorie in Briarwood. Each then slipped into quiet slumber.

*   *   *

The McCallum's neighborhood was a quiet one, particularly at night. No dogs barking, no traffic noise, no late night parties, just a few porch lights up and down the streets silently pushing back the darkness here and there.

About 2:00 am a car entered Briarwood — not the kind of car usually seen in Briarwood. An older model GM sedan, rather dirty, but nice wheels. It slowly cruised up and down the streets almost aimlessly. The car then pulled over to the curb and stopped. No movement, no activity. Maybe the driver was lost, maybe he was just looking for a quiet place to sleep for the rest of the night. It again began to move, slowly making its way down the street. It stopped again. Several minutes elapsed and finally the vehicle's lone occupant exited the passenger side of the car and hurried across the McCallum's front lawn. The side gate next to the garage provided easy access to the backyard and rear of the house. Once in the backyard the man paused — no need to hurry. No lights, no dogs, just a motionless swing set standing in the backyard. Almost casually, the dark figure walked toward the sliding glass doors that led from the patio into the house.

"Why not just walk in if I can," he thought.

Incredibly, the door was not securely fastened and easily popped open with a little tug. The door slid open silently and the man reached in, sweeping the curtains to the side as he stepped through the door into the house. He scanned the interior of the house quickly. Only one small night light shown in the entryway near the front door.

"This place reeks of money," he thought, as he made his way through the family room past the kitchen. On the counter he noticed a tray of brownies still sitting out. "Why not," he thought, as he stuffed a couple of whole brownies in his mouth.

As he cautiously moved toward the entryway, he noticed a family picture. "What a fox!" he mused, as he focused his eyes on Valorie. He then glanced at Lloyd's image in the dim light — no sign of recognition — his warped mind failing to make any connection. Alright, enough site-seeing. It was time to get to it — whatever crime of opportunity happen to present itself.

As he stood in the entry way at the bottom of the stairs, a light appeared upstairs. Quickly, he reached down and unplugged the night light. Emily McCallum came out of the upstairs bathroom and headed toward her parents' bedroom.

"Mommy," she called out, as she approached the master bedroom. Instantly, Valorie was awake and sitting up in bed. As Emily's little silhouette appeared in the doorway, Valorie slid out of bed, walked over and knelt down next to her.

"What's wrong, honey?" she asked.

"My tummy hurts," replied Emily.

"Oh, too much hamburger and French fries maybe?"

"I don't know, but it just hurts!"

"Well, let's you and me go and see if we can find some Pepto-Bismol in the bathroom."

"I already looked," said Emily.

"I bet I can find some," said Valorie.

Sure enough, once in the bathroom mom quickly laid

B. L. McCoy

her hands on the desired medicine and administered a small dose to her daughter.

"Okay," said Valorie. "That should do the trick. Let's go tuck you back in bed and I'm sure you'll feel fine in the morning."

"Thanks mom," said Emily, as they walked toward her bedroom. "I want dad to be home," she said. "I miss him."

"Me too," said Valorie, "but guess what, he'll be home tomorrow."

In the shadows downstairs, the slightest trace of a smile crossed the intruder's face. He couldn't believe his good fortune as he stepped back to the family photograph, picked it up, and studied Valorie in the dim light shinning through the front window. Upstairs, Valorie finished getting Emily into bed, made her way back to her own bedroom and crawled into the sack wishing Lloyd were there to snuggle up to.

Step by step, the man downstairs ascended the circular stairway toward his unsuspecting prey. His hand lightly stroked the banister as he carefully maneuvered upstairs, being careful not to make a sound. He began to fantasize in anticipation of his encounter. The excitement of such a lucky find — a beautiful woman home alone, like a choice piece of meat gratuitously left unguarded for him to devour. He could hardly contain himself. Slowly, methodically, he made his way up the stairs and down the hallway toward the master bedroom. The door was slightly ajar. He gently pushed it open and peered inside the room scanning the entire area at a glance. There she lay, on her side facing away from the door. Her brown hair floating on the surface of the satin covered pillow. Without a sound, he crept toward the bed.

As he stood over her breathing heavily, Valorie instinctively detected a presence in the room, opened her eyes and looked in the direction of the door. She managed to get out about half a scream before the intruder pounced on her like a wild animal. Flailing and struggling under the weight of his body, she kicked and scratched and grabbed at whatever she could. He jerked her head back by her hair, while clamping his other hand firmly over her mouth. Using both hands like a vice, he squeezed her head with sustained force. For what seemed like several minutes he just held her there on the bed with an iron grip on her head, like a predator with its prey.

Lying there helplessly, Valorie was vaguely aware of her attacker leaning down and whispering in her ear, "I'll do you and your little girl both. Do you want that? Cuz, hubby's not home and I can do whatever I damn well please."

Realizing that her daughter, Emily, lay asleep in the room next door, completely unaware of the violent terror Valorie was experiencing, she nodded her head as best she could. The man then released his grip with a questioning look on his face. Valorie hesitatingly whispered "Okay, just don't hurt my daughter." Whereupon the unwelcome intruder proceeded to do whatever he pleased, i.e., take full advantage of the fortuitous opportunity to satisfy his basest appetites.

CHAPTER 3

Reconstructing the Crime

The phone rang unusually early in Lloyd McCallum's hotel room and caught him still in bed asleep. A little groggy he picked up the phone to hear an unfamiliar but earnest voice on the other end. Lloyd wasn't quite awake enough to catch the name, but his eyes popped open when the male voice informed him that he was calling from Saint Mary's Hospital on behalf of Valorie McCallum. As Lloyd listened to the brief report, his eyebrows knit together in a concerned frown and his lips pursed together tightly. He shook his head in disbelief.

"Is she going to be alright?" he probed. The caller assured Lloyd that her condition was not life threatening but the full impact of the ordeal was still uncertain.

"What about the kids?" queried Lloyd.

"They're taken care of," answered the caller.

"Can I talk to Valorie?" asked Lloyd.

"No," was the answer, "she's sedated and pretty out of it for the time being."

"I'll be there in just a few hours," Lloyd said. "Please

tell her I'm on my way."

Lloyd hurriedly hung up the phone, literally threw his clothes into his suitcase, papers into his briefcase and ran out of the room disheveled and unshaven.

It was almost noon when Lloyd rushed into the hospital looking for Valorie. Obviously distressed and agitated, he ran to the information desk to find out where she was. The receptionist typed her name into the computer and before she could say the room number, Lloyd read the information off the monitor, repeated the number out loud and raced for the elevator. The instant the doors opened on the fifth floor, Lloyd flew out looking for Valorie's room number. Rushing down the hallway toward her door he was met by a nurse coming out of her room.

"Is this Valorie McCallum's room?" he gasped.

"And you are?" responded the nurse.

"I'm her husband. Is she in there?" pressed Lloyd, reaching for the door.

"Yes she is, but she's heavily sedated. She's been severely traumatized. Please don't awaken her yet."

Nodding his acknowledgement, Lloyd slowly opened the door and quietly stepped into the room pulling the door closed behind him. There she lay with IV's strung up over her and an oxygen tube taped to her face. Lloyd slowly walked toward her bedside and just stood there looking down at her swollen face. The sounds of the oxygen machine and heart monitor pulsated in the background as Valorie lay there motionless in a near comatose state. Lloyd could not believe his eyes. How could his beloved Valorie be lying in the hospital thoroughly thrashed like some homeless bag lady? What kind of animal could do such a thing? Who in the world would want to hurt Valorie? Lloyd reached down and touched her hair, which felt sticky to the touch. Pulling his hand back and rubbing his thumb and fingers together, Lloyd began to carefully survey the damage. Valorie's lower lip was cracked, her forehead scratched, and her cheeks swollen. He was afraid to look at the rest of her body, but he noticed what appeared to be tiny traces of skin under her fingernails.

All of Lloyd's training and experience, both in the Army and as a lawyer, now came into play. His mind began soaking up every detail and shred of evidence. What little information he already had all pointed to a violent encounter. Lloyd circled around to the other side of Valorie's bed to look at her from a different angle. She looked just as bad from the other side. Shaken to the very core, he stepped back and tears began to run down his cheeks and drip on his shirt. Finally, he could stand it no longer and turned away to stare out the hospital window, grieving and trying to control the anger welling up inside of him. Outside, his eyes focused on a few white fluffy clouds in the otherwise clear blue sky and his mind raced for answers as to why his pleasant, perfect life had suddenly been invaded.

Unaware of how long he'd been standing there, suddenly a nurse's voice interrupted him. "Mr. McCallum, the doctor is free now and would like to speak to you for a moment."

"Sure, by all means," muttered Lloyd as he followed the nurse out of the room.

Just as Lloyd closed the door to Valorie's room, a relatively young man in his mid-thirties approached and introduced himself. "Hello, I'm Dr. Crawford. You must be Mr. McCallum?"

"Yes," said Lloyd with searching eyes.

"I don't know how to soften the blow," the doctor began, "but it appears your wife's been raped."

Lloyd just stared at the doctor, his worst fears having been confirmed.

"As you can see, she's been abused pretty badly," continued the doctor, "but, I have thoroughly examined her, taken x-rays and there are no broken bones or internal injuries, other than . . ." The doctor paused as Lloyd looked at him, dreading what he might hear next. "The vaginal canal is lacerated and there may be damage to the uterus. There are contusions on her thighs and pelvic area."

Lloyd just stood there numb, listening to the report. The doctor continued, "I'm afraid there was penetration. A sperm sample was taken and she's been given antibiotics, but no other lab tests have been completed as yet."

"HIV?" queried Lloyd weakly.

"We don't know yet," answered Dr. Crawford.

Lloyd's mind clouded over. What a nightmare! How could this be happening to him? Violent crime is something that happens to other people. He tried to collect his thoughts, suddenly his children came to mind and he blurted out, "Where are my kids?"

"They're fine. They're staying with your neighbor," interjected a nurse nearby. "If you'd like, we can arrange to have them brought here to the nursery so you can stay with your wife. In fact, you can all spend the night here if need be."

"Thank you," mumbled Lloyd as he contemplated all the arrangements that would have to be made to accommodate this horrific trauma and disruption in their lives. "Would you mind calling our neighbor and ask them if they could bring our kids over here after dinner?" asked Lloyd.

"Sure, no problem," replied the nurse.

"I don't want to leave my wife, but I don't want my kids to be alone tonight either. Is there a phone handy that I could use?" Lloyd asked. "I ran in here and left my cell in the car."

"Sure, right over here, Mr. McCallum," said the nurse pointing to the counter.

Lloyd then called his friend and partner, Gerald Everett, to tell him the bad news. Everett took the call in his office and listened intently with the cool detachment of a seasoned lawyer and the sympathetic indignation of a close friend. Gerald Everett had walked his protégé, Lloyd McCallum, through many a battle, but never one like this. This wasn't a client, some stranger paying him to care. This was Lloyd on the other end of the phone and Lloyd was hurting big time. He and his family had been brutalized. What could he do to help? How could he ease the pain?

"I'm so sorry," began Everett. "What kind of animal would do such a thing? You have my complete support. Take as much time off as you need. I'll have Sally brief me on the status of your cases and farm them out to some of the associates."

"I'm a little worried about that arson case," protested Lloyd.

Everett cut him off saying, "Don't you worry about any of your cases, my friend, we've got it covered. You just take care of your family."

"Thank goodness for people like Gerald Everett," Lloyd thought. "Thanks, Gerald, I appreciate your help," Lloyd said as he hung up the phone. Turning around, he found the doctor and nurse gone — on to the next emergency, someone else's tragedy, leaving Lloyd alone to deal with his own tragedy. Slowly he walked toward Valorie's door trying to muster the strength to walk in there again and face the results of senseless brutality visited upon his dear wife.

Slowly he entered the room and closed the door behind him. Privacy, he needed privacy. He needed to shut the world out while he tried to cope with what had happened. He walked over to Valorie's bed and just stared at her, again surveying the damage. Touching her hair, he thought of the many times he had touched her hair before as he kissed and caressed her face. Lloyd then stroked her arm, working his way down to her hand, taking it in his own and kissing it gently, somehow wishing he could make it all go away and heal her right then and there. Slowly he knelt on the floor next to Valorie's bed and lay his head next to her hand weeping over the hurt and horror his wife had experienced in his absence.

Eventually, Lloyd collected himself enough to crawl into the over stuffed chair in the corner of Valorie's hospital room where the exhausting effect of the whole ordeal finally overcame Lloyd and he fell asleep. Hours later he awakened with a start to find Valorie looking at him with an expression of gentleness and peace which confused Lloyd. After all, his wife had just been through the most traumatic experience he could imagine. Yet there she lay in calm tranquility. He was amazed as he sat there staring back at her. She then lifted her hand slightly and with her fingers motioned him to come to her. As he had done many times before he approached her submissively, kneeling on the floor beside her bed. He placed his face in the palm of her hand and kissed it gently over and over. Looking up at her face, their eyes met again as she said "I'm glad you're here."

"Oh Valorie!" he responded. "I'm so sorry. How could I let something like this happen to you?"

"It's alright," whispered Valorie as tears began to well up in her eyes, realizing she was safely back in the arms of her husband.

"I'm so glad you're safe," whispered Lloyd. "I can't believe this happened. The doctor told me you were attacked, and apparently raped?" said Lloyd with a contorted face and cracking voice.

Valorie just closed her eyes and tears ran down her cheeks as she struggled to recount the horrible experience for Lloyd. Questions began to flood his mind. How did he get in? Why didn't the security system sound an alarm? Who was this guy? Why attack Valorie? What were the kids exposed to? What long term effects on his wife? Their relationship? Their life in general? What kind of publicity would there be? How would they catch this guy and what would happen to him once he was caught? Who would defend him? Would he get off? At that moment, Lloyd became keenly aware of the fact that he was now the victim of a brutal crime, but if and when the perpetrator was caught, his lawyer would do everything he could to defend and protect him against the consequences of his brutality. Lloyd instantly became enraged thinking that whoever had done this horrible thing to his wife might get away with it. He now knew what it felt like to be a victim. And he didn't like it one bit. Suddenly he came face to face with the reason people look at lawyers in disgust and ask how they can defend criminals. The criminal justice system — the sophistry he'd dedicated his life to — suddenly was inadequate to deliver the punishment this guy deserved. Lloyd then looked at Valorie as though in a trance and said mechanically, "That S.O.B.'s going to pay!"

All of the McCallums spent that night at the hospital. Lloyd and Valorie in her hospital room and the kids in the hospital nursery. The next day, Valorie was officially discharged home to rest and recuperate. However, there was one nagging question still left unanswered — the results of the STD test. Finally, late that afternoon a call from the hospital brought some measure of relief. The results were negative. At least Valorie was spared the agonizing torture of eventual death from AIDS or some other horrible desease. Nevertheless, the physical and emotional scars were already beginning to manifest themselves. Lloyd stayed home the rest of the week nursing his wife and tending the children without even calling the office. By Monday however, he was feeling the pressure to get back to work, though he didn't want to leave his wife alone.

Valorie, recognizing her husband's dedication to duty, finally interceded with, "Why don't you go ahead and go to work. It's probably the best thing you can do for both of us at this point." Valorie smiled slightly, "It's alright, I'll be okay. Just keep your cell phone handy." Lloyd and Valorie both needed to regain some normalcy in their lives as soon as possible.

*   *   *

Then there was the police investigation. Detective Mark Hammer, a rape specialist, came to the McCallum's home and questioned Valorie extensively. Sure, he was only doing his job, but it required her to relive the whole experience again. She had to somehow protect herself, disassociate herself from the pain, and protect her family's standing and reputation in the community. Thus, at the outset of the detective's questioning she spontaneously identified herself by a pseudonym — Val Sheppard.

"The report here identifies the victim as a Valerie McCallum," said Hammer. "That's not you?" he asked.

"That's a mistake," said Valorie sharply. "I'm the victim, but that's not my name."

And with no further questions regarding the issue, the detective simply blotted out Valerie McCallum and inserted Val Sheppard on the report. But the most troubling part of the investigation was Detective Hammer's questions about exactly how, step-by-step, the sexual encounter occurred. He even came right out asked her if there was anything she said or did that could've been construed as consent.

"What do you mean?" demanded Valorie. "You think I let that black creep into my house just so I could have sex with him while my husband was gone? What's the matter with you? How dare you even suggest such a thing?"

"Did you fight him every step of the way?" persisted Detective Hammer, "or were you cooperative?"

"Well, yes, I cooperated, if you can call it that, after I was beaten into submission and the guy threatened to kill my daughter! What would you do if you were being strangled?"

"Please, Ms. Sheppard," said Detective Hammer, "I'm not the enemy. I'm trying to nail this down as tight as possible so this guy doesn't get away. I need to know all the details, and that means everything. This might become a pretty high profile case and we don't want any surprises — rape cases always provide fodder for the media, especially so-called black-on-white cases. I think we can conclude it for today though. If I can have my team go through your house for any physical evidence, we can wrap this up. Thank you for your cooperation. I know this has been very difficult for you."

"You don't know the half of it," snapped Valorie with eyes aflame.

Detective Hammer looked at her, slightly nodded his head and went about his work. Two hours later, his team was done and about to leave the premises when he stopped to share some good news with the victim.

"Ms. Sheppard," said Hammer. "I just want you to know that one of my techs found a very good thumb print on your family photo. Hopefully it'll turn up something when we run it through the system. I'm truly sorry this has happened to you. We'll do all we can to catch this guy."

"Thank you," responded Valorie softly. And with that, Detective Hammer left the house and Valorie was again left alone with the filthy aftermath of her ordeal.

CHAPTER 4

Persistent Trauma

After a couple of weeks at home, Valorie felt strong enough to venture out of the house. Lloyd was back to work, the kids were restless, and the bruises on her body had finally faded away.

"Well, there's no school today, so . . . who would like to go shopping?" Valorie asked little Emily playfully.

"I would, I would!" she squealed. "Does Gerald have to come?"

"Well, I don't think we want to leave Gerald home alone do we?"

"Why not?" asked Emily.

"Yeah," said Gerald. "McCaullie Caulkin stayed home alone and he beat the robbers all by himself."

"Well," cautioned Valorie, "you know that was just a movie." And then, starring blankly past her children, she said firmly and deliberately, "Nobody's going to stay home alone, not now, not ever."

Gerald and Emily looked at their mother for some clue as to why the sudden change in demeanor. All three of them just stood there staring until Valorie recovered from her flashback and was able to continue with their plans.

"Where shall we go?" she finally asked.

"To the mall, let's go to the mall!" said little Gerald. "We can go and have lunch and shop for a long time."

"Didn't we just have breakfast?" queried mom.

"But I'm hungry already," said Gerald.

"I think little boys your age are always hungry."

"So are little girls," said Emily.

"Alright, alright, we can have lunch at the mall." And with that, they all trooped out to the garage, got in the car and headed for the great American pass-time — recreational shopping. In route they stopped at the bank and this time decided to go in rather than use the drive-thru. Once inside Valorie waited patiently in line while Gerald and Emily busied themselves checking out the latest promotional display in the lobby. Finally, Valorie stepped up to the counter, took off her sunglasses and presented her transaction to a familiar teller.

"Oh, hello Mrs. McCallum," said the young woman. "May I help you?"

"Yes, I'd like to just cash this check please."

"Of course," replied the teller.

"Oh, and I'd also like a cashiers check made out to Equity Finance for $1,000. We have a little bill we would like to pay off."

"Sure," replied the teller as she turned away and walked over to the back counter to prepare the cashier's check. While there, Valorie noticed another bank employee come up and say something to the teller, who turned around and glanced at Valorie. When the teller was finished she returned to the counter where Valorie was waiting, counted out her cash, presented her with the cashier's check, and then said, "Hope everything's alright."

Looking at the papers in front of her, Valorie responded, "Everything seems to be in order."

"I mean are you feeling okay?" queried the teller.

"Me?" questioned Valorie.

"You seem a little preoccupied is all." Valorie then put her sunglasses back on and from behind their protective shield, almost growled at the young woman.

"Yes, I'm more than a little preoccupied, alright. As you apparently know, I was raped in my own home, and I'm not okay. Does that satisfy your curiosity? Do you want to know what it's like? I don't think so!" Valorie's rage began to take over, but as suddenly as it appeared she swallowed it and turned to walk away, but stopped, leaned back toward the teller and said in a subdued, sarcastic tone of voice, "By the way, it's not contagious."

"I'm sorry, Mrs. McCallum, I didn't know," stammered the teller.

Valorie stalked out of the bank with her two little ones in tow, stuffed them in the car, climbed in, started the engine and gripping the steering wheel, just sat there with tears running down her cheeks from under her sunglasses.

"People can be so insensitive," she thought. People who haven't experienced it can't begin to grasp the magnitude of the assault, the humility, the degradation, the brutality, the raw fear. It's like you've been permanently soiled and other people treat you like some kind of leper, wondering at the same time whether it was really rape or maybe something else. Not everybody acted that way of course, but it seemed to Valorie like the whole world was aware of her ordeal and somehow treated her differently. No more going into the bank, the grocery store, or elsewhere as the sparkling young lawyer's wife and getting the royal treatment.

The days seemed to drag into weeks and still no word from Detective Hammer or anyone else on the progress of the investigation. Valorie began to wonder if her case had been lost among the scores of violent crime cases the police department had to try and solve. All the stories she had heard or read about women being brutalized suddenly came into sharp focus in Valorie's mind. She was no longer an observer, a bystander, a casual onlooker when it came to violent crime. She now had first-hand experience as a victim. She wondered how those other women coped? How they went about their daily activities? How they dealt with their friends, took care of their children, went shopping, or made love to their husbands? How did they ever escape the constant burning pain deep inside? Could anybody ever feel safe after something like that? Would life ever be right again?

Lloyd arrived home from work around the usual time, about 6:30 p.m. "Hello, anybody home?" he announced as he walked in the front door.

"In here," came Valorie's reply from the kitchen. "We're just about ready to sit down. How was your day?"

"So-so," replied Lloyd. "That arson case I've been working on is coming loose at the seams. Remember the one where the guy was accused of torching those nursing homes?" Valorie looked up from stirring the vegetables on the stove and nodded her acknowledgment. "The prosecutor's got witnesses, physical evidence and forensics that are going to make it tough to beat. I'm probably going to have to go with some kind of insanity defense to keep the guy from frying."

"Would you mind mixing this fruit drink for dinner please?" asked Valorie.

"Sure," replied Lloyd as he shed his coat and draped it over the nearest chair. "I mean, what do you do with a guy that systematically burns down nursing homes, cremating little 'ole Ma and Pa Kettle?"

"Ma and Pa Kettle?" questioned Valorie with a blank look on her face.

Suddenly little Gerald burst into the room "Hi dad!" he cried, with Emily right behind him.

"Hey, well if it's not Jack and Jill, Hanzel and Grettle, Little Boy Blue and Little Red Riding Hood all rolled in together. So what have the fearsome twosome been up to today?"

"Ah, nothing," replied Gerald.

"Gerald had to stand by the wall during recess today, dad," volunteered Emily.

"How do you know, Emily?" countered Gerald.

"Cuz Mary Ann told me, that's how. She said you got in trouble at school today."

"What happened?" questioned Lloyd in his best lawyer-like demeanor.

"Well," began Gerald, "me and Jason were playing soccer and he was almost going to make a goal, so I didn't want that to happen and I tripped him."

"You mean you were on opposite teams?" asked Lloyd.

"Yeah, and they were going to beat us, so I tripped him and the playground duty saw it and made me stand by the wall for the rest of recess."

"Well, did Jason get hurt?"

"I don't know. I didn't even care. I was just mad 'cuz the duty made me miss the rest of the game."

"Didn't you even say you were sorry later or anything?"

"No, I didn't even see Jason the rest of the day. Besides they usually always win and I get tired of it."

At that point Valorie stopped what she was doing, dropped her clenched fists to her side, turned and faced Gerald and said sternly, "When you hurt somebody, you make damn sure you say you're sorry, do you hear me?!"

Lloyd, Gerald, and Emily all just stared at Valorie incredulously. They had never heard their mother talk to them quite like that. Tears began to well up in Valorie's eyes as she fought to control the anger spilling out of her. Then she abruptly marched out of the room.

Gerald looked at his father who said, "It's okay. Mom's just not feeling very well, but she's right, you should have told

Jason you were sorry." And with that, Lloyd hurriedly dished up their plates, got them started eating dinner and went upstairs after Valorie. He expected to find her on the bed, but she sat stiffly in the swivel rocker in the corner of their bedroom. Lloyd carefully approached her and knelt down next to the chair. Without even acknowledging his presence, Valorie muttered, "Maybe the creep should fry!"

"What?" asked Lloyd.

"That serial arsonist you're defending. Maybe he ought to rot in jail!"

"Wait a minute, not so fast, the jury's got to convict him first," protested Lloyd.

"To hell with the jury!" snapped Valorie.

"What's that got to do with our son, anyway?" questioned Lloyd.

"When people hurt other people, they ought to take responsibility and at least say they're sorry and if our son doesn't understand that, I'm going to make sure I teach him. And what's going to happen if they catch the guy that raped me? Is some defense lawyer like you gonna manipulate the jury so he gets off? Maybe plead the insanity defense, like your arsonist?"

The thought of Valorie's rapist getting away with it hit Lloyd again right between the eyes. Valorie's feelings of rage then made sense to him and sort of metaphysically transferred from her to him. So there they both sat, motionless, victimized emotionally all over again.

Both Lloyd and Valorie individually then came face to face with not only their own brand of horror, but what it is Lloyd did for a living — defend criminals who committed all kinds of hideous acts of debauchery. The one thing that had enabled Lloyd, and by extension his wife Valorie, to compartmentalize their thinking was the jury. Twelve people randomly chosen from the community determined guilt or innocence. It was not Lloyd's job to make that determination, but it was his job to do all in his power to persuade them that his client wasn't guilty, which he willingly and expertly did — for money. But the thought of a jury releasing his wife's rapist suddenly impaired Lloyd's ability to compartmentalize.

Valorie broke the thick silence with, "I'm not very hungry. I think I'll just go to bed."

Lloyd nodded his acquiescence and went back downstairs to help the kids finish up their dinner and get to bed early that night. There was not going to be any pleasant dinner conversation tonight. He wondered whether his wife would ever be able to function normally again. But life goes on. All the demands of everyday life continue to bear down regardless of what happens. The McCallum's coping mechanisms were already being tested to the limit. Raw emotions lay just under the surface and could erupt at any moment.

CHAPTER 5

The Line-up

Valorie had just walked in the house after dropping Gerald off at school when the phone rang. Cautiously she answered, "hello?"

"Hello Ms. Sheppard, this is detective Hammer. Would you be able to come down to the station and witness a line up for us?"

"When?" queried Valorie.

"This morning about 11:00. We think we may have your man, but we'd like you to ID him and if so, fill out a little paperwork for us so we can formally arrest him and file charges."

"Where do I go?" asked Valorie.

"Just come on down to the courthouse and we're in the building right next door."

"What's the best way to get there?"

"You've never been to the courthouse, Ms. Sheppard?"

"No, I'm afraid not," she replied, even though Valorie had in fact been there with Lloyd on occasion.

Valorie dutifully took down the directions, nervously

got ready and tidied up the house before it was time to go. She hated the thought of possibly seeing the man who had assaulted her, yet deep down her rage motivated her with an intense desire to confront him.

Valorie arrived downtown about 10:30 a.m. and had to wander around to find a parking place. She hated trying to find her way around unfamiliar places. Finally, she found a parking spot and carefully sandwiched her new van in between two other vehicles. She wore a dark red suit, black nylons, and heels. Without really trying, she looked like she just stepped out of Glamour magazine, yet nervously and cautiously she walked toward the entrance of the police station. Once inside she was surprised to see how businesslike the environment appeared. Not the messy, chaotic police station scene portrayed on TV. Valorie approached the reception counter, identified herself and advised the girl that she was there for an 11:00 o'clock appointment with Detective Mark Hammer.

"If you'd like to be seated for a moment, ma'am, I'll page him for you," said the receptionist.

Valorie immediately turned to sit down hoping to somehow disappear. A moment later Detective Hammer appeared in the lobby and walked over to where Valorie was seated.

"Thank you for coming, Ms. Sheppard. I know this probably isn't your most favorite activity."

"No, it certainly isn't, but I hope you have the right guy, so I can have some peace of mind that he's not still out there running around."

"Well, why don't you follow me this way and I'll explain the procedure to you."

Valorie followed Detective Hammer down what seemed like an endless, sterile corridor until they reached the witness observation room. Detective Hammer opened the door for Valorie who walked into what appeared to be a small gallery with a large window in front. The room was dark, but on the other side of the glass, bright lights lit up the small stage.

"We're gonna bring out five men in single file from left to right," explained Detective Hammer. "Look at each one carefully. We'll then tell them to face front. Look at them again, each one individually. Then we'll have them turn to their right so you can see their profile from the left side. Finally, we'll have them turn to the front again and repeat the words you told us the guy said to you. Do you have any questions?"

"No," replied Valorie. "Let's just get it over with."

Valorie sat there in the darkness waiting for the procession to begin. Nervously she looked around worrying that somehow they might be able to see her. She felt exposed, vulnerable. All there was between her and possibly the man who had raped her was a sheet of glass. It reminded her of visiting the zoo with no more than clear glass separating her from a wild animal. Yet with a kind of dogged determination she wanted to face her personal animal and nail him to the wall.

Eventually, five men lumbered through the door, out onto the brightly lit stage in front of Valorie.

"OK, stop," ordered Detective Hammer. Each man came to a halt facing to the right. "Look at the right profile," instructed Detective Hammer. Valorie scrutinized each face carefully. First, number 5, then 4, 3, 2, and 1. Detective Hammer looked at Valorie who looked back and simply nodded her head.

"Alright, face front," ordered the detective.

Again, Valorie searched each face carefully, moving from one man to the next and back again.

"Can you dim the lights in there at all?" asked Valorie.

"Cut the lights in half," instructed Detective Hammer. Instantly, the lights on the men's faces dimmed to about the equivalent of dusk outdoors. The shadows on the men's faces became less apparent. Valorie continued to carefully inspect them, then looked at Detective Hammer and nodded again.

"Face right," commanded the detective.

At once the men turned to their right allowing Valorie to examine their left profiles. Again, she looked at each one individually, after which Valorie said, "Can I see them straight on again and hear their voices?"

"Face front. Number 1, step forward and repeat the words on the reader in front of you.

Number 1, a non-descript man in his mid-thirties, took one step forward and slowly read the words, "I'll do you and your little girl both. Do you want that?"

Detective Hammer looked at Valorie for some response. She sat motionless staring at the man. Finally, the detective ordered Number 2 to step forward and repeat the same words. Again, Valorie stared and listened intently with no apparent reaction. The same procedure was followed for Number 3, then 4, who appeared to be quite young, but rather muscular. He too repeated what Valorie distinctly remembered her attacker saying just before she slipped into semi-consciousness. "I'll do you and your little girl both. Do you want that?" At that point, Valorie got up and walked over to the glass and stared right into the face of suspect Number 4, who, though only six feet away from her, did not know she was there.

"Have him tilt his head back," requested Valorie.

"Number 4, look up at the ceiling," ordered Detective Hammer.

Valorie stepped to her right so she could see the left side of his face from that angle.

"Have him read the words again," instructed Valorie.

"Read the teleprompter again," said Hammer.

Valorie listened intently to the voice as she stared at his face in the dim light. She wanted to be absolutely sure, and

41

at that point she was. Turning toward Detective Hammer, she said resolutely, "That's him. That's the guy that raped me."

"Are you sure?"

"I'm absolutely sure. And if I had a gun in my hands and access to him, he'd be dead right now."

"Alright, step back Number 4," commanded Detective Hammer. "Everybody turn to your right and exit through the door."

As the men shuffled out, Detective Hammer showed Valorie out of the room and back down the corridor to his office.

"Please have a seat, Ms. Sheppard," invited Hammer. "Let me just fill out this positive ID sheet, which I'll ask you to sign and then you can be on your way."

Valorie sat next to Detective Hammer's desk staring straight ahead. Without moving her eyes, she finally asked, "How'd you catch him?"

"We ran the prints we lifted at your house through the system and sure enough, he had a prior."

"Prior what?"

"Arrest for rape, but no conviction."

"Does he have a name?"

"Yeah, William Roundtree."

"So what happens next?"

"We'll gather up all the evidence we've compiled, to include his prints found in your home and your positive ID and submit it to the prosecuting attorney's office for formal charges and off we go to the circus."

"The circus? What's that supposed to mean?"

"That's what I call the criminal justice system once you turn it over to the lawyers."

"Yeah, I used to feel different about lawyers too, but I'm not so sure anymore," mused Valerie.

"Why do you say that?" queried Detective Hammer.

"Because now I know from first-hand experience the

kind of people they represent."

"I wouldn't be too hard on them, Ms. Sheppard. Not everybody they represent is guilty, just 95% of them."

"I don't know," snapped Valorie. "None of it seems very clear anymore. These people, like the guy that raped me, are accused of doing horrendous things, but then the jury lets 'em off. Either they did it or they didn't. What's so hard about deciding that?"

"I don't know, but it shouldn't be too hard in this case. We have this guy's prints in your home and a positive ID by a credible witness."

"Well, like you said Detective, off we go to the circus," Valorie said with a trace of cynicism.

The Detective and Valorie finished up the paperwork and she was ushered back to the reception area where polite formalities were exchanged and Valorie was left alone to walk back to her van and for the moment leave the unpleasant downtown environment behind her. As she hurried to get away, she couldn't help but wonder how Lloyd could go down there so often. What was it about the place that attracted him? Of course it was the courthouse where he spent most of his time, but Valorie wondered whether that had any different feel about it than the police station. She knew someday soon she would find out, but in the meantime she hurried back to suburbia trying to collect herself as best she could before meeting her children.

The freeway seemed to envelop her as she sped faster and faster toward home and yet it was there that the horror had happened. Even as she raced along in seclusion, she was reliving the experience all over again. The stench, the brutality, the pain, the terror, all of it. She became oblivious to the beautiful green landscape of her native Washington and mentally was back in the hospital, just regaining consciousness, realizing that it was not a dream, that she had been raped. Suddenly, Valorie's cell phone rang and jerked her out of her flashback.

"Hello," she said nervously.

"Hi sweetheart, how ya doin?"

"Okay I guess," replied Valorie. "I'm on my way home from the police station. Detective Hammer asked me to come down for a line up. Looks like they got the guy, at least I told them one of them looked and sounded exactly like the guy that . . ." Valorie's voice stopped.

"Are you okay, darling?" asked Lloyd.

"I guess that's the question of the year, isn't it? No, I'm not okay, but hopefully someday I will be."

"So did they catch the guy? Did you identify him?" Lloyd asked.

"Yes, it was him, number 4. No doubt in my mind. He didn't even look like he remembered or cared what happened yesterday, much less what happened to me several weeks ago."

"Well, we don't need to talk about this now," interrupted Lloyd "I just wanted to check in with you and see how things were going. I'll be home a little early tonight and we can just have something quick and easy for dinner with the kids. No fuss, no muss, and no stress."

"That sounds good to me," replied Valorie.

"Well, better get back at it here," said Lloyd. "Love you. See you at home a little later."

"Goodbye," said Valorie.

But it was a rather hollow sounding goodbye. Valorie felt hollow inside. Somehow things were never going to be quite the same again.

True to his word, Lloyd arrived home a little early that night and helped get together a simple dinner of soup and sandwiches. Valorie however, was not her usual cheerful self and both of the kids could sense the difference. There wasn't the light, bouncy conversation. The whole atmosphere was rather subdued. Valorie mechanically responded to her children's comments and questions during dinner — obviously she was pre-occupied with the events of the day. After dinner, Lloyd could see that it was his job to divert the kids and keep them out of Valorie's hair for a while. Eventually it was bed time and again Lloyd took over, making sure the kids didn't miss out on their bed time routine, finally getting them quietly tucked in for the night.

By the time Lloyd reached the master bedroom, Valorie was just coming out of the bathroom in the subdued light wearing Lloyd's favorite shear beige negligee. She moved gracefully toward the bed as Lloyd traded places with her in the bathroom. A few minutes later he came out, walked across the room and slipped into bed next to Valorie. As he snuggled up to her he asked, "Are you going to be okay?"

Valorie whispered, "I hope so."

Lloyd wanted to fool around. Slowly and gently he began his efforts to arouse Valorie. He kissed and caressed her in ways she had readily responded to numerous times in the past. This time however, it seemed more mechanical and labored. It was not happening naturally like Lloyd had become accustomed to. He persisted in the hopes that a little more time and effort would finally put Valorie at ease and they could once again experience the intimacy they both so thoroughly enjoyed before everything happened.

Finally Valorie abruptly exploded, "I can't! I can't do this. I'm sorry. Please don't touch me." She sat up in bed and put her hands over her face, rigid and tense all over. Lloyd lay on his back starring at the ceiling completely dumfounded. It had been months since Valorie's rape and they had yet to make love. Lloyd couldn't help but wonder what was happening and how much longer it would be before Valorie would permit him to express his love for her and she for him. Each time they tried to make love, it failed. Lloyd was becoming frustrated and angry over what was becoming a real obstacle in their marriage.

"What's happening?" he finally asked.

"Nothing's happening," replied Valorie. "You don't understand. It's not like it used to be."

"What do you mean it's not like it used to be? You mean I'm not like I used to be or you're not like you used to be?" questioned Lloyd.

"I don't know," answered Valorie. "Maybe neither one of us is like we used to be."

"What's that supposed to mean?"

"Sex just doesn't interest me anymore. I can't get into it."

"Sex in general or sex with me?" queried Lloyd.

"It's not you," said Valorie pausing. "I don't know, maybe it is you. Who knows?"

"Who cares, right?" added Lloyd.

He just lay there staring at Valorie shaking his head wondering what else was going on that he wasn't aware of. It's easy for a man to become suspicious when his wife repeatedly rejects his advances. Of course he knew the rape had had a devastating effect on Valorie, but somehow suspicions began to creep into his mind as he saw his relationship with Valorie deteriorating. Indeed, his mind went back to around the time they were married.

He and Valorie had such a whirlwind courtship they hardly had time to catch their breath. They had both been in serious relationships with other people which were abruptly broken off when things began to heat up between them. Lloyd wondered even then if Valorie didn't some times look back wistfully at her previous relationship. In fact, even after they were married he'd stumbled onto a couple of text messages on Valorie's phone between her and her old boyfriend. They seemed innocent enough, but it gave him pause then and now even more so. Had she been in contact with him again? Lloyd had to wonder what was really going on. Was Valorie pulling away from him and using this so-called rape as an elaborate cover-up? Wow! He could hardly believe he was even thinking that way about his beloved Valorie.

CHAPTER 6

The Pro Bono Client

The presiding department of the criminal division
of Superior Court was a buzz with activity. Sitting in the
busy crowded courtroom was Mr. Brent Jamison, a young
attorney who was just getting his feet wet doing criminal
defense work. He was from the highly respected firm of
LANCASTER, VERNON and EVERETT, which like many
firms, participated in the pro bono program providing free
legal counsel for indigents. Jamison sat in the courtroom
a little nervous, not having been in court, at least criminal
court, very many times before. Suddenly his nervousness
peaked when he heard the judge call out his name above the
din in the courtroom.

"Mr. Jamison, are you here on the pro bono docket?"

"Yes, your Honor," replied Jamison as he stood up
and walked toward the bar.

"The clerk here has several files for you. Each of
the files has a Notice of Arraignment already in it. Please
promptly file your Notice of Appearance. I don't know how
many of these defendants are in custody, but I'll leave that to

you to figure out from the files and advise them that you've been appointed to represent them."

"Thank you, your Honor," responded Jamison dutifully as he took an armload of files from the clerk and made his way out of the courtroom.

Back at his office, Jamison began going through the half-dozen files he'd been given and found among them a few felony cases, to include a first degree burglary and rape case. Setting the other files aside for the time being, he began reading what little bit was available about the case of State v. William Roundtree. The first thing Jamison looked at was the Information — the prosecutor's official charge sheet. Apparently his newly acquired client, Mr. Roundtree, simply walked into a house in a suburban subdivision and pounced on the alleged victim — a Val Shepard. From what Jamison could tell reading between the lines, the burglary charge was already looking pretty weak. He wanted to get his discovery request right out so he could see just how strong a case the prosecution had.

Jamison picked up his dictaphone and immediately issued instructions to his paralegal to prepare the necessary pleadings to obtain all of the evidence and documentation in the prosecutor's possession. That of course was required in any criminal case. The prosecution had to give the defense copies of any and all evidence available to enable the accused to prepare his defense. It didn't work that way in reverse, however. The defense didn't have to give the prosecution much of anything. It's the State's burden of proof to establish guilt beyond a reasonable doubt and all the defense has to do was create that little doubt.

Within a week, Jamison had the requested discovery — all the police reports, including victim's statement, forensic reports, fingerprints, hair, semen matches, and a line-up positive ID. Looked like a solid case — for the other side. Jamison poured over the documentation searching for any weaknesses or mistakes on the part of the police. The next step was to interview the client. Jamison threw everything into his briefcase and headed for the jail. That was always an experience in itself. The place always gave him the creeps. It was like going to the zoo, only the animals in the cages were human.

Jamison walked into the huge stone building with tiny windows and took the elevator to the second floor. As the doors opened, he could almost smell the stench of human captivity, even though there was stainless steel everywhere and the place was spotless. He made his way to the reception counter and produced his bar card in exchange for a visitor's pass and signed in. The jailor pushed the button, there was a loud click and Jamison reached over and pulled open the heavy steel door, stepped through and let it slam behind him. Walking down a narrow corridor he heard another loud click and a large door with steel bars slowly slid open. Immediately upon stepping through, the door slid back and locked behind him. He made his way down another corridor into the bowels of the cold facility, finally reaching another reception desk encased behind thick glass. The officer on duty spoke through the intercom. "What can I do for you?" he asked impersonally.

"I need to see a William Roundtree," replied Jamison.

"Go to Conference Room A just to your left and someone will bring him to you."

Jamison proceeded down still another corridor to the first door on the left marked Conference Room A. He opened the door and stepped inside. It was bleak, absolutely nothing in the room except a small metal table and two chairs. Everything was concrete — the walls, floors, ceiling, except a 4x4 window next to the door to enable the roving guard to keep an eye on things in the room. Jamison took a seat facing the door, which a few minutes later abruptly opened and Roundtree was thrust into the room and the door shut behind him. He just stood there for a moment staring down at Brent Jamison, a young, clean cut, nicely dressed attorney. In contrast, William Roundtree wore only his drab, gray jailhouse pajamas and sandals.

"Who are you?" demanded Roundtree.

"I'm your lawyer," replied Jamison.

"I didn't hire no lawyer."

"I was appointed by the Court."

"Are you one of those public defender types?"

"No, I work for a private law firm and we represent people like you pro bono."

"Pro what?!"

"It's a program where attorneys help out people in need for little or no pay for the good of society, supposedly."

"Well, society never did no good for me!"

The two men just stared at one another while Jamison thought about the lofty purposes of the pro bono program and his own idealistic reasons for going to law school. And here was Willie Roundtree, the ungrateful beneficiary of both.

"Why don't you take a seat, Mr. Roundtree, and let's talk about your case."

Reluctantly, the accused sat down and again took up his snide little stare at his court-appointed lawyer.

"I've read the police reports and . . ."

"What you wanna know?" interrupted Roundtree.

"Well," replied Jamison, "why don't you just tell me what happened."

"I went huntin'," said Roundtree as he swabbed the inside of his lips with his tongue.

"You went hunting?"

"Yeah, I just got in my car and decided to prowl around a little."

"What led you to . . . uh," Jamison hesitated and opened the file to find the name of the subdivision.

"Nothin' in particular. I really don't know how I ended up over there."

"So go on, tell me what happened."

"Well, I just started drivin' down the street and stopped in front of this one house, big house, nice place. Got out, walked through the side gate to the backyard and decided to try the sliding glass door. Sure enough, it wasn't even locked, so I just walked in, helped myself to some goodies . . ."

"What do you mean goodies?"

"I mean some brownies. And then, I heard this kid upstairs talking about how daddy was out of town and momma was there all by her-lonesome. So, why not? I went on upstairs and persuaded her to do it my way. You know, like they say in the TV commercial."

"Maybe you could be a little more specific," urged Jamison, making notes to the file.

"What's there to be specific about? We just made love, ya know."

"You made love? Did you choke her or threaten her?"

"No, I never did no such thing. I think she liked it."

"And how did she demonstrate that she liked it?"

"Well, I whispered in her ear and she just rolled over and spread 'em."

"What did you whisper in her ear?"

"I don't remember. I guess her man was out of town and she was just lonely 'cuz she didn't put up much of a fuss."

"She didn't put up much of a fuss? How come she was hospitalized then?"

"I don't know nothin' about that. I didn't beat her up, but it did get a little rough."

"Well, what happened after you were done making love?"

"She just laid there almost like she was sleepin' so I just pulled up my pants and left. Probably wasn't there more than 30 minutes total."

"Could she have been unconscious?"

"No, no way! Like I say, I think she liked it."

"What's your history?" asked Jamison.

"What do you mean what's my history?"

"Any priors?"

"No. But I was accused once."

"Accused of rape?"

"Yeah. But I got off."

"And how did you get off?"

"I don't know. Had a good lawyer I guess. You a good lawyer?"

"I think so," said Jamison with some reservation. "Anything else you can tell me about this?"

"No, that's about it."

"Did you break anything to gain entry into the house?"

"No. Like I said, the door was open. I just walked in."

"Alright, I guess that'll do it for now. I'll get back in touch with you. In the meantime, don't say anything to anybody in here. You understand?"

"Yeah, I understand. You gonna get me outta here?"

"Well, there's a bail hearing in a couple days. Do you have a job, a place to live, or any family in the area?"

"Yeah, I got a sister over on the east side."

"Can you stay with her if the Judge grants bail?"

"Sure," nodded Roundtree.

"Alright, I'll see you at the hearing," concluded Jamison.

And with that, both men stood up and Jamison motioned for the officer to come get his client and usher him back to his cage. As Jamison made his way out of the jail he was already formulating his defense. Consent. He knew enough about criminal law to know that during the commission of a crime, things can change and what starts out as resistance sometimes morphs into acquiescence, especially in cases of this nature.

CHAPTER 7

State v. Roundtree

It was time for the regular monthly meeting of LANCASTER, VERNON and EVERETT, usually held the first Monday of every month. All attorneys and paralegals attend for the purpose of coordinating administrative matters and discussing pending cases. Two dozen lawyers and about that many paralegals typically gather for the meeting. The senior partner present conducts. This morning it was Gerald Everett, a seasoned lawyer with 30 years experience trying both civil and criminal cases. He was not unlike Lloyd McCallum, having burst on the scene as a young lawyer, distinguishing himself as a lawyer's lawyer and worthy adversary in any legal battle. That is why Lloyd looked to him for guidance in the early years of his own career and still did. There was an air of confidence and quiet aggressiveness about Gerald Everett that captivated Lloyd and most other people familiar with Mr. Everett.

It was sort of an informal tradition that lawyers and their paralegals sat around the large conference table at these firm meetings more or less in order of seniority. So that was usually the order of discussion in the meetings as well. The first attorney to Mr. Everett's left was Frank Brennan, also a very good lawyer only a few years younger than Everett. Brennan specialized in commercial litigation, a sub-specialty of general civil litigation. He knew contract law and the Uniform Commercial Code better than any lawyer in town and represented most of the firm's corporate clients. He had a lot of clout both in the firm and around town.

"What's on your list today?" Everett asked Brennan.

"Well," paused Brennan pensively. "We need a new can of air freshener in the men's room." That's what made Brennan such a good shmoozer. He could always figure out a way to lighten the mood and put people at ease. At the same time it had the effect of disarming opponents.

"I've got a pretty heavy-duty trial right around the corner and could use a little help with last minute witness preparation."

From across the table an eager young woman lawyer spoke right up, "My schedule looks pretty clear. I'd be happy to help any way I can."

"Done," replied Brennan. "I'll get you the names and phone numbers so you can schedule interviews and I'll tell you what I basically need from each one." The young woman was visibly pleased that her offer was so readily accepted by one of the heavy-weights in the firm.

"That's it for me," said Brennan. And so it went around the table until it was Brent Jamison's turn.

"Well, sir," began Jamison. "I picked up several files from the courthouse yesterday for our criminal pro bono program. They all seem pretty routine, although I'm probably going to be looking for some help on a first degree burglary and rape case I got. The facts are all over the place. The State has charged our man with burglary in breaking into a private residence and then raping some gal. But I've met with our client and he says the door was open and he just walked in and found the woman, who consented to the sex. The only problem however, is that she later turned up at the hospital pretty worked over. Our man says he had nothin' to do with that, though he does admit that it got 'a little rough.' After they made love, he zipped up and walked out and that was it. So, we have a major discrepancy in the facts."

Mr. Everett then looked at young Jamison and asked, "How many criminal cases have you handled, Brent?"

"Not very many, sir."

"Less than half a dozen maybe?"

"That's a fair estimate," admitted Jamison.

"Well, then you should already realize that there is nearly always a 'major discrepancy' in the facts. Officially, accept your client's story but privately question everything he says. Remember in the last analysis the State must prove every element of the crime beyond a reasonable doubt. Your job as the defense attorney is simply to create some doubt with regard to one or more of those elements. First, thoroughly research the corpus delicti, then closely examine police procedure and development of their evidence, and finally, carefully examine and develop the facts and evidence from the defense prospective. One of the best in this town is one of ours, Lloyd McCallum. Take the case as far as you can before you bother him, then enlist his considerable expertise and you'll do yourself and your client proud. By the way, where is our man McCallum this morning?"

"He's in a deposition on that arson case, Mr. Everett," came the reply from somewhere at the other end of the table.

"Fine," concluded Everett. "Unless there is any other business we need to cover, let's adjourn and get to work." And with that, everybody folded their papers and shuffled out of the room to their respective cubicals.

Back in his office, Jamison began in earnest to examine the case of State v. Roundtree. He carefully reviewed again the Information and statement of probable cause outlining the prosecution's basic charges. Initial discovery included a witness statement that Roundtree's car had been seen parked in the alleged victim's neighborhood the night of the crime. Discovery also included the forensics report identifying Roundtree's thumb print on a family portrait. The report also included evidence of hair and semen in the master bedroom matching that of Jamison's client. And finally, there was the victim's statement and positive ID in a line-up. All the evidence definitely pointed to Roundtree being in the house on the night in question, but one important issue was very much in dispute — whether there was consent. This Val Shepard, the victim, said that Roundtree broke into her house and raped her. The client however, maintained that Ms. Shepard was in the mood for some rough love and consented. But that still doesn't explain how the victim ended up in the hospital all battered and swollen. The client says when he left the house she was basically fine. He doesn't know how she got so thrashed and wound up in the hospital. Jamison concluded that he needed to interview the victim. He also wanted to see the scene of the alleged crime himself.

Jamison picked up the phone and called the deputy prosecutor assigned to the Roundtree matter — a Vicki Davis whom Jamison knew had been prosecuting cases longer than he had been defending them. They had become acquainted as members of the Young Lawyers Division of the local Bar Association.

"Hello, Vicki, this is Brent Jamison."

"Hi, Brent. Let's see, we crossed paths at a Bar meeting or something recently, didn't we?"

"Yeah, I think we got into a discussion about police misconduct or something," Jamison joked.

"Of course," said Ms. Davis. "You view every case as an opportunity to critique the police rather than defend your client."

"That's part of defending my client," responded

Jamison. "But, as you probably already know, I haven't actually handled all that many cases."

"So did you call for a little free advice?" questioned Davis.

"Well, I'll take it wherever I can get it, even from a prosecutor, but actually I did call on business."

"So, what can I do for you, Mr. Jamison?"

"I'd like to talk to your victim in the State v. Roundtree matter. That's one of your files isn't it?"

"Well, let me check here. Yeah, it looks like that's one of mine. A Val Shepard is our lady?"

"Yeah," said Jamison, "I've got your initial discovery, but I'd really like to talk to your gal if I can."

"Okay," said Davis. "Give her a call and if she's agreeable, set it up. You realize though, this sort of thing doesn't usually happen. We don't typically turn our victim over to the defense attorney without somebody from our office being present. But we're just swamped and my gut tells me that you'll behave yourself."

"Promise to behave myself," replied Jamison. "Do you happen to have her address and phone number?"

"Isn't it in the discovery we gave you?" asked Davis.

Jamison took a moment to flip through his file and sure enough there it was. "Yeah, here it is."

"You're right, you haven't handled very many of these cases, have you?" Davis poked.

"Okay, chalk one up for you," replied Jamison. "If I have any trouble, I'll set up a formal interview through your office."

"Alright, hope I don't hear from you," said Davis. "I got plenty to do without sitting through defense attorney interviews."

"Well, thanks," said Jamison. "See you at the next bar meeting."

"Not if I see you first," joked Davis.

And with that, the two lawyers hung up the phone and Brent punched another line to call Ms. Val Shepard.

This was another first for Brent — actually talking to the victim of a brutal rape, if indeed that's what it was. Of course, his objective was to find out from the victim herself what happened and ultimately whether he could make a case for consent — without abusing the latitude he'd been given by the prosecuting attorney. Brent punched in the number and listened to the phone ring several times before someone finally answered.

"Hello," said a small voice on the other end.

"Hello," said Brent. "Is this the Shepard residence?"

"No," came the reply.

Jamison quickly double checked the phone number and was sure he had dialed correctly. "What's your name?" asked Brent.

"Emily," said the little voice. "My momma's home. Do you wanna talk to her?"

"Yes please," said Brent.

After a few moments, Brent heard a woman's voice on the other end say, "Hello, who is this?" in a somewhat defensive tone.

"My name is Brent Jamison. I'm an attorney here in town and I represent a defendant in a criminal case by the name of William Roundtree."

"Why are you calling me?" demanded Valorie. "I've told the police everything several times, and I really don't want to discuss it again with you."

"I can appreciate that," said Brent, "but I have spoken to the prosecuting attorney, a Ms. Vicki Davis, and I would prefer to speak with you informally if possible. If you insist however, we can arrange for a formal interview downtown at the prosecutor's office. As you can appreciate, my client has been charged with a serious offense and I would like to hear your version of the story."

"My version of the story?" echoed Valorie.

"Yes, there seems to be a few discrepancies in the reports," pressed Jamison, "and I'd like to give you an opportunity to clarify exactly what happened."

"Why don't you just ask your client? I'm sure he can tell you what happened."

"I have asked my client, Ms. Shepard, and that's where some of the discrepancies come from. May I arrange a time to come out to your home, to make it convenient for you?"

"You mean come out and inspect the scene of the crime, don't you?" queried Valorie.

Jamison knew then that he was not talking to some dummy, but this woman could read between the lines. It made him feel a little uneasy.

"Well, yes," admitted Brent. "If you don't mind, I would like to see where all this stuff happened."

"Don't you mean allegedly happened?" pushed Valorie.

"Well, I guess what exactly happened, or if anything happened, is what the jury will ultimately have to decide. So, yes, to be perfectly honest with you, Ms. Shepard, I'm interested in seeing the scene of the alleged crime and talking to you about what allegedly occurred."

"Might as well put all the cards on the table," Jamison thought.

"Well, Mr. Jamison," said Valorie, "You come on out and I'll tell you what happened, not what allegedly happened. How about tomorrow morning at 10:00 o'clock?" And she hung up the phone before Brent could say another word.

Brent slowly hung up the phone and looked out the window of his small office. It wasn't much of a view, just the building next door, but he stared anyway. "This is real life stuff," he thought. "Law school doesn't prepare you for this." He contemplated the seriousness of what he was involved in. Defending a man charged with multiple serious crimes, to include first-degree rape, versus an obviously intelligent woman, whose anger over what happened to her rises to a boil at the mere thought of it. Jamison felt himself being torn between his client and the victim already. But how could that be? He owed the alleged victim nothing and owed his client his total and undivided loyalty. Again, Jamison reflected on law school and how academia doesn't begin to prepare a lawyer for the real life practice of law.

Jamison arrived at the office a little early the next morning having thought about State v. Roundtree well into the night and ever since he woke up that morning. He again reviewed the file and all the discovery obtained from the prosecutor and then began to prepare his outline of questions and things he wanted to cover with Ms. Shepard. That was one thing at least law school did teach him — preparation, preparation and preparation. Brent figured it was about a half hour drive out to the suburbs where Ms. Shepard lived. It was kind of nice to get out of his cubical once in a while.

The offices of LANCASTER, VERNON and EVERETT were definitely plush, but it was a pressure packed environment, especially for young associates like Brent Jamison. He was expected to bill out at least 2,000 hours annually, which breaks down to about 40 billable hours a week, which sounds easy enough, but in reality a lawyer has to work 50 to 60 hours per week in order to produce 40 billable hours. In other words, not everything a lawyer does during the day can or should be billed to a client. But at 2,000 hours a year billed out at $250 per hour equals $500,000 per year, about half of which goes to pay office overhead leaving $250,000, less $70,000 to $90,000 in salary to the junior associate, which equals $160,000 to $180,000 clear profit for the firm's senior partners. Then multiply that times a dozen or two junior associates and you have a nice little business built on the backs of the junior associates (on top of what the senior lawyers earn themselves). Why do these bright young law graduates do it? Experience, prestige, and the hope of someday becoming a partner themselves.

So, as Brent checked out of the office, he knew that every minute he was gone, including travel time, would be billable time, except in this particular case, there would be no revenue for the firm since he was doing it pro bono. But the firm certainly received other benefits from this sort of community service. It heightened their image in the legal community and among the judiciary. And when it came to currying the good will of judges, LANCASTER, VERNON and EVERETT was among the most astute.

As Jamison jetted out of the parking lot in his older model Honda, he began to imagine what it would be like to interview a rape victim, no, alleged rape victim. He mustn't forget his role in this whole thing. The sights and sounds of the city on this gray overcast day in western Washington made Jamison feel almost as closed in as he did at the office. A light drizzle sprinkled the windshield as Jamison drove out of the city. It was obvious when he left the city and entered the suburbs, the whole mood changed. There was space, grass, trees, shopping malls and big expensive homes. He'd never been to this particular area before but had heard that it was definitely a ritzy neighborhood.

As he arrived at the entrance there was a large brick monument with Briarwood spread across the front in what appeared to be brass letters. Jamison instinctively slowed down as he entered the uncommonly nice neighborhood. Without much trouble, he found his way to the object of his search — Ms. Shepard's home. What a beautiful place. Professionally manicured lawns and shrubbery, a huge 8,000 square foot split-level home with brick facade, cedar siding and shake roof, all expensive features. Reverently, Jamison extracted himself from his little car and approached the front door. Just as he stepped toward the front door he was surprised by a man's voice.

"May I help you, sir?" Jamison turned to see the McCallum's gardener, Norm Macintyre, approaching from around the corner of the house.

"Well, I'm here to see the lady of the house," said Jamison. "In fact, I have a 10:00 o'clock appointment. I'm an attorney."

"So you gonna sue somebody?"

Jamison just stared at the man for a moment. Macintyre continued, "I don't usually go around screening my customers' visitors, but the lady of the house just asked me to keep an eye out whenever I am around."

"And why is that?" asked Jamison.

"Because she was attacked a couple of months ago and has felt pretty insecure ever since."

"Attacked? Are you talking about when she was raped?" asked Jamison.

"Yeah, that's exactly what I'm talking about," said Macintyre.

"You didn't happen to be around when that happened, did you?"

"No, but if I had, that man would be dead!"

"Well, so you don't have any first-hand knowledge of what happened?" pressed Jamison.

"No, but I sure know how it's affected her."

"How about before all this happened?" asked Jamison. "Did these folks get along okay?"

"Absolutely," replied Macintyre. "They were like the all-American family."

"Well, every couple has problems," said Jamison. "Does the mister travel much?"

Macintyre knew exactly where Jamison was going with that question.

"No," he snapped. "And the Mrs. isn't the lonely type either. She's not one of those flirtatious women that plays around on the side while her husband's out of town, if that's what you mean."

"I'm not trying to imply anything. I'm just asking a few questions, okay?" assured Jamison. "Maybe I better talk to her since she was there that night. Thanks anyway for the information."

And with that, Jamison turned on his heel, marched up to the door and rang the doorbell. Even the sound of the doorbell conveyed wealth and status. It wasn't really a doorbell at all, but a series of melodic chimes. Jamison stood waiting, feeling fidgety. He looked over at Macintyre who was still standing in the yard watching him. Finally the door opened crisply and there stood one of the most attractive women Jamison had seen in a long time. About 5'6" tall, long brown hair draped around her shoulders, beautifully contoured facial features, and full figure all packaged in a very nice maroon pants suit complete with heels. Jamison was stunned.

"Ms. Val Shepard?" asked Jamison.

"Yes," replied Valorie.

"How do you do? I'm Brent Jamison."

"Come in, Mr. Jamison."

Brent obediently stepped through the door as Valorie shut it behind him. His eyes immediately panned the spacious entryway taking in the spiral staircase to the left, hallway directly in front of him, and the beautifully furnished sunken living room to his right. "This place definitely did not look like a crime scene," he thought. Meanwhile, Valorie stepped back around in front of Jamison and motioning toward the living room said, "We can talk in there, Mr. Jamison."

"Actually, before we get started, could you please show me around your house so I have some familiarity with where things were and what happened that night?" asked Jamison somewhat cautiously.

"Oh yes, that's right. You wanted to see the scene of the crime. As far as I know, he came in through the sliding glass door in back," explained Valorie pointing down the hallway toward the back of the house. "He made his way down this hallway, up the stairs and snuck into my bedroom."

"I know this is distasteful for you, Ms. Shepard, but could you walk me through this step by step?"

Valorie just looked at him and then without saying a word walked down the hallway toward the sliding door. Jamison quickly followed as she led him through the door out onto the back patio. Then turning back toward the glass door she almost mechanically described what she knew.

"I think he came in through this door, which must have been left unlocked. Why he picked my house I'll never know. I don't know how long he was downstairs here, but nothing was stolen or even disturbed. The first thing I was aware of was someone standing over me in the bedroom shortly after I had gotten up with our daughter and put her back to bed. As I turned over, he pounced on me and grabbed me by the throat."

"Before we get into those details, Ms. Shepard," interrupted Jamison, "Could you show me around the rest of the downstairs area of your house?"

Valorie abruptly stopped her description, swallowed hard and dutifully showed Jamison the rest of the downstairs. The spacious kitchen, adjoining dining room and entertainment area, library/office on the other side of the kitchen and of course the living room. Everything was exquisitely furnished and decorated. By this time, Jamison was curious about who paid for all of this."

"May I see the family picture the police lifted the thumbprint from?" asked Jamison.

"No," replied Valorie. "The police took it to their forensics lab and said they were going to run some more tests of some kind or another and haven't given it back to us yet."

"Oh," responded Jamison, hoping to see a photo of the guy this woman was married to. Maybe he could begin to get some clues about their marital relationship. On more of a hormonal level Jamison wondered whether the guy really appreciated what he had here.

"Maybe you could show me the upstairs now, Ms. Shepard, if you don't mind," suggested Jamison. Valorie immediately made her way to the bottom of the circular stairway and walked up to the second floor with Jamison right behind her. He glanced up once to see her buttocks swishing back and forth at about eye level and just about stumbled. Once upstairs she led him to the master bedroom. What a layout, he thought. Decorated in gray and mauve colors, a huge king size bed in the middle of the far wall, a couch under the window to the left, with a large walk-in closet and master bath to the right.

"I know this is difficult for you," began Jamison, "but could you kind of reenact things as you describe what happened?"

Valorie began explaining that her daughter, Emily, had gotten up in the night complaining of a tummy ache. Valorie had gotten up, given her some Pepto-Bismol and put her back to bed, then returned to the master bedroom where she lay down on the right side of the bed on her right side. She had just about drifted off to sleep when she somehow sensed a presence in the room, and as she looked over her left shoulder a man pounced on her, grabbed her by the head and clamped his hand over her mouth.

"Sounds like you struggled?" observed Jamison.

"You bet I struggled!" replied Valorie, "until he threatened me and Emily."

"What exactly did he say?"

"As best I can recall, he said be quiet or I'll do you and your little girl both. I remember he said something about my husband being out of town too. I don't know how he knew that."

"Did he hit you?" questioned Jamison.

67

"Not exactly. Not that I remember."

"You were admitted to the hospital in pretty bad shape, weren't you, Ms. Shepard? But you don't remember this man hitting you?"

"I remember his hand on my face and not being able to breath and feeling like my head was in a vice."

"So you don't remember being struck but you do remember a threat. Did this guy produce a weapon or anything?"

"Not that I saw," admitted Valorie.

"Did he take any steps to carry out this threat?"

"Well, if practically suffocating me means carrying out his threat, then yes."

"What did you do after he supposedly threatened you?"

"He did threaten me, Mr. Jamison. And then I let him have his way."

"What does that mean? What happened next?"

"By that time I was on my back and he was on his knees straddling me, he unbuckled his belt, pulled his pants down, forced my legs apart with his knees and . . ." Her voice trailed off as she closed her eyes and pursed her lips in silence.

Jamison mentally noted that she did not cry but became tight lipped which could mean most anything. He quickly reviewed her story in his mind. She claims to have been threatened but admits there was no weapon. There were signs of physical abuse, yet she doesn't remember being struck, and admits to just lying there, having given him his way, as she put it. Was there some truth to Willie Roundtree's story? Could this woman have been in the mood for some rough love as he described it, and essentially consented to the sex? Maybe she suffers from some latent masochistic desires, which were played out at Willie Roundtree's unwitting invitation. She later felt contrite about the whole thing, added a few bruises of her own and reported it as a rape. A plausible theory at least, Jamison mused.

"Would you tell me about your husband, Ms. Shepard?"

"There's nothing to tell," answered Valorie. "He's a good husband and father and he's been hurt by this almost as much as I have."

"Do you two get along okay?" pressed Jamison.

"Yes, we get along fine and that's all the questions I'm going to answer today."

Jamison figured he'd pushed about as far as he could and thanking Valorie, he excused himself, made his way downstairs and out the front door. Back in his car he couldn't help but wonder what really happened in that bedroom that night.

Simultaneously, Valorie wondered why she had consented to talk to Jamison and relive the whole ordeal over again. Maybe she just needed to tell her story to somebody who could influence the outcome of her case. Maybe this defense attorney could be persuaded that she was telling the truth and agree to just plea bargain his client. If she could convince the defense attorney in the case, she was home free!

B. L. McCoy

CHAPTER 8

Napalm and Cosmopolitan

Lloyd McCallum sat slouched down in the large leather chair behind his desk, which was covered with papers about his serial arsonist case. It was only 10:00 a.m., but Lloyd had already been on the job for three hours and had his tie undone and sleeves rolled up. In his hands he held a copy of the prosecution psychiatrist's deposition in which the doctor testified that Lloyd's client was perfectly sane and deliberately murdered the eight people who died in three different fires. "How in the world was he going to refute this evidence," he wondered.

The elements of first-degree arson are (1) knowingly and maliciously causing a fire; (2) which is manifestly dangerous; (3) to human life. McCallum's client was also charged with first-degree murder based on the felony murder rule, which holds that if a homicide occurs in the course of commission of a felony, the perpetrator is not only guilty of the felony, but guilty of murder as well. Lloyd always viewed the felony murder rule as kind of a "piggy back" way of pinning a homicide on someone when they really didn't commit a homicide. But before ever getting to the felony murder rule, the prosecution has to prove beyond a reasonable doubt every element of the underlying felony — in this case, first degree arson. That's of course where Lloyd had to concentrate his efforts.

There didn't seem to be much doubt that the prosecution could prove his man did it — that is, started the fires. But what was his state of mind at the moment he committed the act? The prosecution had its hired gun ready to testify that Lloyd's client was perfectly sane. Lloyd knew he could go out and hire his own doctor to evaluate his client and render an opinion that the guy was nuttier than a fruitcake, but would the jury buy it when weighed against eight charred corpses? Lloyd decided he had to go talk to his client again.

"Sally?"

"Yes," replied his secretary on the intercom.

"I don't have anything scheduled between now and lunch, do I?"

"No," she said. "You're clear until about mid-afternoon actually, which is your only appointment."

"Well, I'm going to run downtown and see Mr. Goldstein again," advised Lloyd. "I'll be back after lunch, probably around 1:30."

"Okay," replied Sally.

Lloyd gathered up the entire file, particularly the state psychiatrist's evaluation and headed downtown to his second office — the county jail. Once there, he went through the usual routine of flashing his bar card, signing in and getting a visitor's pass. Strange as it was, Lloyd got a bit of a rush every time he went into the jail. It was like a close encounter of the weird kind. The only way to describe it was like going to the zoo and letting wild animals eat out of your hand. It was a controlled situation, but still a little spooky being that close to vicious criminals — wild animals of the human kind.

"Can I help you?" questioned the uniformed guard

from behind the glass.

"Yes," replied Lloyd. "I'm here to see Harold Goldstein."

"Go down the hall there to Conference Room A and we'll bring him to you."

"Thank you," said Lloyd, as he turned and headed toward the stark conference room, furnished with only a small table and two chairs. The room didn't look much different than a jail cell, except there was a metal door instead of bars. Lloyd walked over and sat down on one side of the table and waited. But instead of thinking about his interview with Harold Goldstein, his mind wandered back to Valorie and the ordeal they were both still dealing with. He wondered again whether things were ever going to be normal. Somehow deep down inside, Lloyd realized he had lost something forever. That miserable rapist, that scum of the earth had taken something from him and his wife that they could never get back. At that moment, the door of the room burst open and Harry Goldstein was thrust into the room and the door immediately shut behind him. Neither man moved or said anything. After what seemed like several minutes, Lloyd finally suggested Goldstein take a seat.

Lloyd struggled silently. He sat there just looking at Goldstein mentally picturing another criminal — his wife's attacker. He had difficulty concentrating on the task at hand, realizing possibly for the first time, in very personal terms, that his client had deprived someone else of something they would never get back — their loved ones, who had died in Goldstein's fires. Lloyd forced himself to focus on the question of culpability which depended upon Goldstein's state of mind when he set the fires. A person is not to blame if they really don't know or appreciate what they are doing. Still, Lloyd found it difficult to segregate such questions when his own wife had been victimized by some clown who would use every device and excuse available to avoid culpability.

Finally, Goldstein brought Lloyd back to earth with "What do you want? Haven't we already been over everything before?"

Lloyd was not in the mood for any caustic ingratitude. "There are four methods of capital punishment: hanging, lethal injection, gas, and the electric chair. Which do you prefer?" Lloyd sneered. Goldstein looked a little stunned, but didn't say anything.

"We need to go over it again," continued Lloyd. "I have the prosecution psychiatrist's deposition here and he says you were perfectly sane and rational when you set those fires. Unless we come up with something pretty heavy-duty to rebut this, you're dead and I'll have to put your case in the L column. We can go hire our own shrink to say you were nuts when you did it, but the prosecution's going to show photos of eight charred corpses to the jury. Then they are going to look at you and say fry him. So let's go over it again. Let's start at the beginning. How old were you when you went to Vietnam?"

"The first time?"

"Yeah."

"I just turned 19."

"How soon after arriving in country were you assigned to a long range reconnaissance patrol?"

"Immediately."

"What did you do?"

"We re-conned."

"No, what did you do?"

"Basically, I was the forward observer for the air assault teams. I could even sometimes ask for the type of ordnance I wanted."

"So what did you ask for?"

"I'd get Napalm."

"Why?"

"So I could see the SOB's burn!"

"Anybody in particular?"

"Yeah, those miserable wenches that produced those gooks."

"You mean the women?" asked Lloyd incredulously.

"Yeah, the women! It's called zero population growth. No females, no kids, no gooks."

Lloyd had had some experience himself as a Green Beret in Central America, but this was a whole new philosophy of war that he'd never encountered before — one man's personal war on women.

"So is that basically all you did your first tour?" questioned Lloyd.

"Yeah, that's all I did. Napalm is great stuff. You can probably buy it on the internet nowadays."

"So what was your turn around time before you went back to Vietnam the second time?"

"Less than a year. I wanted to go back. Napalm. It was a rush. I could rain down hell fire on those gooks and they were just gone, disappeared, poof!"

Lloyd began to wonder just what he was dealing with here. "So did you do anything else with fire while in Vietnam?"

"Lit a lot of cigarettes."

Lloyd just stared at Goldstein, un-amused by his lame attempt at humor.

Realizing his lawyer didn't appreciate his levity, Goldstein acknowledged, "Oh, you want to know whether I burned anything?"

"Yeah, any incidents of arson?"

"No, other than I set fire to a couple of cat houses the second time I was over there."

"You mean brothels?"

"Yeah, but somebody caught it in time and there wasn't much damage."

"Anybody hurt?" asked Lloyd.

"No, and nobody even suspected me," said Goldstein.
"Honorable discharge?"
"Yeah, I did my job in the Army."
"I understand you accumulated quite a pile of money after you got back home."
"Yeah," said Goldstein. "I qualified for and got every kind of pay I could while I was in the Army and never spent a dime. After I got back to the states, it all went into the stock market and I managed to hit it pretty big."
"Tell me about your folks," inquired Lloyd.
"Nothing to tell," said Goldstein.
"There's always something to tell," pressed Lloyd. "I know a little bit about your background having talked to your step-father."
"Did you say father? That creep is no father, certainly not mine."
"What about your mother?"
"Now there's a piece of work," began Goldstein. "I hope she rots in hell."
For the next 20 minutes Lloyd listened to pure acid as it spewed from the mouth of his client, describing his relationship with his mother. It was pure and simple verbal matricide. Then it became obvious. The fires this man set were only incidental and the mostly elderly women who died represented his mother burning in hell. This was a mindset that started way back in childhood and was fed and enhanced while in the military.
Lloyd wondered whether he could sue the Department of Defense as a defense to arson. After all, the Army had taken an emotionally unstable and vulnerable teenager and turned him loose in an environment where he developed, indeed was almost encouraged to develop, an unrestrained liking for killing. Each time he called in Napalm, he got to send his mother to hell again. Over and over for two solid years, fire became his ally, his narcotic, an escape from his

childhood. Lloyd knew now just what kind of shrink he needed, a specialist in Vietnam War post-traumatic stress disorder. Maybe, just maybe, he could sell it to a jury.

"We're done," announced Lloyd. "Stay out of trouble while you're in here and I'll see what I can do about arranging bail." The words were barely out of Lloyd's mouth when he realized that maybe Harold Goldstein should stay in jail. Was he the kind of guy that ought to be out on the street? These were the kind of conflicts Lloyd hadn't worried much about before. Lloyd stepped to the door, opened it and motioned for the guard to come get his client. Outside the jail Lloyd stared up at the bright blue sky, a rarity in western Washington. He breathed in the fresh outside air and was glad to be a free man — free in more ways than one.

McCallum got back to the office about 1:30 pm and happened to walk by Brent Jamison's office on his way to his own coveted corner office.

"Mr. McCallum," called out Jamison as Lloyd walked by. "Can I bend your ear for a second? I got this pro bono case I've been working on and I was wondering if I could chat with you a little about it?"

"Sure," replied McCallum as he stepped into Jamison's cubicle and plopped down in the chair in front of his desk.

"I just came from another room just like this," said Lloyd. "Why don't you put something on the walls?"

Jamison was a little taken aback and quickly agreed to dress up his office a bit, in deference to Lloyd who was a full partner in the firm.

"Have you ever been in one of those interrogation rooms down at the jail?" continued Lloyd. "It's enough to give you claustrophobia."

"Well, as a matter of fact," replied Jamison, "I was just down there recently on this case. At least my office has a window," joked Jamison. Already tiring of their chitchat, McCallum prodded, "Well, what can I do for you?"

Sensing the need to get right to it, Jamison said, "The issue is consent. The victim said she was raped and even has some physical evidence of assault, but the client says the gal was in the mood for some rough sex and it was all consensual."

"You've talked to both of them?" questioned McCallum.

"Yes."

"So who do you believe?"

"I don't know," replied Jamison.

"What's your gut tell ya?"

"I don't know. That's why I'm talkin' to you."

"What's this gal's prior history?" asked McCallum.

"Clean as a whistle as far as I can tell," said Jamison. "Your basic suburban housewife, from all appearances."

"Your basic suburban housewife," repeated McCallum, drifting off into private thoughts about Valorie as he stared out the window behind Jamison. "Suburban housewives have all kinds of reputations nowadays," he thought. "Everything from absolutely faithful to promiscuous as a dog in heat."

Lloyd's ability to compartmentalize was uncanny. One minute he was thinking about Valorie's case, the next minute he was talking to Jamison about his, it never occurring to him that the two might somehow be connected.

Directing his attention back to the task at hand, McCallum assumed the role of law school professor and queried, "What are the elements of first degree rape?"

"Sexual intercourse with another person by forcible compulsion where the perpetrator uses or threatens to use a deadly weapon, kidnaps the victim, inflicts serious physical injury, or breaks and enters into a building where the victim's at," responded Jamison like he'd memorized the statute.

"Well, consent is not forcible compulsion," said McCallum. "Sounds like that's where you need to focus your efforts."

"Well, I kinda knew that," said Jamison boldly. "I need help with how to prove it."

McCallum flashed his sharp eyes at Jamison as though he had been insubordinate. "You've got to focus on the physical evidence of assault and turn it into physical evidence of rough but consensual sex. I think some of these suburban housewives sit around reading Cosmopolitan a little too much and first thing you know, their fantasies get the best of them and when an opportunity comes along, they grab it. Problem is how do they explain the glaring crack in their facade? Easy, they point the finger at someone else and call it rape. So you have to break her story down, Brent. You have to go after the victim with a vengeance and show her for the fraud she is. I assume you've been through the police investigation file thoroughly?"

"Several times," replied Jamison.

"Get the medical records and let's have a forensic expert go over them with a fine tooth comb looking for any evidence that would support our theory of rough love. After you've done that much, we'll take another look at it and go from there." And with that, Lloyd McCallum jumped up and was out the door almost before Jamison could say thanks for the help.

Back in his own office, Lloyd mulled over in his mind the counsel he'd just given his young associate. As the hard charging criminal defense lawyer he'd come to be, he had told Jamison to attack the victim. He had learned over the years that almost every piece of evidence can be interpreted differently and in Jamison's case even so-called physical evidence of assault could be interpreted as physical evidence of rough but consensual sex. It might be a stretch, but if the victim didn't hold up under close scrutiny that could be enough to establish reasonable doubt. So all they had to do was create some doubt as to whether the sex occurred by "forcible compulsion." If not, if it was consensual to any degree, then the jury had to acquit their client.

Lloyd had learned well how to think like a lawyer. As he sat there thinking he began to retrace his thought processes, not as a lawyer but as a husband. Valorie's unsoiled image came to mind, their perfect life together. Everything was going so well until that night. How could Lloyd and Valorie ever recover what they'd lost? Lloyd realized that some defense lawyer somewhere would probably be going through the same thought processes he'd just gone through to try to get his wife's rapist acquitted. He'd probably focus on the victim too and maybe try and show it was consensual despite the physical evidence. He might even try to turn that evidence around to say that Valorie was acting out some secret sadomasochistic fantasy. Not Valorie. Impossible.

All at once Lloyd's tender feelings as the husband of a rape victim crashed head-on with his sterile analysis as a lawyer defending an accused rapist. He felt like his mind was going to implode. What if the analysis he explained to Jamison was tried on Valorie? Would it fit? Could there be a secret side of Valorie that not even he knew about? He shuddered at the thought. Lloyd felt like his own mind was playing cruel tricks on him and he began to realize just how devastating an effect this whole ordeal had had on him. Thoughts of raunchy infidelity on the part of Valorie had never entered his head. A rape was a rape, not some sort of one night stand. But that's exactly what it was if consent was any part of the scenario. How could Lloyd ever be absolutely sure? He felt the foundations of his life shifting and cracking as his training not to accept anything at face value prompted close scrutiny of his own marriage. He felt himself sinking into an abyss.

———— ❁ ————

CHAPTER 9

Preparation For Trial

Brent Jamison was in his office early pouring over the forensic pathologist's report he'd just received. He took Lloyd McCallum's suggestion to have a forensic expert thoroughly review the case from a medical standpoint to see if they could pick apart the victim's story and at least raise a reasonable doubt as to whether the injuries were consistent with an assault or more indicative of very physical but arguably consensual sex. Like any good hired gun, Jamison's expert concluded, based on his review of the medical records and police reports that a strong case could be made for consensual sex. Jamison felt an adrenalin rush. His mind raced ahead and he envisioned himself in the courtroom methodically walking his expert through his testimony with the jury totally transfixed.

Jamison had received the report just in time for the omnibus hearing at which both the prosecution and the defense officially disclose the basics of their case. The forensic pathologist's report would have to be produced for the prosecution. Jamison actually relished the thought and imagined the look on the prosecutor's face when he read the expert's report. Jamison began to appreciate more and more Lloyd's suggestion to get a forensic expert involved. These guys were really something. It didn't matter what the subject area was, you could find someone who could divine some scenario that would explain things the way you wanted them explained. The good ones were worth every penny and they definitely charged a pretty penny for their expertise, which incidentally, included the ability to wow a jury. In fact, some of these guys were more of an expert witness than a legitimate professional in a particular field. But Jamison didn't care about that — he was an advocate and if a forensic pathologist could sell the story that this "encounter" between his client and Ms. Shepard did not involve "forcible compulsion", that's all that mattered. It was time for Jamison to get the case ready for trial.

It seemed like a pretty simple and straightforward case. There were no eye witnesses, it basically boiled down to a question of credibility. Even though a bit of a stretch, could it have happened the way Willie Roundtree said it did? He admitted to entering the house unlawfully, fully intending to have his way with whomever he found inside. But once in the bedroom, did things change? Did Ms. Shepard suddenly decide to take advantage of the situation herself and act out a secret fantasy of her own? "It was certainly plausible," Jamison thought, and he had a forensic pathologist's report to back it up.

Jamison wasn't prepared however, for the sheer tedium of trial preparation. There was the substantive law which outlines what the prosecution has to prove. There are the facts of the case as developed through investigation. There are procedural rules. There are evidentiary rules. The challenge of preparing and scheduling witnesses, outlining your witness' testimony and preparing for cross examination of your opponent's witnesses. Preparing exhibits. Drafting proposed jury instructions. And finally, trying to orchestrate it all and tell a believable story to the jury. Sometimes it seemed to Jamison like trying to herd cats.

His respect and admiration for Lloyd McCallum grew considerably with each day he spent getting everything ready for trial. Lloyd was the consummate trial lawyer. He seemed to know intuitively how to marshal the evidence to put the best spin possible on his client's story, and he seemed to posses the trial lawyer's most effective quality — credibility. It doesn't matter how airtight a case you have, if the trial lawyer doesn't come across as believable and personally committed, there is no way the jury is going to buy it. Jamison definitely understood that much and went about preparing his case with credibility as the central theme. Indeed, this case was all about credibility from top to bottom.

Jamison was excited. This was his first significant felony case and he looked forward to the confrontation, though he had the luxury of knowing that all the responsibility didn't rest on him — Lloyd McCallum would be the lead trial attorney. He would be able to sit next to Lloyd and observe and learn from one of the best. He had to make sure everything was airtight. Not just to impress his boss but Jamison wanted to win. He had already been seduced, as it were, by the narcotic of big time competition. Two lawyers going at it head-to-head where the stakes are high. In this case, a man's freedom and a woman's integrity and self-image hung in the balance.

At last, Jamison felt he had the case ready for trial. He had been over everything numerous times — the law, the facts, the evidence, the medical records, the police reports, and he'd gotten helpful input from Lloyd. Most importantly, he felt his client was as ready as he would ever be if he had to testify, but Lloyd left that part of the case entirely up to Jamison. Knowing how to handle the client was crucial and the only way to learn was by doing it. Of course, in a criminal trial the defendant does not have to testify at all if he chooses not to.

That decision was typically made after the prosecution rested its case in chief, so Jamison prepared Roundtree thoroughly just in case they made the tactical decision to put him on the stand. Their decision would largely depend upon how the prosecution's main witness came across. Just how good a witness would she be? Would she be confident, articulate? Would she invoke sympathy? And most importantly, how credible would she be? Could they shake her on cross-examination? Would that in itself, be sufficient to raise a reasonable doubt in the minds of the jury? Could they provoke her into an angry outburst? All of these considerations had to be explored in anticipation of courtroom combat.

Finally, the case was ready, and even if it wasn't, time had run out. It was Saturday afternoon and trial was scheduled to start first thing Monday morning. Coincidentally, both Lloyd McCallum and Brent Jamison were packing up getting ready to leave the office about the same time Saturday afternoon. Both had been there working as usual on the weekend preparing cases for litigation. Other than an occasional conference with Jamison, Lloyd really hadn't paid much attention to his young associate's rape case scheduled to go to trial the following week. He figured Jamison had a good handle on who the witnesses were going to be and basically what their testimony would consist of. He realized this was one of those cases that basically boiled down to a question of credibility and they had enough ammunition with the forensic pathologist's testimony to create some doubt about the victim's story.

"Well, we ready to go, Brent?" questioned Lloyd as they walked toward the door together.

"I think so," replied Jamison. "I've been over this stuff several times now and I think we're as ready as we're going to get."

"Well, are we ready enough to win?" questioned McCallum. "Do you feel confident about this?"

"Yes, I do," replied Jamison recognizing that now was not the time to express doubts about the strength of their case.

"Well, good," said Lloyd. "This should be an interesting trial. Take tomorrow off, Brent, and we'll see you here bright and early Monday morning." And with that, both men walked out, made their way to their cars and headed home. Lloyd was thinking a lot more about his arson case than the rape case he and Jamison would be trying next week. Indeed, his mind hardly paused on next week's court appearance. He was consumed with what he considered to be more important matters.

As he cruised out of the city past the high-rise office buildings out of the reach of inner city congestion, he mentally laid his work aside and turned his thoughts toward his family. He tried to relax. He pictured each of his loved ones individually starting with Emily and her bright uninhibited smile, then his son, Gerald, with all his boyish exuberance, and finally his wife, Valorie, with all the pressures and problems they had experienced recently.

He still couldn't wait to get home to her. It seemed like only a few minutes later Lloyd was driving into his quiet suburban upper-class neighborhood, which used to provide some measure of security and protection from the grimy world in which Lloyd worked. He pulled into the driveway, reached up and pressed the garage door opener and waited for the garage door to open. As soon as he could, he pulled his BMW into the garage and again pressed the garage door remote to close the door behind him. Lloyd sat there in his car wishing he felt the same piece of mind he used to when he came home. Now there was that nagging feeling that something was wrong. Something was amiss. Life didn't fit neatly together anymore. He got out of the car and went into the house trying to be cheerful, pretending everything was alright.

"Hey, anybody home?" shouted Lloyd. Lloyd could hear the washing machine going nearby in the laundry room, but no one answered. He walked toward the family room in the back of the house where he found Emily and Gerald transfixed in front of the TV.

"Hey, what are you guys up to?" Neither child moved, totally absorbed in their cartoons. Lloyd tried again, "Hey Emily, Gerald, how about a hug?"

"Dad, we can't hear!" replied Emily, still staring at the TV.

"Yeah Dad, be quiet," Gerald chimed in.

Lloyd just stood there looking at his children for a moment. He wasn't used to being ignored by anyone. He felt a certain amount of irritation well up inside him. He considered his options. Finally, Lloyd walked over, picked up the remote, and turned the TV off.

"Hey Dad, turn it back on!" protested Gerald.

"Yeah, we want to watch it!" cried Emily.

"Well, I'd like at least a hello when I get home."

"Okay," agreed Gerald reluctantly. "Hi! Now would you turn the TV back on?"

Simultaneously, Emily got up and ran out of the room crying, "Mom, Daddy won't let us watch TV."

Valorie met Emily and walked back into the room with her.

"Is there some reason they can't watch TV?" questioned Valorie as she reached over and turned it back on.

"Well, no," responded Lloyd. "But I didn't think I had to compete with the TV for a mere hello."

"Well, it keeps them quiet and out of my hair," replied Valorie as she turned to walk out of the room. Lloyd got up and followed her into the kitchen.

"Rough day?" he asked.

"Not particularly," answered Valorie.

Lloyd pressed further. "You seem upset over something."

"Really!" Valorie shot back.

"What is it?" asked Lloyd, pushing a little harder.

"What do you mean, what is it?" echoed Valorie sarcastically. "I have this simmering anger just under the surface all the time and you don't seem overly understanding."

"You act almost like what happened was my fault," Lloyd retorted.

"See? That's what I mean," said Valorie, her eyes aflame. "It's not about you and whether it was your fault, this is about me and it's not going away. I'm not a happy camper, okay?"

"Alright, I'm sorry. I'm trying to be understanding," assured Lloyd. "But you seem to be awful defensive about it."

"You think I'm hiding something?" questioned Valorie.

Lloyd and Valorie just stared at each other. Her eyes were defiant, his probing. The air between them was almost palpable. Lloyd was seeing a side of Valorie he had never seen before. Her question echoed over and over in his mind. He struggled to formulate an answer. He genuinely hoped she wasn't hiding something, but he had to confess that he wondered. He couldn't bring himself to say that though, so he finally articulated the answer he had to give.

"No, I don't think you're hiding anything." Valorie continued to stare at him, almost daring him to question her. Finally, she turned around and resumed preparing food for the evening meal.

After dinner, which was tense, with little conversation, Lloyd went into the living room to just sit and think. His conversation with Valorie before dinner kept replaying itself in his mind. Her question thrust at him — "Do you think I'm hiding something?" — troubled him. Not only was Valorie not getting over it, but she was becoming more defensive about it. Lloyd had a lot of experience with people and knew that questions like that were sometimes a declaratory admission of guilt masked as a question. Was there something that Valorie wasn't telling him? Was she feeling guilty and that's why she was keeping him at a distance?

Lloyd couldn't believe he was analytically slicing and dicing his wife. There was never any reason to distrust her before, other than those seemingly innocent texts he'd found on Valorie's phone years ago. But now it was like this rape was a cancer eating away at the life and vitality of their marriage. Lloyd sat in the living room of his beautiful home feeling numb. He needed to sort some things out but there was no time. He was scheduled to be in trial Monday morning and he had to be focused. At the moment however, Lloyd felt exhausted. All he could do was veg out and watch TV.

The next day, Sunday, was much the same. There was an uneasy tension in the McCallum home all day. That night, as they were both getting ready for bed, Lloyd tried to ease the tension between him and Valorie. He hoped that if he could get her talk about things a little, maybe that would help.

"Has the prosecutor told you when your case is going to trial?" queried Lloyd.

"Yes, it's supposed to this coming week some time," answered Valorie.

"Do you know what day you're scheded to testify?" asked Lloyd.

"No, not yet. I think some time around the middle of the week," said Valorie.

"Well, I'm supposed to start a trial Monday — actually just be there to mentor an associate, so I'll figure out a way to make myself available when you have to testify," said Lloyd, trying to reassure his wife.

"It would be nice if you could be there," admitted Valorie. "But if you can't, I'll survive. I have this long."
What did she mean by that? wondered Lloyd. "Just survive?" he questioned out loud. Was she was referring to the rape or something broader like their marriage in general? Again, Lloyd felt confused about their relationship and verbally flicked even while trying to console and offer support for Valorie, who didn't bother to respond to his question.

"Well," he finally said, "if you'll let me know when you're supposed to testify, I'll do my best to be there."

Valorie wasn't sure she even wanted her husband in court, so she decided she probably wouldn't tell him when she was going to testify. That way there would be no "post-game analysis." She wouldn't have to explain her testimony or rehash everything with her lawyer husband. Nevertheless, she replied with a simple "okay" and both husband and wife rolled over in opposite directions and drifted off to sleep.

CHAPTER 10

Motive and Opportunity

Early Monday morning found the McCallum's already up and at it. Lloyd was getting ready to head to the office, then to the courthouse, and Valorie was trying to get a head start on her day before Gerald and Emily got up for school. There wasn't much conversation as they maneuvered around the bedroom and bathroom getting showered, dressed, and ready for the day.

"Do you want any breakfast before you go?" Valorie finally asked, knowing full well that Lloyd usually didn't eat much if anything for breakfast when he was in trial.

Not wanting to discourage her offer however, Lloyd said, "Sure, a piece of toast and glass of orange juice would be good."

Valorie got down to the kitchen just enough ahead of Lloyd to have his toast and juice ready and waiting for him on the kitchen counter.

"Thank you," he said as he quickly consumed the toast and orange juice. Then looking directly into her eyes he said, "Have a good day, I love you."

She glanced away briefly and dutifully answered, "Love you too." And with that Lloyd grabbed his briefcase and marched out the door to the garage, backed down the driveway, and drove away. Meanwhile, Valorie walked into the living room and stood stoically watching Lloyd until he disappeared from sight. Even though Lloyd had gotten up and left for work thousands of times over the course of their marriage, Valorie felt more alone now then ever. She felt alienated from her best friend — her husband. And strangely, she felt an eerie discontent and combativeness beginning to sweep over her.

Lloyd arrived at the office by 7:00 a.m. to find his junior associate, Brent Jamison, already there.

"How ya doing, Brent?" called out Lloyd as he marched by Jamison's office. "You ready to knock 'em dead today?"

"Yes sir," replied Brent briskly. "I think we actually have a pretty strong case," he added.

"Well, good! I'm counting on you," encouraged Lloyd. "Why don't you gather up your stuff and come in my office and let's run through what's going to happen today."

A couple of minutes later Brent appeared in Lloyd's door and waited to be motioned in to sit down in front of the huge desk. "Well, you've done all the work-up on this case," began Lloyd, "so as you know, you'll be doing most of the work in the courtroom. I'll be there of course to help out if you get in a bind, but I think you'll do fine. You just got to jump into the water sometime and this is as good a case as any to do it."

"I guess so," replied Brent with a kind of forced smile. "We may or may not get to any witnesses today with jury selection and opening statements. We might get to the investigating officer's testimony, but that's probably about it."

"You're right," said Lloyd. "You have thought through this, haven't you? You have your voir dire questions ready

90

and opening statement? By the way, who's our judge in this case?"

"Myron Steiner," replied Jamison.

"Oh yes, Judge Steiner," said Lloyd thoughtfully. "He's a good judge. In fact he was the judge in the last rape case I had. He usually gives you quite a bit of leeway in voir dire, which is nice. Gives you the opportunity to develop rapport with the jury and subtly sway them toward your theory of the case. By the way, what's the theme of this case? Have you capsulized that in a single phrase that you can repeat over and over to the jury?" queried Lloyd.

Brent was a little taken aback by that. This was getting into trial techniques that were still a little beyond Jamison. "Well, no, I guess I haven't," admitted Jamison. "Any suggestions?"

"What's at the core of this case?" probed Lloyd. Jamison thought for a moment and said, "Motive and opportunity."

That one even surprised Lloyd a bit. "You sound like a prosecutor," he said.

"Exactly," admitted Brent with a sly smile. Both attorneys just sat there looking at each other, Brent giving his mentor a moment to catch up.

"Alright! Describe her as the 'criminal'," said Lloyd, marking quotations in the air with his fingers.

"Exactly," replied Brent.

"Prosecutors work on the basis of motive and opportunity all the time, don't they," added Lloyd.

"Yes," nodded Brent.

"So why can't we turn the tables on them and make that our theme song? Sure, our client may be guilty of breaking and entering, but once he was in the bedroom that night, did our alleged victim suddenly became motivated and seize the opportunity to act out her own dirty little fantasy? And having done so, she cries wolf, and our man takes the fall. Sounds plausible to me," said Lloyd.

"And there you have it. A theme and a catch phrase — motive and opportunity — that we can turn around and use on the prosecution."

"I like it," said Lloyd, smiling smugly. This is what he relished the most — the strategy and tactics of hand-to-hand courtroom combat. "Okay, let's run through the investigating officer's anticipated testimony real quick and make sure you're ready for cross-examination," prodded Lloyd.

Brent dutifully laid out what he expected the officer to say based on a thorough analysis of the police reports.

The forensic evidence placing the client in the victim's house that night included his thumb print on a family photo, and hair and semen matching that of the client's. On the crucial issue of consent, however, the officer was vulnerable on cross-examination. Sure, he could say the defendant was in the house that night, but on the issue of consent, he couldn't say, nor could he testify concerning the alleged victim's background and whether she harbored any secret fantasies that she simply acted out that night while her husband was gone. This case was shaping up to be a real soap opera — written and directed by the defense lawyers for the benefit of the jury.

"Well, I guess we're about as ready as we are going to get," announced Lloyd.

Brent dutifully nodded his agreement and began gathering up everything he would need for the first day of trial — his voir dire questions, opening statement outline, and everything he would need to cross-examine the investigating officer. As he gathered up the tools of his trade and the time for combat drew closer, Jamison could feel the tension mount. This was it, the real thing. The time for preparing was over. The time to go to battle was now.

It was State v. William Roundtree — his client. It might as well have been State v. Brent Jamison. He felt intense pressure building within him. Everything was on the line. His client's life was in his hands. His skill and reputation as a lawyer was at stake. It seemed as though Jamison's whole life hung in the balance. What if he'd overlooked something? What if he had misinterpreted the law? What if the judge excluded crucial evidence or admitted especially damaging evidence? What would he do to protect his client? How would he fare against an experienced prosecutor? Would he embarrass his mentor, Lloyd McCallum? What would the secretaries and staff think if he bungled it? On the other hand, what would they think if he won an acquittal? How impressed would the Judge be with this new upstart, Brent Jamison? How grateful would his client be? How impressed Lloyd would be. All of these conflicting thoughts and feelings rushed through Jamison's mind simultaneously. He couldn't wait to get out of the office and into the arena just to be doing something — implementing his plans rather than just making plans.

The ride to the courthouse seemed short. Before he knew it, Jamison was marching into the courthouse beside Lloyd like two gladiators striding into the coliseum. As they walked down the hallway, Jamison imagined all of the battles that had been fought in this particular arena, all the people who had come here and bled as it were, all the lawyers who had fought valiantly for their cause. And now Jamison was one of them.

As they walked into Judge Steiner's courtroom, they were the first to arrive. Since Judge Steiner was one of the more senior judges, he had one of the older, more ornate courtrooms. The bench seemed high above the floor with a large black swivel rocking chair where the judge sat. To the right was the jury box with 14 chairs — 12 jurors, and two alternates. In front of the bench were two huge tables, one for the prosecution, one for the defense. Then there was the gallery — several rows of benches for any interested onlookers who in most cases were few in number. Between the judge's bench and the jury box was the focal point of the courtroom, the witness chair. This was in every sense of the word the hot seat. This was the place from which the story of every case unfolded. This was the fountain of truth in the courtroom. This was where the lawyers plied their skills and elicited testimony or attacked witnesses in their mortal struggle to conquer. In short, this was where the blood flowed.

Since Lloyd and Brent were the first to arrive, they selected the table closest to the jury box. Lloyd preferred that table. He liked being closer to the jury where he could observe their reactions to various pieces of evidence and they too could observe his reaction unobstructed. For Lloyd, the courtroom provided a stage in which to maneuver and act out the story's plot — his story, the one he tried so carefully to choreograph for the jury. Every gesture, every facial expression, every voice intonation, every question was designed to persuade the jury to favor his client, a flesh and blood person over the prosecution's incorporeal client, the government.

In Lloyd's experience, most jurors were some combination of trust and suspicion. He also knew that most people believe that where there's smoke there's fire. The government wouldn't just charge an innocent person with a crime, would they? So Lloyd's job, as he saw it, was to force the government to prove beyond a reasonable doubt that there was indeed fire behind all the smoke and not let the jury convict on the strength of smoke alone. Lloyd simply relished the thrill of combat as it were, and that was all he thought about once in the ring with his opponent. His own case, or rather his wife's case, never entered his mind — all he could see was what lay directly in front of him — winning this case!

About the time Lloyd and Brent had finished setting out their papers getting ready for voir dire, in walked the prosecuting attorney — Franklin Cartwright. This was a man Lloyd was well acquainted with, at least professionally. They had tried several cases against one another and so far Lloyd had won just about all of them. But he respected Cartwright as a professional and worthy opponent. Cartwright was dressed in his usual conservative dark suit and marched over to the prosecution's table like the soldier he viewed himself. Without looking at Lloyd or Brent, he began removing his file and other paperwork from his large leather briefcase.

"How ya doin', McCallum? What brings you down here today?" ventured Cartwright.

"We're pro bono. My man Jamison here is trial counsel on this one. I'm just along for the ride. By the way, have you ever met Brent of our office?"

Looking up for the first time, Frank Cartwright said, "No, I don't guess I have," while stepping toward Brent with hand extended. As they shook hands, their eyes locked, each man trying to size up the other in the few seconds available to them. Lloyd was not a casual observer of this ritual but noted a certain amount of cautious innocence in Jamison in contrast to Cartwright's seasoned aggressiveness. Cartwright didn't waste any time trying ever so subtly to intimidate his opponent. Lloyd smiled to himself, reliving some of his own early experiences in the courtroom. He was amused by Cartwright's maneuvering so early in the game and yet in high stakes competition like this, both sides understood that the slightest edge can sometimes make the difference. Of course, that's exactly why Lloyd McCallum was there, to make sure his protégé was not taken advantage of by Cartwright or any other government hatchet man.

"I thought Vicki Davis was the prosecutor on this one," said Brent.

"Yeah, she was, until some family emergency took her out of town. So I guess you get me," replied Cartwright as he smiled at McCallum.

At 9:00 a.m. sharp, Judge Steiner called the attorneys for both sides into his chambers. He liked doing that to informally touch base with the attorneys and make sure the case was ready to go.

"Good Morning, Gentlemen," opened Judge Steiner.

"Good morning, your Honor," all three lawyers said almost in unison.

"Have a seat. Are there any last minute matters that we need to take up before beginning voir dire?" Judge Steiner asked.

"I don't believe so," offered Cartwright.

Jamison looked at McCallum apparently wishing to defer to him, but when Lloyd remained quiet, Jamison offered, "I don't think there is anything on the defense side, your Honor."

"Any wrinkles in this case that I need to be aware of in advance, counsel?"

"Don't believe so," replied Cartwright.

"I don't think so," mimicked Jamison.

At that point, McCallum decided to inject the defense theory of the case. "The whole case is about consent, your Honor. We admit our man entered the house, but it's our position the lady was not forcibly raped. It was consensual."

"You really think you can sell that?" probed Judge Steiner.

"Well, we're going to give it our best shot," replied McCallum.

"Alright, sounds pretty straight forward to me," said Judge Steiner indicating that their little discussion was over.

"Let's get on with voir dire and move this case along. I've got a very full calendar." And with that, all four men stood and the three attorneys exited the Judge's chambers while he slipped on his black robe — the vestments of infallibility, or so was the intended image.

In the courtroom, the attorneys studied the jury list which provided basic demographic information about each prospective juror.

"All rise, the Superior Court of the State of Washington in and for the County of Pierce is now in session, the Honorable Myron B. Steiner presiding," announced the bailiff.

As Judge Steiner ascended the bench, peering over his spectacles, he directed, "Please be seated. In the matter of State of Washington v. William Roundtree, are the parties ready?"

"Yes, your Honor," responded Cartwright.

"Yes, your Honor," replied Jamison.

"Ready to proceed with voir dire?" inquired the Judge.

"Yes, we are, your Honor," responded both attorneys.

"Then why don't both counsel swing your chairs around to this side of the table, face the gallery and prospective jurors and let's get started."

Both the prosecutor and defense attorneys dutifully complied rolling their swivel armchairs around to the other side of the table so they could face the jury pool seated in the gallery. The judge's assistant had already placed the prospective jurors in numerical order, 1-35, so the attorneys looking at their jury list could identify prospective jurors by name and number.

"We'll alternate voir dire questions, 20 minutes each side, beginning with you Mr. Cartwright," instructed Judge Steiner.

Frank Cartwright and Lloyd McCallum both understood the importance of this phase of the trial, though Brent Jamison was a little less tuned in. Lloyd took the opportunity again to remind Brent that there's only three times an attorney has the opportunity to address the jury directly — once during voir dire, then during opening statement, and finally, closing argument. Thus, an attorney must use these opportunities to maximum advantage. Frank

Cartwright's voir dire went smoothly as he subtly looked for anyone who might have a bias against police officers or the criminal justice system. Then it was Brent Jamison's turn. He too was not looking for objective jurors, but those who would be sympathetic, even if subconsciously, toward his client, who he wanted to portray as the victim of a closet vamp. Thus, his questions about whether any of the prospective jurors knew anyone who loved playing the martyr role. Or whether they or anyone they knew had ever been falsely accused.

Thus, back and forth the two attorneys went, questioning the prospective jurors until twelve men and women were seated in the jury box. It's actually a misnomer to call it "jury selection" since all the lawyers can do is try and get the worst jurors (worst from their perspective) removed, either for cause or through what's called pre-emptory challenges. Each side is usually given three "challenges" with which they can have a prospective juror excused for any reason or no reason at all. So having gone through that process, the twelve that survive represent the collective wisdom of the community — theoretically. But from each attorney's perspective, hopefully they represent the ones most sympathetic to their side. Just as Jamison thought, voir dire took all morning. So after lunch came opening statements.

"Ladies and gentlemen of the jury, I'll be brief," began Franklin Cartwright in a crisp polished manner. This case is a simple one. It's simple because we have undisputed forensic evidence found at the scene and we have a confession from the Defendant. He admits breaking and entering the victim's home late at night while her husband was gone and she was home alone with her two little children. He admits coming in through the rear sliding glass door and casing the place, even helping himself to some brownies sitting on the kitchen counter. He then walks down the hall toward the front door and picks up a family picture, staring at his would-be victims and leaving an identifying thumbprint on the glass. It was then one of the children woke her mother up complaining of a tummy ache, and in the course of their conversation, inadvertently disclosed to the defendant hiding downstairs, that her daddy wasn't home. Mr. Roundtree here," Cartwright gesturing toward Jamison's client with a look of utter contempt, "then snuck upstairs to the master bedroom where he literally pounced on his prey like an animal. She resisted until he choked her into submission, whereupon he raped her. In the process, he beat and bruised her requiring her to be hospitalized. Ladies and gentlemen of the jury, this is a heinous crime, and I am confident that upon hearing the evidence you will return a verdict of guilty. Thank you."

Lloyd didn't hear a word Cartwright said. He'd heard prosecutors' opening statements so many times he could practically recite them verbatim. His mind was somewhere in the future — immersed in his arson case.

Meanwhile, Brent Jamison sat in his chair not realizing how much Cartwright's brief but powerful opening would impact him too. It was now his opportunity however, to take over the director's job and sketch out the story he wanted the jury to accept.

"Ladies and gentlemen, motive and opportunity," he began, followed by a long awkward pause. He left the words hanging there in the air. Finally, Lloyd looked at Brent wondering if that was going to be the extent of his opening statement. Even the jury began to look a little uncomfortable, wondering if Brent had maybe forgotten what else he was supposed to say. Finally, Jamison repeated the same words,

"Motive and opportunity." Then he continued, "Those are words most often used by the prosecution to describe criminal behavior. A perpetrator must be motivated by some criminal intent, and when the opportunity presents itself to commit the crime, his intent is carried out. But remember what I asked you in voir dire?" queried Jamison, as he looked intently at each of the jurors. He paused, allowing them time to run a quick memory search and then provided the answer.

"How many of us know people who seem to love to play the martyr role? They're motivated by some distorted view of the world, or fantasy, if you will, and take advantage of opportunities to act out their little script to their own detriment. It's a sick little game that some people play. Some play it all the time, some occasionally, some maybe only once. We believe the evidence will show and you'll be persuaded that the alleged victim in this case was, in reality, acting out a dark little fantasy which, having done so, she had to explain by calling it a rape. As Mr. Cartwright said, my client was in the house that night and he did eat some brownies," said Jamison with a trace of a smile. "And," paused Brent, "he admits to having sex with the woman of the house. But, from the moment he got on the bed, what really happened between these two people differs dramatically from what Mr. Cartwright told you. To prove rape, the prosecution must show that intercourse occurred by forcible compulsion. If it was consensual, no rape. If the alleged victim decided to act out some secret little fantasy and then later thought better of it, no rape. We believe the evidence will show that the sex itself was indeed consensual, thus requiring you to find my client not guilty. Thank you."

Jamison briskly walked back to the defense table and glanced at Lloyd as he sat down. Lloyd nodded his approval. Jamison knew he was off to a good start.

"Please call your first witness, Mr. Cartwright," announced Judge Steiner.

"The prosecution would call Detective Mark Hammer," intoned Cartwright.

Detective Hammer who had been sitting in the back of the courtroom arose and made his way forward to the witness box. He was a lean man of average height and build with sharp features. His years in law enforcement had produced a street-wise skepticism combined with unwavering confidence in his own abilities as an investigator. Not only that, he had testified in criminal trials numerous times and was the consummate professional in the hands of a skilled prosecutor.

Just as Detective Hammer reached the witness chair, Judge Steiner directed, "Please raise your right hand. Do you swear that the testimony you give in this matter will be the truth, the whole truth, and nothing but the truth?"

"I do," replied Hammer.

"Please be seated," instructed the Judge. "Proceed, Mr. Cartwright."

"Thank you, your Honor. Would you please state your full name and business address."

"Mark Hammer, Detective, Sexual Assault Division, Pierce County Sheriff's Office, 930 Tacoma Avenue, Tacoma, Washington."

"Would you please describe your duties as a Detective in the Sexual Assault Division, Mr. Hammer."

"Yes sir, it's my job to investigate crimes of a sexual nature and report the results of my investigation to the prosecuting attorney's office."

"Do you have anything to do with the charges that may or may not result from your investigation, Mr. Hammer?"
"No sir, I don't. I simply gather the facts, perform a thorough investigation, and turn over my results to you folks."

"Do you have any kind of vested interest in what happens with the results of your investigation?"

"No, I try to remain as objective and impartial as I can. It's up to you, the prosecutor, to decide whether to file charges. That's not my job."

At that point Lloyd McCallum leaned over to Brent Jamison and whispered, "Objective and impartial? Right! These guys might as well be blood brothers."

"Alright, Mr. Hammer," continued Cartwright, "directing your attention to the matter at hand, did you have occasion to investigate a rape that occurred . . ."

"Objection," interjected Jamison, "Alleged rape, your Honor."

"Sustained," responded Judge Steiner.

"Alright, alleged rape," continued Cartwright.

"Yes I did," replied Hammer.

"Please describe for the jury how you conducted your investigation and summarize the results for us."

"Sure," began the Detective, "I was called in to investigate a reported rape a day or so after the uniforms had answered the 911 call."

"Why did you necessarily respond rather than someone else, Detective Hammer?" queried Cartwright.

"Well, I'm a specialist in rape cases and this one looked like it might need a little extra attention."

"Why's that?"

"Because of where it occurred and the circumstances. It happened in a pretty high-class neighborhood with no apparent evidence of breaking and entering or other criminal activity."

"Does it make a difference where a rape occurs?"

"Well, it could. We are obviously concerned about every sexual assault that happens on our watch, but when it happens in a high-end neighborhood, that tends to get people's attention because it's not the kind of activity we typically see in that kind of neighborhood."

"Did that change the way you conducted your investigation?" asked Cartwright

"No, we just tend to be a little more careful under those circumstances. That kind of criminal behavior is usually associated with certain areas of town. So when it leaks out to the suburbs, we want to know why."

Jamison was listening intently and taking notes furiously for his cross-examination of Detective Hammer.

"So is it fair to say you were extra careful in this case?"

asked Cartwright

"Objection, leading the witness," interrupted Jamison.

"Sustained," responded Judge Steiner.

"Did the fact, Detective Hammer, that this crime occurred in an area not typically known for these types of offenses prompt you to conduct your investigation any differently than usual?"

"Well, not really, but I was a little more conscientious because of where it happened. We know that the media typically makes a bigger deal out of things that happen in the more high-class neighborhoods. I guess everybody expects things like this to happen in the inner city."

"Very well, please continue Detective Hammer, and explain to the jury what you did."

At that point Detective Hammer repositioned himself in the witness chair slightly so he could look directly at the jury like he had been instructed to do by attorneys many times before. Eye to eye contact with the jury is supposed to increase the witness's credibility and impact.

"First," began the detective, "I gathered some basic information concerning the date, time, and location of the rape. I learned that there were two children in the house at the time but they were unharmed, at least physically."

"Objection," barked Jamison, "Detective Hammer is not a child psychologist or psychiatrist so he can't even imply that either of these children may have been harmed emotionally or psychologically as a result of this alleged rape."

"Sustained, but you don't have to make a mini speech," responded Judge Steiner.

Lloyd looked at Brent and smiled his approval thinking that for a novice, Brent was doing pretty darn good. By now Lloyd was paying closer attention — this case also happened in a high-end neighborhood? For the first time, he actually looked at Jamison's client, who hadn't said a word since entering the courtroom, and searched for a connection. Nothing came. Lloyd made it a deliberate practice to forget his criminal clients. More than once over the years he had run into former clients and had to admit that he couldn't remember them. He didn't remember Willie Roundtree either. Of course, Willie's previously boyish appearance had long since disappeared.

"Please go on," urged Cartwright.

"Well, after that I conducted a thorough inspection of the scene from the sliding glass door in the back, through the house and up the stairs to the master bedroom. On my way to the residence I had called for a finger print team who arrived shortly after I did and began to dust for prints everywhere. We didn't find very many, though we found a very distinct thumb print on a family photo in the hallway at the bottom of the stairs. In the master bedroom we found several hair samples which turned out to be those of the victim and the defendant."

"Can you be more precise, Detective Hammer? Besides the victim, whose hair was it?"

Detective Hammer then, right on cue, pointed directly at Jamison's client and said, in his best police officer's voice, "Mr. William Roundtree, seated there at that table."

"We also did a DNA analysis," continued Hammer, "which confirmed that the semen found on the bed was Mr. Roundtree's."

"Did you talk to the victim, Detective?" asked Cartwright.

"Yes, I did. I've talked to her several times, the first time being a day or so after the reported rape."

"What did she tell you?"

"Objection, hearsay," interjected Jamison.

"Sustained," responded Judge Steiner.

Cartwright wasn't quite prepared for this young upstart Jamison so he had to back up and get the evidence in another way. "Detective Hammer, did you make out a report contemporaneously with the statement given to you by the victim?"

"Yes sir, I did. I took careful notes and went right back to my office and typed it up the same day."

"Does that report represent your best recollection of the statements made by the victim, as well as an official government record kept in the regular course of your official duties?"

"Yes, it does," replied the detective.

"Then handing you what's been marked as state's Exhibit 1, can you identify that?"

"Yes I can. This is my initial report summarizing the information I obtained from the victim."

"Please share its contents with the jury."

Detective Hammer then perusing his report testified, "Ms. Val Sheppard was home alone with her two children and had gone to bed about 11:00 o'clock that night. She and her husband, who was out of town, had a brief phone conversation and she then went to sleep. About two or three hours later, she was awakened by her little girl who needed some motherly reassurance in the middle of the night. After going back to bed, but before she fell asleep again, the defendant appeared in her bedroom and literally pounced on her, placing his hand over mouth in an apparent effort to suffocate her."

"Objection," barked Jamison, "Speculation."

"Sustained," replied Judge Steiner.

"Please continue, Detective Hammer."

"The victim reported that the defendant then threatened her and, having subdued her, proceeded to rape her. In fact, he didn't just rape her, he put her in the hospital." Jamison thought about objecting, but he let it go figuring he could work this guy over on cross-examination.

"Could you be more specific, Detective Hammer?" prompted Cartwright.

"Well, the victim had various scratches and bruises on her and was pretty strung out emotionally."

"How do you know that?" asked Cartwright.

"Because when I visited the home, the injuries were still evident."

"Describe her physical appearance for the jury."

At that point, Lloyd leaned over to Brent and asked, "Do you see what's happening?"

"Yeah, he is trying to evoke sympathy."

"Well," began Hammer "she's an attractive woman in her early thirties, but I noticed some bruising on her arms. And she was still really frazzled and angry. So I had to kinda reassure her just to get her statement."

"And that's the statement you just shared with the jury?"

"That's right."

"So when was the next time you had an occasion to speak to Ms. Sheppard?"

"A few weeks later we rounded up the defendant and called Ms. Sheppard in to see if she could identify him in a line up. She scrutinized the five subjects very closely and picked out the defendant as her rapist. She was absolutely sure."

"What happened next?" prodded Cartwright.

"We arrested Mr. Roundtree here, read him his rights and held him for questioning."

"Who handled the interrogation?"

"I did," replied Detective Hammer.

"Please tell the jury how that went."

"Well, I started with the basics and asked him what he was doing the night this rape occurred. He was kind of evasive and said he was just out cruising around. I asked him where, and he said 'What's it to ya?' So I explained to Mr. Roundtree that he had been ID'd as a rapist. He denied it, of course, so I asked him if he would be willing to give us a sample to do a DNA analysis. He then asked if he should have a lawyer and I told him again he was entitled to one if he wanted, but if he didn't do it, he could just give us a sample and we'd eliminate him as a suspect. So he reluctantly agreed to give us a sample. We did the analysis and it came back a positive match with the evidence we collected at the scene."

"What evidence specifically?"

"The hair and semen."

"So the sample you got from Mr. Roundtree here matched the DNA found at the scene of the crime?"

"That's right, without question."

"Did you later confront Mr. Roundtree with the results of your DNA test?"

"I sure did and he still denied it."

"Thank you, Detective Hammer. I don't have any more questions."

Brent Jamison sat motionless for a moment, trying to heighten the jury's anticipation of his cross-examination. Slowly he stood up and looking directly at Detective Hammer, began, "Let's start where you left off, Detective. You say the hair and semen found at the scene matched my client's and after you confronted him with that evidence he still denied it. What exactly did he deny, Detective?"

"He denied that he did it."

"He denied that he raped her?"

"That's right."

"Did he deny that he was in the house that night?"

"No."

"Did he try to argue that the samples you found didn't match his?"

"No, how could he?"

"In fact, he admitted being there, didn't he, Detective?"

"Yes, eventually."

"So what he denied was actually raping her, isn't that right?"

Detective Hammer paused, "If you say so."

Jamison knew he was beginning to get under his skin already. "Now you weren't there when this alleged rape occurred, were you Detective?"

"No, of course not," replied Hammer.

"So you don't have any first hand knowledge of what actually happened between these people, do you?"

"Well, if you're asking me if I actually saw it, no, but I've got a credible victim's statement including a positive ID, and I observed the bruises and scratches on the victim myself."

"So what we really have here is a woman with scratches and bruises on her arms saying that she was raped."

"Look," replied Hammer somewhat agitated, "we know your guy was in the house, we know he was in the bedroom, and we have a beat up woman swearing that he raped her. You put it all together and it's a slam dunk, counsel."

"I don't think so," challenged Jamison. "It looks to me more like a he said-she said situation, Detective."

"Objection," barked Cartwright. "Is that a question, your Honor?"

"Sustained," droned Judge Steiner. "Ask your next question, Mr. Jamison."

"How long does it take someone to consent to sexual relations, Detective Hammer?"

"Well, not very long I suppose."

"Not very long indeed," mimicked Jamison.

"Would a simple yes do?"

"I suppose."

"How about a nod of the head? Could that constitute consent?"

"Maybe."

"How long before the sex act actually occurs, must consent be given?"

"I couldn't tell you," replied Hammer, anticipating the obvious.

"What if two people are wrestling around and playing pretty rough with one another and the woman agrees to sexual relations just before it happens. Would that constitute consent, Detective?"

"I suppose it could, unless the victim is under duress like she was in this case," replied Detective Hammer, trying his best to derail Jamison's line of questioning.

"But again, that depends entirely upon the victim's version of what happened, right?" pressed Jamison. "If my client says there was no threat or other intimidation and the alleged victim says there was, then we're right back to the he said-she said situation, aren't we Detective?"

Somewhat chagrinned, Detective Hammer agreed, "I suppose that's true. But I'll tell you what, when you put it all together with the fact that Ms. Sheppard was beaten up, I'll take her word that she didn't consent to it."

"Are you familiar with sadomasochism?" questioned Jamison.

Lloyd sat at the defense table wondering where Jamison got such machismo.

"Yes, of course," replied Hammer.

"Isn't it true that some people enjoy getting roughed up, shall we say, during sex?"

"Yes," admitted Hammer.

"In fact, some people enjoy more than just getting roughed up. They actually beat one another don't they, Detective?"

"Some do, I suppose."

"How well do you personally know the alleged victim in this case?"

"I know her fairly well. I visited with her several times, both in her home and downtown, and view her as a respectable, credible person."

Jamison was irritated with Hammer's gratuitous evaluation of Ms. Sheppard.

"You really don't know her at all, do you, Detective Hammer," challenged Jamison. "Have you ever known a closet sadomasochist?"

"What do you mean, closet?" questioned Hammer.

"I think you know what I mean, someone who has sadomasochistic ideation but keeps it hidden."

"I suppose there are those types of people," admitted Hammer.

"Objection," interjected Cartwright, "this is really getting far a field, your Honor. Everybody knows there are all kinds of weirdoes out there. This case is about Val Sheppard, so could we ask counsel to stick to the matter at hand?"

"Sustained," intoned the Judge. "Stay on course, Mr. Jamison."

"Yes, your Honor," responded Jamison dutifully.

"Anyway, Detective Hammer," continued Brent. "You really don't know whether or not Ms. Sheppard harbors any of these aberrant fantasies, do you?"

"Well, I am not a psychologist, if that's what you mean, but I've dealt with a lot of rape victims over the years and Ms. Sheppard is about as straight as they come."

"Have you ever been surprised to find out later that someone had some closet fetish that you didn't know about?"

"Of course, everybody has seen things pop up later in people that they didn't know were there. But that certainly doesn't mean . . ."

Jamison cut Hammer off, "Please just answer the question, Detective. So you have had that experience, haven't you?"

"Yes. So what? This case is about Val Sheppard and I just don't think she's some closet weirdo."

"But you really don't know for a fact, do you?" pressed Jamison.

Detective Hammer just sat in the witness chair with a little smirk on his face but didn't answer.

Jamison produced his own little smirk in return, then said, "I don't believe I have any more questions for this witness," and sat down, feeling triumphant.

Frank Cartwright thought about asking a few follow up questions on redirect but decided to let it go, thinking his detective held up pretty well under Jamison's cross examination. He already knew the case revolved around the issue of consent. He would rely on Ms. Sheppard to carry the day.

"Call your next witness, Mr. Cartwright," instructed Judge Steiner.

"Yes, your Honor. The prosecution would call Ms. Val Sheppard."

At that point the bailiff stepped out into the hallway and motioned for Valorie to come in. As she walked through the large double doors at the rear of the courtroom, she was stunning — dressed in a deep red suit featuring a knee length skirt, black nylons and high heels, with her light brown hair gently flowing down around her shoulders, and a face that belonged on the cover of Cosmopolitan. She was an exquisite specimen of female beauty.

As she strode toward the front of the courtroom, the attorneys didn't turn to look, but every one of the jurors was transfixed. As she walked past the lawyers sitting at their respective tables, only Cartwright glanced up from the papers in front of him. Jamison and McCallum were both focused on one last look at their preparation for the prosecution's star witness. They made sure they had copies of all of the police reports, statements, and the pathologist's report at their fingertips.

Judge Steiner instructed Valorie to raise her right hand and directed his standard question to the witness. "Do you swear that the testimony you give in this matter will be the truth, the whole truth, and nothing but the truth?"

"I do," responded Valorie.

"Please be seated. You may proceed, Mr. Cartwright," instructed the Judge.

At that moment Lloyd looked up as an expression of utter shock and disbelief began to disfigure his face. His eyebrows spontaneously flexed downward as his eyes grew narrow, squinting at what couldn't possibly be true. Simultaneously Valorie scanned the courtroom, her eyes eventually locking on her husband seated at the defense table. "What was he doing sitting at the defense table," she wondered. She continued to stare at Lloyd with a confused look on her face.

CHAPTER 11

Conflict of Interest

McCallum quickly leaned over and pulled on Jamison's shoulder, "What the hell is this? Why is she on the witness stand?"

Jamison was surprised by his boss's sudden, agitated query. "That's Val Sheppard," responded Jamison, "the alleged victim."

"What do you mean? That's my wife sitting there!"

"What?" replied Jamison incredulously.

Willie Roundtree just sat there taking it all in as he listened to his attorneys trying to figure out what was truly an unanticipated surprise.

"What are we going to do, Mr. McCallum?" questioned Jamison.

Lloyd just sat there paralyzed, staring at his wife. Why did she use the name Val Sheppard? What the heck was going on?

Meanwhile, Franklin Cartwright stood up to approach the witness and begin his direct examination. "Would you please state your name and address for the record."

"Yes, Val Sheppard, and my address is 1436 Briarwood Lane, Lakewood, Washington."

McCallum could not believe what he was hearing. That was his wife, Valorie McCallum sitting there reciting his home address, but using the name Val Sheppard. His mind began to spin. Suddenly he couldn't stand it any longer and jumped up, "May we have a recess your Honor?"

"Why, your Honor? We're just getting started with this witness," complained Cartwright.

"Indeed," replied the Judge. "Why a recess right now, Mr. McCallum?"

"May I approach the bench, your Honor?"
Without answering, the Judge nodded, motioning the attorneys forward. Once there, Lloyd simply blurted out in a half-whisper half-gasp, "That's my wife sitting there on the witness stand, your Honor."

"What?" responded the Judge. "What is going on here? How can you be defending a case in which your wife is the victim?"

"I don't know, your Honor. I don't know how this happened. I think we need a conference in chambers."

"Indeed we do," replied Judge Steiner, who, lifting his head announced, "We'll be at recess until further notice. The jury will be excused for the time being. Bailiff, take the jury into the jury room for a break and instruct the witness to wait out in the hall."

"Of course, your Honor," replied the bailiff, as the Judge and all three attorneys trooped into the Judge's chambers.

As soon as Jamison cleared the door, Judge Steiner ordered, "Shut the door and sit down. Somebody better explain to me what's going on here."

"This is a rape trial, your Honor, and I'm trying to question the prosecution's chief witness, the victim in this case," offered Cartwright.

"That seems pretty obvious, Frank," snapped the Judge, "but clearly there is more going on here than meets the eye. Mr. McCallum?" questioned Judge Steiner, looking at Lloyd for an explanation.

Again, he just sat there trying to collect himself.

"I don't know your Honor. Mr. Jamison here of our office worked this case up pro bono and I provided some guidance here and there on trial technique. And then I come to court and see my wife taking the stand as the prosecution's complaining witness, introducing herself as someone else."

"So was this woman, whoever she is, raped or not?" probed the Judge.

"Yes, she was," insisted Cartwright. "That's why we're here. We have the evidence, and we think we can get a conviction."

"Wait a minute," interjected Lloyd, "there's been a terrible mistake here. I don't know how this happened your Honor, but that Val Sheppard sitting out there is my wife, Valorie McCallum."

"Well, that's real interesting," offered Cartwright, "and here you are defending the guy that raped her. No supper for you tonight."

Ignoring Cartwright's sarcastic attempt at humor, McCallum continued, "Your Honor, my wife was raped several months ago, but she pretty much dealt with the investigation herself. I wasn't involved, nor have I been involved in this case. Brent here has done all the work up. So I don't know how we came to represent the guy who apparently raped my wife. I need to talk to her.

May I be excused, your Honor?"

Before Judge Steiner could react, Cartwright practically shouted, "No way, your Honor, she is the prosecution's prime witness in a rape trial and I don't want her having ex-parte contact with one of the defense attorneys in the middle of her testimony!"

"Take a hike Cartwright," replied McCallum. "She's my wife. I'll talk to her if I want to."

"Wait just a minute," intervened Judge Steiner. "She may be your wife, but she is also the prosecution's witness whose testimony has been interrupted at the behest of defense counsel. Moreover, Mr. McCallum," continued the Judge, "you have a serious conflict of interest, which obviously compromises your ability to represent your client."

"I need to talk to my wife," repeated McCallum.

"I object," responded Cartwright. "I don't know how he got into this mess, but it's not my problem. We have a rape trial going here and my prime witness is sitting out there waiting to testify," urged Cartwright.

By this time Judge Steiner was sitting in his chair behind his large desk with his arms folded, just shaking his head. "How in the world could something like this happen?" he questioned rhetorically.

"She may be your wife, Mr. McCallum," began Judge Steiner, "but you're going to have to talk to her on your own time. She's been sworn in as a witness in a felony jury trial and I'm going to allow her to testify without your talking to her privately before-hand. Frankly, I think you need to be more concerned about your client.

This obvious conflict of interest situation in which you find yourself, Mr. McCallum, could result in your disbarment. Do you understand that?"

Lloyd looked at the Judge with a blank stare. Once again he was painfully reminded of how difficult life had become since Valorie was raped. Not only had his serene family life been shattered, but now the career he'd worked so hard to build was threatened as well.

"Then may I have a moment to confer with my client?" Lloyd finally asked.

"I think you better," agreed the Judge. "You can use the small conference room just outside the courtroom."

"Thank you, your Honor. I'll be back as soon as possible. Let's go Brent," instructed McCallum.

All three attorneys then stood up and stiffly walked out of the Judge's chambers into the courtroom, which was empty except for William Roundtree, who was still sitting where Lloyd and Brent had left him — at the defense table. "Come on, we need to talk," said McCallum as he walked past their client.

As they opened the double doors at the rear of the courtroom, headed toward the conference room, Lloyd caught sight of his wife, Valorie. Instinctively he started toward her, at which time Brent grabbed his arm as a gentle reminder of the Judge's instructions not to have ex-parte contact with the prosecution's witness. Valorie nevertheless started toward her husband, "Lloyd, what's going on? Why are you going in there with that guy?"

Lloyd just held up his hand to stop his wife's approach saying simply, "I'm sorry, I can't talk to you right now," as he ducked into the small conference room with Brent and Willie Roundtree.

"Have a seat, Mr. Roundtree," ordered McCallum. "I know you. I represented you once before on a rape charge," said Lloyd with disdain. Then, looking at Jamison with eyes aflame, he yelled, "How did this happen? Didn't anybody do a conflict of interest search?"

"Yes sir," replied Brent. "I'm sure that was done when we first got the case and opened our file."

"Well, didn't anybody notice that my wife was the victim?"

"Well no, Mr. McCallum. Val Sheppard was ID'd as the victim on everything we saw."

"Well, you interviewed her didn't you? Didn't you connect the dots?" demanded Lloyd.

"No sir, I've never met your wife."

"So where'd the name Val Sheppard come from? Why

would my wife change her name?" pressed Lloyd.

Both attorneys lapsed into silence, confused and bewildered by this inexplicable series of events. Finally, Lloyd said to Brent, "We've got to get out of this. We can't continue to represent this guy," referring to their client as though he weren't even there.

Willie Roundtree, who had been sitting quietly, enjoying watching the two attorneys squirm, then spoke up.

"Wait a minute, if you two bail out, what happens to me?"

"We don't have any choice," McCallum shot back.

"You're our client and the victim's my wife — an obvious conflict of interest, which makes it impossible for us to represent you."

"Why can't Jamison here continue on as my lawyer? He seems to know what he's doing," replied Roundtree.

"He works for me," said McCallum. "The rules of ethics prohibit attorneys from representing someone under circumstances that would undermine the lawyer's ability to zealously protect his client's interests."

"So this whole conflict of interest thing is suppose to protect me against you guys screwing me, right?"

"That's it in a nutshell," agreed McCallum.

"So what if I don't care? What if I want you to represent me anyway?"

"You'd have to sign a waiver of conflict of interest," offered Jamison.

"There is still no way," objected McCallum. "Do you understand that's my wife out there saying you raped her? I should be trying to castrate you instead of defend you," said McCallum with teeth clenched, bending over practically nose-to-nose with Roundtree.

Willie Roundtree just sat there staring back at McCallum, unflinching and unintimidated. His devious mind then hit upon a way to play both ends against the middle. "You know this thing about consent," he began, looking first at McCallum then Jamison. "That's my defense, right? Well, it's the truth. I hate to say it, man, but your wife wanted it."

"You miserable liar. I oughta take your head off right now," threatened McCallum.

"Hey, I'm just telling it like it is, man. She kind of fought it at first but that didn't last long."

Jamison was dumb-founded. Here his client was explaining to his boss how he did his wife and how she let him. That's how Jamison figured it happened and how he'd built his defense, but to think that his boss's wife was the one who'd engineered this whole thing blew his mind.

Lloyd couldn't stand it. "Are you telling me that my wife consented to sexual relations with you?"

At that point, Roundtree knew he had him.

"That's right," he said, "this whole thing about consent, that Mr. Jamison here told the jury, is the truth. I want you guys to represent me. I'll sign a waiver or whatever it's called. I don't want to start all over with some other lawyer."

Lloyd looked at Jamison and just shook his head incredulously, wondering how this happened and how it was all going to play out. His mind began to call up the many times Valorie withdrew from him and seemed distant. He recalled their attempts to make love — unsuccessfully.

What was really going on? Was it her encounter with Roundtree that changed her, or had she begun to pull away before then? The more Lloyd thought about it the more he believed his wife may be using what happened as an excuse to keep him at arm's length. But why? They'd always had such a close relationship. Could there be some truth to the defense Brent had put together? Finally recovering from his private musings, McCallum announced, "Let's go talk to the Judge."

Lloyd threw open the door to the conference room

and marched out seemingly in slow motion as he glanced toward Valorie, still waiting in the hallway. Their eyes met momentarily, Valorie's questioning, Lloyd's resolute. He had made a decision. The three men walked into the courtroom. Lloyd instructed his client to take a seat at the defense table and asked the bailiff to notify the Judge that he was prepared to address the court on the record.

In a few minutes Judge Steiner appeared from back stage — his chambers — and ascended the bench. "You wish to put something on the record, Mr. McCallum?" questioned the Judge.

"Yes, your Honor, I do. I've had an opportunity to confer with my client regarding this matter and he is prepared to execute a waiver of conflict of interest and has requested that we continue to represent him as defense counsel."

"I don't think I've ever seen a situation quite like this," remarked the Judge. "We have a defense attorney representing the man accused of raping his wife. I thought I'd seen everything. Mr. Roundtree, are you prepared to waive this egregious conflict of interest and have Mr. McCallum and Mr. Jamison here continue to represent you in this trial?" Without allowing Roundtree to respond, Judge Steiner continued, "You have every reason to be concerned about your attorneys' loyalties and you need to give this matter serious consideration. It's your life and liberty that's at stake here."

"Yes sir," replied Roundtree as he stood up, sensing an opportunity to curry the Judge's favor with a show of proper decorum. "I'm not worried about it, your Honor," continued Roundtree. "Me and my lawyers had a chance to talk about it and I still want them to represent me. I agree to waive this conflict of interest thing or whatever it's called."

Judge Steiner then leaning forward, his eyes fixed firmly on William Roundtree, explained, "Do you realize that your lawyer is married to the victim — the woman you're accused of raping? Mr. McCallum here could pull the plug on you and send you down the river for a long, long time."

"Don't matter, your Honor," replied Roundtree. "I've been telling the truth through this whole thing and my lawyers know that." Roundtree was deliberately messing with McCallum's mind, reinforcing his own consent defense.

"Mr. McCallum?" queried Judge Steiner, in a final attempt to let Lloyd McCallum out of the case.

"As I explained to my client," began Lloyd, "the conflict of interest rules are designed to protect the client against actual or potential divided loyalties on the part of the attorney. If the client, after full disclosure, is willing to waive the conflict, then I guess we're prepared to proceed, your Honor."

Judge Steiner could still hardly believe it. "What about your wife, Mr. McCallum?"

Pausing for a moment, Lloyd looked at the Judge with the look of a man resigned to his fate and said simply, "A trial is designed to ferret out the truth, your Honor, whatever that truth may turn out to be."

"Alright then," said Judge Steiner. "Mr. Cartwright, do you have anything to offer on the matter?"

Franklin Cartwright, slowly standing up, cautiously offered, "Well, your honor, I've never seen anything like this either. But I have two concerns. First, this conflict of interest could actually work to the benefit of the defendant. His lawyer knows more about the victim than anybody and could conceivably use that knowledge unfairly. Secondly, if this doesn't turn out the way Mr. Roundtree here would like it to, he could still cry foul and maybe claim a mistrial."

"Your concerns are noted," replied Judge Steiner, "but we're going to go ahead with this circus. We're into it this far, we might as well finish it. Are you prepared to proceed with direct examination of your witness, Mr. Cartwright?"

"Yes I am, your Honor."

"Then let's proceed. Bailiff, bring the jury back in and go get Ms. Shepard or whoever she is, and bring her back in here."

"Yes, your Honor," replied the bailiff, as he went to retrieve the jury, who knew nothing about the legal maneuvering that had occurred in their absence.

At the bailiff's invitation, Valorie then entered the courtroom and, obviously distressed, retook the witness stand.

Cartwright sensing her uncertainty and vulnerability, decided to capitalize on it for the benefit of the jury. He began, "I apologize for the interruption in your testimony, Ms. Shepard. I'm sure this is uncomfortable for you. Are you feeling a little anxious?"

"Yes," replied Valorie, rather weakly. "I don't really understand these things and I just want it all to be over with."

"I'll try to make it as painless as possible for you," reassured Cartwright, knowing full well there was no way he could do that. He wanted Valorie to exhibit the full spectrum of her agony for the jury. He decided to focus a laser right on her anxiety.

"Did you feel anxious the night you were raped?"
Before Jamison could object, Valorie shot back, "I was terrified."

"Now, Ms. Shepard," continued Cartwright, "we've heard an account of what happened from Detective Hammer, but the jury I'm sure wants to hear it in your own words. So, if you would start at the beginning and tell us what happened to you."

"Well," began Valorie slowly, "my husband," Valorie paused and looked over at Lloyd, still not fully grasping why he was sitting next to her attacker. "My husband," she began again, "was out of town on a business trip and it was just me and the kids home that night."

"What are your children's names, Ms. Shepard?"

"Gerald and Emily."

"How old are they?"

"Now ten and eight. We'd finished our usual dinner routine and the kids went to bed around 8:30 and I went to bed a couple of hours later."

"Before your encounter with Mr. Roundtree here, did you have contact with anybody else that evening?" questioned Cartwright.

"No, other than I got a phone call from my husband just before going to sleep."

"What time was that?"

"Probably around 11:00 p.m."

"How long did the phone call last?"

"Maybe ten minutes."

"What did you talk about?"

"Just the events of the day and when he was coming home."

And when was that?"

"The next day sometime. He was only going to be gone overnight."

"Please go ahead and tell us what happened after that, Ms. Shepard."

Valorie bowed her head in an effort to gather strength. The jury waited in anticipation. Lloyd and Brent focused their full attention on the witness. This time however, Lloyd listened with the critical ears of a lawyer rather than the sympathetic ears of a husband.

"Well, after my husband called, I lay in bed for a while just thinking and then drifted off to sleep. I didn't hear or see anything until about two o'clock when I was awakened by our daughter, Emily. She had a stomach ache, so I got up to give her a dose of Pepto-Bismal, after which we both went back to bed."

"Your daughter went back to her own room?" probed Cartwright.

"Yes, and I lay back down on my bed. I was just drifting back to sleep when I sensed a presence or something in the room and rolled over to look toward the door as a man literally pounced on me."

"What was your first reaction?" questioned Cartwright.

"I screamed, but I didn't hear anything. I think he already had his hand over my mouth before I could get it out. All I really remember is him on top of me holding me down. His hands were gripping my head and his face was right next to mine."

"So did you get a clear look at him?"

"I sure did."

"Do you see him in the courtroom?"

"Yes, that's him right there," said Valorie pointing at Willie Roundtree.

"Do you remember if he said anything, Ms. Shepard?"

"He said some things. I said some things. But what I really remember is him saying something like, I'll do you and your little girl both, cuz hubby's not home and we can do whatever we please. I don't know how he knew my husband wasn't home, but I didn't want him to hurt my kids."

"So what did you do, Ms. Shepard?"

"Well, I reluctantly went along with it."

"Only after he threatened you and your daughter?"

"That's correct."

"Ms. Shepard, tell the jury what he did to you," instructed Cartwright.

Valorie again bowed her head and paused, "Well," she began slowly, "he basically spread my legs with his knees, undid his pants and . . ." her voice trailed off into silence. The entire courtroom was completely quiet and all eyes were on Valorie. Everyone in the courtroom just sat there, mesmerized by her quiet dignity in the face of excruciating pain.

Cartwright hesitated asking his next question, savoring the moment and allowing the jury to imagine the worst. Finally, he broke the silence with, "Your medical records indicate you were hospitalized with various injuries. Can you describe what those injuries were and how you got them?"

"I had scratches and bruises in the pelvic area. The doctors told me I had some internal injuries. I had some scratches and bruises on my arms. My face was swollen."

"How did you sustain bruises on your arms, Ms. Shepard? Did your attacker strike you?"

"I don't believe so, but he was gripping my upper arms really tight and then all of a sudden he rolled over on his back and pulled me on top of him."

"So how long did that go on?" probed Cartwright.

"I don't remember. It seemed like a long time."

"So how long did you remain in the hospital, Ms. Shepard?"

"It was just over night."

"What was your condition upon discharge from the hospital?"

"Physically, I guess there wasn't much more they could do for me. The tests they ran on me came back negative so they let me go home. The scratches and bruises healed pretty quickly, but emotionally I'm still pretty much a wreck." Cartwright then abruptly concluded his questioning with,

"Thank you, Ms. Shepard. No more questions."
Lloyd McCallum and Brent Jamison sat there momentarily immobilized by Valorie's first-hand account of what she described under oath as rape. Jamison started to get up to begin his cross-examination of the witness but Lloyd reached over and pulled him back down in his chair. "I'll do it," he told Jamison.

Before he could stand up however, Willie Roundtree confirmed Lloyd's worst fears. "She not only wanted it, she liked it," whispered Roundtree. Lloyd just stared at him as he stood up to approach his wife on the witness stand.

CHAPTER 12

Cross Examination

McCallum maneuvered his way around the defense table with his eyes fixed on Valorie, but stopped, right in front of the jury box. He was on now. It was show time. He brought all of his training and skills to bear on the moment. Valerie sat motionless, staring at her husband as he assumed the attack position. Lloyd looked at the jury, silently inviting them to participate in the spectacle that was about to take place.

Lloyd's mind raced, this was his opportunity to get at the truth. How many times does a suspicious husband have the opportunity to question a possibly unfaithful wife under oath in public? Those seemingly innocent text messages Valorie exchanged with her old boyfriend after they were married now loomed large in his mind. Did something happen then that's been hidden all this time? Did something happen between Roundtree and Valorie that she wasn't willing to admit? — even to herself?

"You said your name was Val, is that right?" began Lloyd.

"Yes," answered Valorie quickly.

"Val Sheppard, is that how you identified yourself?"

"Yes," came the reply.

"Would you agree that a name is something personal?"

"Yes."

"Your name is who you are. It tells everybody who they're dealing with, right?"

"Yes, I guess that's right," replied Valorie.

"Do you know what's required to legally change one's name?"

"No."

"Do you know why people have to go through the court system to change their name?"

"Not really."

"It's so people can't defraud the rest of the world. So they can't pretend to be somebody they aren't," Lloyd inserted acidly. "Have you ever legally changed your name?"

"No."

"But Val Sheppard, the name by which you identified yourself here in court today, is not your real name, is it?" pressed Lloyd with an obvious edge in his voice.

"No, it's not," replied Valorie.

Lloyd paused, allowing the admitted discrepancy to hang in the air for the jury. "So what is your real name? Who are you?" demanded Lloyd, more as a husband than a lawyer.

Valorie just stared at Lloyd, her bewilderment turning to anger. "My real name is Valorie McCallum," she declared.

"And I think you know that," she added.

Ignoring the post script, Lloyd pursued his interrogation. "So you lied to this court and to this jury about your identity?"

"No, I was embarrassed."

"People eventually are when they lie, Ms. McCallum," interjected Lloyd.

"That's not what I mean," reacted Valorie. "I mean I was so embarrassed about being raped I didn't want it to become common knowledge. I didn't want the whole town to know it was me. So when the police came to the house, I decided to change my name."

"So you lied to the police, just like you lied here today."

"No, I didn't," replied Valorie, becoming more angry. "I didn't want to believe something so terrible had happened to me. Maybe it was a defense mechanism. If I changed my name, maybe it didn't really happen to me. It was just some fictitious person's nightmare."

Lloyd couldn't resist this opportunity, "Maybe you're right, maybe this whole thing is fictitious, Ms. McCallum."

"How dare you," growled Valorie, her eyes focused on Lloyd like a laser.

"Well," continued Lloyd, "you fabricated your identity, maybe you fabricated the rest of your story as well."

Valorie bristled as Lloyd stepped to within arms length of her.

"In fact, calling a consensual tryst a rape provides a neat little cover-up for you, doesn't it?"

"You son-of-a...," hissed Valorie.

"Isn't it true, Ms. McCallum, that you and your husband were having marital problems around the time of this so-called rape?"

"We're sure having marital problems now!"

"Indeed," rejoined Lloyd. "Would you describe the nature of your marital problems?"

"Objection," interjected Cartwright, "What does this have to do with this rape case, your Honor?"

Without waiting for the Judge's ruling, McCallum replied, "I'll tie it together, your Honor."

"I hope so, counsel," cautioned Judge Steiner.

"Have you ever entertained fantasies of rough sex with someone other than your husband, Ms. McCallum?"

"I suppose everybody has fantasies of one kind or

another."

"Indeed," rejoined Lloyd. "In your testimony on direct examination you described how the events occurred the night in question. You described rolling over on top of Mr. Roundtree and remaining in that position, on top of him, for a long time. Do you remember that testimony, Ms. McCallum?"

"I said he pulled me over on top of him," snapped Valorie.

"Yes, I know that's what you said, but you also said you stayed on top of him a long time. Is that how you got the scratches and bruises in your pelvic area, Ms. McCallum?"

"Objection," interjected Cartwright. "Her testimony was she was on top for what *seemed* like a long time, your Honor."

"Sustained."

Lloyd was sure the jury at that point didn't care about such delicate distinctions.

"To answer your question," snarled Valorie, "I don't know when I suffered the injuries to my pelvic area."

"Once you were on top, you could have freed yourself and run. Why didn't you?"

"How could I? Gerald and Emily were in the house," yelled Valorie, suddenly personalizing her children.

"So you're saying that for their sake you stayed in the bedroom? Or were you just living out some raucous fantasy?" pressed Lloyd sarcastically.

Valorie closed her eyes and just shook her head in silence. Figuratively her husband was sticking a knife in her and twisting it. Suddenly she burst into tears and screamed at her husband.

"I'm telling you the truth, that animal raped me! It was never a consensual thing. If I could have stopped it, I would have. Sure, everybody has marital problems once in awhile and everybody has fantasies of one kind or another, but this wasn't one of mine and if I could relive that night over again, that man would not be any part of it. He has caused me and my family untold misery." Valorie just sat in the witness chair shaking.

"Well, I guess that's the issue, isn't it Ms. McCallum," Lloyd concluded. "Did he cause all this misery, or did you yourself cause it?" Lloyd paused, then with deliberate disdain in his voice as much for his own satisfaction as for the jury, concluded, "He may have started it, but you sure as hell finished it."

"Objection," snapped Cartwright.

"Sustained. This isn't closing argument, counsel," cautioned Judge Steiner.

Lloyd slowly walked across the courtroom back to his seat at the defense table.   As he sat down, Willie Roundtree started to congratulate his lawyer on a job well done. But before he could get the words out of his mouth, Lloyd snapped, "Shut up." Brent Jamison sat motionless, barely able to grasp what he had just witnessed.

Finally, Judge Steiner barked, "Redirect, Mr. Cartwright?"

Cartwright stood, realizing his prime witness had just taken a severe beating. "As the court can appreciate," he began, "this has been very difficult for," and then he hesitated, "Ms. McCallum. May I suggest that since it's almost quitting time anyway, we just call it a day and I'll defer any re-direct testimony until tomorrow."

"Counsel?" queried Judge Steiner, looking at Brent and Lloyd.

"No objection, your Honor," responded Jamison.
As the Judge stood up, the baliff instructed, "All rise, court will be at recess."

As the jury filed out of the courtroom, Valorie stepped down from the witness stand and hurriedly made her way out of the courtroom without looking at or speaking to anyone.

The officer on duty took Willie Roundtree back into custody and led him out of the courtroom, leaving just the three attorneys alone.

Franklin Cartwright was the first to speak, "Now that's dedication," he said sarcastically. "A defense lawyer willing to sacrifice his wife for his client. I guess winning really is everything to you guys," he concluded.

"I think you better shut your mouth and get out of here," growled Lloyd.

"Or what? You'll viciously cross examine me?" chided Cartwright as he walked out of the courtroom shaking his head.

Meanwhile, Brent Jamison tried to maintain his composure as he stuffed papers into his briefcase.

"Well, what do you think?" queried Lloyd, trying to ease the tension in the air.

"I don't know what to think," admitted Brent. "Law school didn't prepare me for this sort of thing."

"So do you think it was consensual or not?" questioned Lloyd, more as a husband than a lawyer.

"Well, I don't think it necessarily started out that way, but as you brought out on cross, it may have ended up that way," replied Brent. "And all we need is reasonable doubt, right?" Young Jamison then began to fully realize the intense conflict inherent in the situation.

If the sex was consensual, his boss's wife was guilty — of infidelity. If it wasn't consensual, then his client was guilty — of rape. What an impossible situation. "At least he wasn't married to the alleged victim," he thought.

"Let's get out of here," announced Lloyd as he finally stood up from the defense table and strode out of the courtroom. For the first time in his career, he felt disoriented and battered. Before today, he'd always walked out of the courtroom feeling confident and in control. Today was very different. It felt like his whole life was unraveling before his eyes.

"What just happened?" he wondered. He could barely think straight. His finely honed analytical skills escaped him totally. Lloyd McCallum walked through the court house almost in a daze. As he and Brent Jamison parted ways, Brent tried to ask his mentor what he should focus on to prepare for tomorrow. Lloyd just waved him off and kept walking. Finally, just before reaching the outer doors of the court house, Lloyd turned around and yelled at Brent, "Consent. It's all about consent." That much Brent knew. Indeed, that was the whole basis for his defense. He was hoping for something a little more specific.

As Lloyd walked toward his car, his mind, by force of habit, turned to thoughts of home. Ordinarily, those thoughts would include visions of a warm reception and hugs and kisses from the three most important people in his life — Valorie and little Gerald and Emily. Today however, it was a long and tedious ride home. Lloyd actually felt sick to his stomach. As he drove up to his beautiful house, it no longer felt like home. He just couldn't get it out of his mind — the mental image of his wife in their bedroom on top of Willy Roundtree. Did she really do it to protect the children? Was it coerced? Or did it become the consensual re-enactment of a hidden fantasy? How well did he really know his wife?

Questions kept swirling around in Lloyd's head until he felt like he would explode. Would he ever really know the truth?

Lloyd walked into the house cautiously, feeling almost like a visitor in his own home. He passed through the entry way toward the kitchen where he would normally hear and smell dinner in the making. Today was different. There was nothing. Not a sound. No one. Valorie and the children were no where to be seen. It occurred to Lloyd to look in the garage to see if Valorie's car was there. Sure enough, there it was as per usual. Finding no sign of anyone downstairs, Lloyd decided to check upstairs. As he slowly climbed the stairs, he cautiously called out "Valorie?" Nothing, not a sound. He reached the top of the stairs and headed down the hall toward the bedroom, the door to which was closed. Slowly he turned the knob and opened the door. There she was, sitting in the overstuffed chair in the corner, knees pulled up, arms wrapped around her legs, and face down. She sat there, motionless, still wearing the dark pantsuit she'd worn to court. Lloyd felt paralyzed. The last words he had accusingly hurled at his wife in court were, "He may have started it, but you sure as hell finished it." Lloyd knew he'd done some serious damage — to someone he'd vowed to love and to cherish. His doubts about that night continued to haunt him unmercifully. Lloyd knew he had to try and talk to her, this time as his wife and not as the prosecution's prime witness. He slowly and silently moved across the room toward her. She remained curled up in the fetal position, seemingly unaware of his presence. As he approached her, Lloyd reached out and touched his wife on the shoulder. The reaction was instantaneous.

Recoiling like a disturbed rattler, "How dare you touch me?" she hissed at him. Her eyes were aflame with rage. The entire room was suddenly supercharged with emotion.

"I had no idea," offered Lloyd. "How was I to know the Val Shepard in Brent's case was actually you? I was caught totally off guard."

"It didn't seem to matter to you anyway," replied Valorie with tears washing black mascara streaks down her cheeks. "I told you in court why I used a different name. You didn't care. I told you how it happened too. He made me do it. He threatened the kids."

Valorie abruptly stood up. She and Lloyd were now face to face. "Isn't it enough that this ugly thing happened to me?" she demanded with her head cocked to one side. "Would you rather he'd done something to the kids too? Then would you believe me?" she yelled in her husband's face. "How dare you," she snarled with utter contempt. "You can't even imagine what this has done to me. Every time I think about it I feel like I need to take a shower, but it won't wash off. It never goes away. The stench of the whole ordeal makes me sick. I see it. I hear it. I feel it. I smell it. I almost taste it, everyday!" Valorie screamed, her face contorted and red with anger. Lloyd was stunned. He'd never seen his wife so filled with rage.

"And you, you son-of-a — ," continued Valorie. "You don't even believe me. You think I was acting out some fantasy — isn't that what you called it? The one person who is supposed to protect me, doesn't. Where were you that night? Why weren't you home? Why weren't you here with us? Oh no, the great Lloyd McCallum, famous criminal defense lawyer, was off chasing after whatever so you could get some other loser off. But that's not enough, you have to show the whole world that you're the best lawyer in town, even if it means slicing and dicing your own wife! But you're no better than the filthy scum you represent." And with that Valorie suddenly slapped her husband across the face as hard as she could. "Now get out!" Valorie screamed at him. Lloyd was physically shaken by the force of the blow as a large red welt began to appear on the side of his face.

"Please, we have to get to the bottom of this," Lloyd insisted.

"Shut up!" Valorie replied. "I don't ever want to see you again. Get out!" she screamed again, raising both fists above her head.

Lloyd raised his arms to block the blows as Valorie struck at his head. Again and again she pounded downward as Lloyd backpedaled across the room, his back now against the wall. Finally, Valorie's right fist found its mark, crashing down and striking Lloyd just above the left eye. Lloyd instinctively reacted, pushing Valorie away with both hands. She came right back at him, raking her fingernails across his chest, tearing open his shirt. This time Lloyd grabbed her, wrapping his arms around her and holding her tight. Valorie twisted and squirmed trying to break free. Unable to do so, she became more frantic and tried to bite Lloyd. Lloyd shoved her away so hard Valorie went sprawling on the bedroom floor.

"What's wrong with you?" he yelled. "Are you crazy?"

"Maybe I am," screamed Valorie, still on the floor.

"Just get out of here!"

"You can sure as hell fight when you want to, can't you?" Lloyd declared.

"What's that suppose to mean?" demanded Valorie.

"It means you could have stopped it that night if you really wanted to," Lloyd yelled back at her.

"Right, it all comes back to that, doesn't it?" said Valorie.

"Yeah, it does all come back to that," agreed Lloyd.

"You had sex with that black SOB right here in this room. How am I supposed to forget that?!"

"*How am I supposed to forget that?!*" screamed Valorie. "We didn't just have sex, he raped me. Can't you get that through your thick head?!"

"Yeah yeah, so you say, as you're riding him hard."

"Get out!" Valorie screamed again as she struggled to her feet. For a moment they stood there glaring at each other, feeling utter contempt for one another. Finally, Lloyd just shook his head, turned and stepped out of the room as Valorie slammed the door behind him.

As Lloyd stood in the hallway gasping, he could hear his wife weeping through the closed door. What had he done? Would they ever be able to trust one another again? Lloyd decided to just lay low downstairs until Valorie left to pick up the kids at the babysitter's. Within a half-hour she was gone. Lloyd then went upstairs and gathered up a couple days worth of clothes and headed to a motel for the night. He wondered when he would see his kids again.

*   *   *

The next morning Lloyd McCallum and Brent Jamison arrived at the courthouse at about the same time. As the two men walked through the multi-level concrete parking garage toward the entrance to the main lobby, neither said a word. Brent reached the door first and held it open for Lloyd. As he passed in front of him, Brent posed a question, "Any last minute instructions?"

Lloyd ignored his young pupil, apparently viewing the question as an annoying distraction. Brent hurried to catch up as Lloyd marched through the spacious marble floor lobby toward the elevator that would take them to the courtroom. Not a word was spoken on the way up. As the two men reached the heavy wooden doors to Judge Steiner's courtroom, Lloyd flung them open and continued his march to defense counsel's table, discovering that he was the first to arrive. He preferred it that way. He could mentally arrange the arena before the arrival of his adversary. Brent followed Lloyd to the large table and immediately began removing notes and papers from his briefcase and arranging them in front of him. Finally, Lloyd looked directly at Brent, acknowledging him for the first time and answered his question. "We're going to put our client on the stand," he said.

Brent was taken aback. "Why?" he blurted out. "We've got this case won, why risk it? Cartwright hasn't proven his case beyond a reasonable doubt, so why expose our client to potentially damaging cross-examination?"

"Because I want to hear what he has to say, that's why," yelled Lloyd. "I don't know, I may end up cross-examining him myself."

Brent just stared at his boss, then looking down at the table, began to shake his head incredulously. This was too much. He wondered if Lloyd was losing it — if this unbelievable conflict of interest was literally blowing his mind.

"Well," Brent finally said, "We've got the victim's re-direct and re-cross before we get to Willy."

Lloyd paused, and staring straight ahead replied simply, "Alleged victim."

About that time Franklin Cartwright walked into the courtroom and took his place at the prosecution's table. He looked over at Lloyd and Brent, "Morning gentlemen. You sleep okay last night, McCallum?" jabbed Cartwright, picking up right where he left off the day before.

Maintaining his forward stare, Lloyd replied, "Like a baby, thank you very much."

Cartwright chuckled to himself, glad that McCallum's marriage was probably in shambles. Noticing the remains of the red welt still on Lloyd's face, Cartwright couldn't resist,

"Your rosey-red cheek becomes you," he said, as though it were some sort of accessory. Lloyd just ignored the sarcastic insult as an attempt to take him out of his game.

For the next several minutes, the three lawyers sat in silence waiting for the Judge. At nine o'clock sharp, the bailiff and court reporter emerged from the Judge's chambers to announce, "All rise, the Superior Court of the State of Washington in and for the County of Pierce is now in session. The Honorable Myron B. Steiner presiding." The Judge immediately appeared, ascended the bench and without really looking at anyone, intoned, "Morning gentlemen, please be seated."

"Morning your Honor," dutifully replied Cartwright.

"Good morning your Honor," responded Jamison, while Lloyd remained silent.

"Are there any matters to be brought before the court

before we bring in the jury?" questioned the Judge.

"I don't believe so," replied Cartwright.

"Nothing at this time," rejoined Jamison.

"Then bring in the jury and let's get started."

"Mr. Cartwright, is your witness ready for re-direct?" Before he could answer, the twelve member jury began filing into their seats with all eyes in the courtroom looking on. That was always a somewhat anxious moment, watching the jury, trying to divine their feelings about the case. What would it take to persuade them?

"Good morning ladies and gentlemen of the jury," greeted Judge Steiner.

"Morning," came the muffled reply as several jurors nodded their acknowledgement. Just ordinary middle class citizens drawn from the community, doing their duty, but anxious to get back to their own lives.

The next player to enter the arena was Willie Roundtree, dressed to look like a member of the local chamber of commerce – dark suit and tie, obviously not a look he was accustomed to, but he did his best to wear his costume convincingly. It was a hard sell though, his little jive walk giving him away.

Suddenly, the rear doors of the courtroom swung open and in walked Valorie — the picture of grace and sophistication, wearing a knee length dark blue sleeveless dress, which accentuated her perfect figure. She strode down the center aisle of the courtroom like it was a runway, with the eyes of every member of the jury fixed on her. It was as though she glided toward them in slow motion. Indeed, she had the appearance of a consummate professional, her every move designed to persuade her observers that she was authentic, that her story was the truth, the whole truth, and nothing but the truth. As she ascended the witness stand and slid her perfect form into the seat, she slowly turned her head and looked directly at all the jurors with an angelic expression of innocence. Lloyd was irritated by what he viewed as an obvious attempt to sway the jury with her feminine seductiveness.

"Remember, you're still under oath," instructed Judge Steiner. "You may proceed, Mr. Cartwright."

"Thank you, your Honor," replied Cartwright as he got up to direct his star performer. He knew what every good trial lawyer knows — that a trial is a theatrical performance. The witnesses are the actors, the lawyers are the directors, and the jury is the audience. The plot is always the same — good guys vs. bad guys. Somebody did somebody wrong and they were gonna have to pay. And how you weave the plot makes all the difference in the world.

"So," began Cartwright, "did you get a good night's sleep last night, Ms. McCallum?" trying to put his witness at ease while conveying her humanness to the jury.

"Not really," replied Valorie. "I'm afraid I never sleep very well since the night I met Mr. Roundtree there," nodding her head toward the defense table.

"Well, hopefully something can be done about that," rejoined Cartwright.

"Objection, your Honor," snapped Lloyd.

"Sustained," said Judge Steiner. "We don't need you editorializing, Mr. Cartwright."

"Alright, Ms. McCallum, I'd like to follow up on some of Mr. McCallum's questions from yesterday." As he heard the words come out of his mouth, Cartwright realized that he'd used the names of both the witness and the defense attorney in the same sentence and those names were identical — McCallum. Suddenly, he looked at the jury like the cat that ate the canary and wondered if they had put two and two together. He wondered if they realized that the witness and the defense attorney were related, not just related, but very closely related. "Oh well," he thought, "we're into it now and there's no turning back."

"Let's go back to the night you met Mr. Roundtree, then. Defense counsel (better to use the generic title, he thought) asked you among other things, how you sustained the injuries you did. Do you remember that?"

"Yes, I do."

"You described how the Defendant, from his position on top of you, grabbed you by the arms and rolled over on his back, pulling you over on top of him. Do you remember that?"

"Yes," said Valorie softly.

"Did you feel pain in your arms as he did that?" probed Cartwright.

"Yes, I did. I could feel his fingernails dig into my skin."

"So now you're on top of him. Did he let go of your arms?"

"No, he didn't. He just held me there on top of him," Valorie said, her voice trailing off.

"So he had a hold of you and you couldn't get away."

"Objection, leading," interjected Lloyd.

"Sustained," intoned the Judge.

Ignoring the momentary interruption, Cartwright continued.

"Did you try to get away?"

"No. As I said before, the kids were in the house and I wasn't going to just run away and leave them."

"Is that the only reason you remained in the bedroom with Mr. Roundtree here?" asked Cartwright, gesturing toward the defendant.

"Yes," replied Valorie simply.

"No further questions," concluded Cartwright, glancing at the jury as he sat down, hoping he had adequately rehabilitated his witness.

"Re-cross, Mr. McCallum," invited Judge Steiner.

"Thank you, your Honor, I do have a few more questions for this witness," said Lloyd as he stood up, his eyes fixed on Valorie. He walked slowly toward her, across the "stage" in front of the "audience" mentally baring his teeth for the kill.

"Ms. McCallum — that is your name, right? We established that yesterday, didn't we," Lloyd began, wanting to again call attention to the fact that Valorie had lied about her identity.

"You said that your kids were in the house the night of your alleged attack?"

Valorie cocked her head slightly as she looked at Lloyd, realizing that he still doubted her story. "There's nothing alleged about it," she corrected. "And yes, the kids were in the house. He threatened them if I didn't cooperate and go along," insisted Valorie.

Ignoring her postscript, Lloyd went right to the heart of his client's defense. "Right, so you did cooperate didn't you!" thrust Lloyd as he raised both hands and scratched quotation marks in the air. "And you cooperated for a long time too, didn't you. Wasn't that your testimony?"

"Objection, mischaracterizes the testimony, your Honor," inserted Cartwright.

Before the judge could rule, Valorie shot back, "I said, as I'm sure you recall, that it seemed like a long time."

"Because it was a long time, wasn't it," bellowed Lloyd, his face turning red. His heart was pounding now. He was going to get at the truth one way or another. He had to know what was going on in his wife's mind as she was having sex with his client.

"So how long were you on top of Mr. Roundtree?"

"I don't know, until he was done, I guess," replied Volorie almost nonchalantly.

"Until he was done? Or until you were done, Ms. McCallum?" questioned Lloyd acidly.

Meanwhile, Brent Jamison sat at the defense table absolutely astonished. He couldn't believe his eyes and ears.

Here was his hero tearing his own wife apart on the witness stand. Was Lloyd so driven that he couldn't restrain himself even at the expense of his own family? How does stuff like this happen? This was obviously why the conflict of interest rules were established — not just to protect the client, but to protect the lawyer too. It was impossible for Lloyd to separate his feelings as a husband from his duties as a lawyer. He was doing irreparable damage to both, and it didn't matter that the client had signed a waiver of conflict of interest. But the carnage had to be played out to its unholy conclusion.

"I guess until we were both done. Is that what you want to hear?" demanded Valorie.

"I just want the truth!" shouted Lloyd, as though there were no one else present but him and his wife. "Just tell me," he pleaded.

Now Valorie was in complete control. "Just tell me," begged her husband. What she said next would make it or break it — for the prosecution's case as well as her marriage. If she stuck to her story that it was rape, i.e. non-consensual, the prosecution wins and hopefully her husband is satisfied. If she even implies that it was at any time consensual, Roundtree gets off and her marriage is probably over. Talk about a conflict of interest, seems like everybody's got some kind of conflict of interest in this case.

Valorie paused for what seemed like forever. She thought about her marriage and what it used to be like before all this happened. She thought it was strong. She thought her husband trusted her and would stand by her no matter what. But he doubted her. Questioned her honesty. Verbally assaulted her, and even physically assaulted her just last night. Would their marriage ever be the same now? She felt angry at him. Angry that he doubted her. Angry that he questioned her, especially under these circumstances — in open court.

She was repulsed by Willie Roundtree, but what a

wild ride that night — it was almost like she had been given license to let her inhibitions go. But how could she live with herself if she admitted to such an egregious breakdown in the heat of the moment? She had always been so strong. Now she was under tremendous pressure again. Oh well, she thought, what's the use? Everything's gone. Her virtue. Her marriage. Her self-image.

"Ms. McCallum?" Judge Steiner finally said.

"Sorry, your Honor," said Valorie.

"Do you need a minute to compose yourself?" offered the judge.

"No, I think I've made up my mind, or rather I'm ready to proceed."

Valorie looked directly at Lloyd with a resigned expression — resigned to the fact that life as she had known it was never going to be the same.

"To answer your question, Mr. McCallum," intentionally using her husband's sir name in addressing him, "When the defendant was done, I wasn't done. So we kept at it until I was."

The entire court room was absolutely still. Not a sound. No one moved. Everybody just stared at Valorie, as though she had completely disrobed in front of the whole world. There she sat, in the witness chair, exposed to all humanity, having admitted that what started out as a rape ended up just like the defense said all along — a consensual tryst in the middle of the night when no one was around.

Lloyd stood there, just a few feet from the witness stand, motionless, stricken to the very core. His worst fears had just been confirmed. His wife had been unfaithful. She had consented to it, albeit not at first. He couldn't believe it. The expression on his face turned from one of pleading to one of victory, mixed with disgust. He finally got her to admit it. But it was a hollow victory. He'd gotten at the truth, or so he thought, but at what price?

Even Judge Steiner sat in his elevated chair stunned. He'd never seen anything like it.

"Anything further for this witness, or any other witnesses, Mr. Cartwright?"

"No, your Honor. That concludes the prosecution's case in chief."

"You may step down, Ms. McCallum."

Valorie simply walked out of the courtroom, without looking at anyone. But the eyes of every juror were fixed on her all the way out. Many of them just looked down after she left, almost in a reverent moment of silence, realizing that she had publicly sacrificed everything that day — right in front of them.

"Alright, is the defense ready to proceed, Mr. McCallum?"

"Well, your Honor, we were going to call Mr. Roundtree to testify, but in light of what we just heard, we'll forego that and advise the court that the defense rests."

"Very well, gentlemen, are we ready for closing argument, then submit the case to the jury?"

Both attorneys agreed that was the next step. Judge Steiner then laboriously read the jury instructions to the jury, outlining the legal requirements to prove the crime of rape:

"A person is guilty of rape in the first degree when such person engages in sexual intercourse with another person by forcible compulsion..." Both attorneys thereupon waived closing argument.

"Does the jury have any questions before you are dismissed to deliberate?"

"No," came the collective response.

"You are therefore dismissed to begin your deliberations. Bailiff, please usher the jurors into the jury room."

This is always the part of the trial that is the most nerve racking for the lawyers. They put everything they've got into a case and then turn it over to twelve strangers to decide their fate, or rather their client's fate. Waiting was always the worst part. Lloyd and Brent decided to go get something to eat. Before leaving however, they gave their cell phone numbers to the bailiff so he could call them as soon as the jury reached a verdict. They had scarcely finished their lunch at the deli across the street when Brent's phone rang. He answered. The jury had reached a verdict already. As they made their way back to the courthouse and up to the courtroom, both men remained silent. This was a no-win situation for Lloyd. Even if he won, he had already lost.

Franklin Cartwright was getting to the courtroom about the same time as Lloyd and Brent. Lloyd didn't even look at Cartwright, but Brent's eyes met his opponent's for just a moment — long enough for Cartwright to convey a certain amount of sympathy for Lloyd, when ordinarily he felt nothing but contempt for defense lawyers, especially when he lost to them. Cartwright slowed his approach just enough to let his opponents enter the courtroom first, after which all three men sat down at their respective tables. The bailiff buzzed the judge on the intercom and advised that all three lawyers had returned whereupon he appeared from chambers and took his place on the bench.

"Everybody here?" confirmed Judge Steiner. "Then call in the jury."

Dutifully the bailiff retrieved the jury and led them into the jury box where they all stood until invited to sit by Judge Steiner.

"Please be seated. Has the jury reached a verdict?"

"Yes, we have," replied the foreman, a vanilla type guy who was non-threatening, which is probably why he was elected foreman.

"Would you please hand the verdict form to the bailiff," instructed the judge, whereupon the bailiff handed it to the judge who read it without any noticeable reaction.

Handing it back to the bailiff who then returned it to the foreman, the judge instructed him to read the jury's verdict while instructing the defendant to rise.

"In the matter of the State of Washington vs. William Roundtree, as to the charge of rape in the first degree, we the jury find the defendant: NOT GUILTY."

Cartwright was the first to react. Looking down at the table he just shook his head ever so slightly. What appeared to be a slam dunk turned out to be a carnival ride. "What a circus," he thought. An obvious criminal goes free because some frustrated house wife, in the middle of the crime, decides to become a willing accomplice.

Lloyd stood next to his client just staring at the foreman with a dazed look on his face. Normally of course, he would feel a sense of professional pride in a job well done. He would even privately gloat over having beaten his adversary in the arena, in front of everybody. Then he would stride out of courtroom the victor — it was all about winning. But not this time. He had proven his client innocent, but at the same time, proven his wife guilty.

As the realization of it all sunk in, Lloyd slowly sat back down in silence, not hearing the judge politely dismiss the jury or advise his client that he was free to go. Not hearing anything but the final words of his wife as she testified in open court, "I wasn't done, so we kept at it until I was." The image of that scene played over and over in his mind. He felt a stabbing pain in his heart. He was paralyzed. The silence of the moment was then broken with Roundtree talking to his lawyer. His mouth moved but Lloyd couldn't hear him. Roundtree raised his voice. Finally, Lloyd comprehended what was being said to him.

"Thanks, dude. You saved my life — again! I can't believe it. Twice you got me off. We oughta go into business together. I do 'em and you get me off. Such a deal," laughed Roundtree.

Lloyd abruptly stood up so he was nose to nose with Roundtree.

"Shut your foul mouth, you filthy piece of crap." Roundtree just stared back at Lloyd without flinching, knowing he was a free man — at the expense of his lawyer and his lawyer's wife. "It doesn't get much better than that," he thought. He was able to have his way with a beautiful woman and her husband is the one who set him free to do it again. Wow! What good fortune! A criminal's dream come true. "So maybe you better just get the hell out of here while you're still in one piece," continued Lloyd.

"Whoa," mocked Roundtree as he took a step back. "No hard feelings, counselor." He paused, sizing up Lloyd. "I know you want your money, and I'm gonna pay ya ... someday," he said as he did his little jive walk out of the court room, chuckling and shaking his head all the way. Roundtree knew full well that no amount of money would ever make up for what this trial cost his lawyer, and payment of anything would be like thirty pieces of silver — to a Judas husband. "My oh my," he thought. This couldn't have turned out any better if he'd planned it. Meanwhile, Lloyd was left to pick up the pieces of his life, if that was possible.

Brent didn't dare say a word. At last, Lloyd simply commanded, "Let's go," as he started out of the court room, with very different feelings this time. Lloyd didn't go home this time either. How could he? His home had been destroyed in court that day. He decided he'd spend the weekend at a motel. He couldn't imagine what it would be like to see Valorie. Who was she? Who was he? Could he ever forgive her for her egregious lapse of integrity? Could she ever forgive him for making a public spectacle of it? He was exhausted in every way imaginable. All he wanted to do was crash and sink into oblivion.

CHAPTER 13

Forced Sabbatical

Monday morning found Lloyd McCallum at his desk working — as usual. But it was anything but usual. He'd spent a fitful weekend alone at a motel, completely numb. How could such a perfect life come crashing down so quickly? Everything he had worked so hard for was suddenly gone. How was he ever going to recover from such a devastating loss? So he dove into his work, or tried to. He decided to call a meeting of his staff and try and get his bearings. What was the status of all the other matters he'd been working on before the excruciating blood-letting he'd just been through? He would never think of trials the same again. They were not games of cat and mouse. They were not plays with actors trying to sway an audience. They were not gladiator spectacles where only the strong survive. They were in fact very personal confrontations where real people often had everything at stake in a grueling winner take all ordeal. People's lives and fortunes were on the line and now Lloyd McCallum understood that in a way he never did before. There's no way to describe the feelings associated with losing

— not just losing, but losing everything — even sometimes when you "win."

"Sally," Lloyd summoned, pressing the button on his intercom, "would you and Brent gather up your lists and come in here for a meeting?"

"Sure, be right there, Mr. McCallum," replied Sally dutifully. A few minutes later Lloyd's loyal secretary and associate appeared at his door and waited to be invited in and take a seat. Even after several years of working together, they didn't take their relationship with their boss for granted. Lloyd tried to be business-like.

"Alright, where are we?" he questioned.

"Well," began Sally, "you have three trials scheduled over the next six weeks, basically back to back."

"What are they?" demanded Lloyd.

"Well, there's the Malone matter first up — armed robbery. Then there's Patterson — vehicular homicide. And then Goldstein – serial arson."

Lloyd sat there trying to absorb the mental onslaught — what it means to take on the defense of people whose life and liberty are at stake. It is an awesome responsibility. It requires someone who is totally committed to our system of justice. Someone like Lloyd McCallum, or at least someone like Lloyd McCallum used to be. He had been changed — irreversibly.

"What do we have left to do on Malone?" questioned Lloyd.

"Not much," replied Brent, "we're pretty much ready to go, just have to finalize our proposed jury instructions. Our witnesses are ready and subpoenas have gone out."

"Alright," said Lloyd. "Malone gets under way when? — on Wednesday?"

"Yes," replied Sally.

"And we'll be ready," assured Lloyd, as much for himself as his staff. "Let's spend today and tomorrow finalizing our prep for Wednesday and knock 'em dead." Sally and Brent glanced at each other hoping Lloyd's confident manner was genuine. The next two days were however, unsettling. Lloyd was not himself. For the first time in his career, he could not focus. He could not zero in on the pressure points in the case. He could not muster the mental edge necessary to walk into court and throw down the gauntlet. Brent could see it and worried about it. He wanted to help, so he approached Lloyd.

"Mr. McCallum, would you let me do this one? I know it's kind of a dicey armed robbery case, but I think I've got a good handle on it and can do it. Besides, that way you could take a little time off and . . ."

"And what?" interrupted Lloyd, scowling at Brent.

"And recover — from what you've just been through. It's gotta be unbelievably painful," said Brent, shaking his head.

"You don't even know the half of it," replied Lloyd.

"But I'm okay. I've been through a lot of battles and I'll weather this one too."

"Okay," said Brent, somewhat skeptical but realizing he wasn't going to talk his boss out of plowing through the task at hand, whatever it was. "You still want me to assist?"
"Yes I do, so make sure you have the trial notebook ready and we'll meet early and run through it before heading down town."

That in itself was a change Brent noticed. Lloyd never waited until the day of trial to go through the trial notebook. That was too much like shooting from the hip and Lloyd was renown for his thorough preparation before trial. He was already showing the effects of his own ordeal.

Nevertheless, the next morning the two lawyers met at the office, ran through their outline for trial and headed to the court house. It was business as usual. People coming and going, with the gallery full of prospective jurors waiting for voir dire — the tedious process of jury selection. The prosecutor was someone unfamiliar to Brent but Lloyd knew him, and more than likely, his strengths and weaknesses too. He had always made it a point to know his adversary. Soon the judge, a woman in her mid-forties and formerly with one of the big firms down town, called the case of State of Washington vs. Jacob Malone. She wasn't one of Lloyd's favorite judges. The big firms always seemed to have their fingers in the pie, making sure their people got the judicial appointments. It was all about connections and status in big city firms, the senior partners viewing themselves as wheeler-dealers, tight with the political types.

"Counsel ready in the matter of Washington vs. Malone?" queried the judge.

"Ready, your Honor," replied the attorneys almost in unison.

"You may proceed with voir dire," instructed the judge.

"Each of you has twenty minutes, alternating back and forth until we have a jury. Please keep it moving, gentlemen."

Jury selection went without a hitch, Lloyd and Brent feeling satisfied with the panel they ended up with. As the trial unfolded however, it was obvious Lloyd was not himself. Numerous times when Brent thought an objection to the prosecutor's questions would have been proper, Lloyd remained seated. Brent was sure Lloyd hadn't missed it, but he was zoned out. It was like he was on overload and didn't even know it. Signals were getting through but there was no processing of information. Finally, Brent basically took over with Lloyd's acquiescence as the trial stretched over several days. Jacob Malone was well represented, just not by Lloyd McCallum.

Back at the office, rumors began to circulate that Lloyd wasn't up to par. He didn't have that swagger and quick retort any more. But there was something simmering just under the surface that boiled over on more than one occasion. Finally, something needed to be done. Lloyd's mentor and friend, Gerald Everett, called him in for a heart to heart in his spacious corner office overlooking Commencement Bay.

"How's it going, Lloyd?" Mr. Everett asked in his usual easy manner.

"Things are fine," replied Lloyd rather stiffly as his eyes drifted toward the window.

Not to be taken lightly, Everett got right to it. "They don't seem fine."

Lloyd jerked his head back peering at his senior partner with a look of vailed hostility. He knew his friend only had his best interests at heart, but he still resented the intrusion.

"Well, they are fine," insisted Lloyd.

"You should know that I got a call from Judge Morgan, a courtesy call, because I knew her father back in the day," offered Everett. "She said you were off your game in her court the other day and just wanted to let me know so I could intervene if necessary. Were you off your game?"

Lloyd paused, "Maybe a little," he admitted.

"Maybe a little?" repeated Everett. "What the hell does that mean? You know as well as anybody that all it takes is a little to make all the difference in the world!"

Lloyd sat there stunned. He'd never been talked to like that before.

"Do you know what a major claim of malpractice would do to this firm?" demanded Everett. "Do you know what 'ineffective assistance of counsel' means?"

Lloyd's mentor was talking to him like a junior associate and pulling no punches.

"Ineffective assistance of counsel means your representation fell below the constitutionally required standard of lawyering necessary to protect people accused of crimes in our society."

"I know that," offered Lloyd.

"I know you know that," shot back Everett. "And I know you're one of the best trial lawyers in town. But if you're in need of our lawyer assistance program, then get help."

Lloyd knew what that meant. That was a program for lawyers who were having major problems with some sort of addiction or disability. Those were lawyers who were a liability to themselves and their clients, and thus to their partners, and Gerald Everett was not one to work all his life just to have some rising star burn out and come crashing down in his lap.

"I know you've been through a terrible ordeal recently with your family and all, and I sympathize, but I hope you can appreciate our position here," said Everett. He then paused, "We're lawyers," he said with pride. "We're warriors. If we can't do our job, if we can't protect the people, we're all vulnerable!"

Lloyd always understood that, but now he was being treated like a wounded warrior — someone who couldn't be trusted to carry his share of the weight in the on-going battle over civil rights. And of course, there was the matter of money. Law firms are like any other business — they're in business to make money. And whether it was the threat of a malpractice suit or simply loss of profits due to lack of productivity, it was the same — less money. So Lloyd knew his boss wasn't only concerned about protecting civil rights, he was also concerned about the bottom line.

"I'm going to suggest you take some time off and collect yourself," Everett finally said. "As you know, we have a sabbatical program and you're a prime candidate. You've earned it, so take as much time as you need, up to twelve months if need be. We've got the resources to cover it, so don't worry about it."

Lloyd wondered deep down if he'd have a job when

he got back, but it didn't sound like he had much choice.

"Alright, if you think that's the best thing for all concerned," agreed Lloyd, not wanting to antagonize the situation any further. He couldn't help but wonder though, if back to back marginal performances were what really earned him his "sabbatical." Oh well, he thought, he'd always landed on his feet. That was something he'd learned to do back in the Army — as a result of his Special Forces training. You do what you have to do. At least now he could focus on trying to repair his marriage, if that was possible. He decided to dismantle his office before he left that day. He figured Brent Jamison would probably use his office until he got back, assuming he came back. Why did it feel like he was being fired? It seemed like Lloyd McCallum's life was over in more ways than one. Right in the middle of a very promising career, he was out of work, or rather on involuntary "sabbatical." It felt weird to be putting away personal things, like pictures of his family, for an extended period of time, maybe forever.

CHAPTER 14

True Confession

Meanwhile, what was going on with Valorie? Lloyd hadn't even seen her for over two weeks, having decided to rent a motel room until he could sort things out. But his trial schedule didn't allow much time to sort anything out. He'd finished the Roundtree trial and went right into the Malone trial with hardly a break. He had no idea where things stood with his wife after their horrendous confrontation in court. He knew he had to contact her. What would he say? What would she say? Lloyd decided he would go home rather than back to the motel room, and see what happened.

It seemed like a very long drive this time. Everything in Lloyd's life had basically taken a one-eighty in a just a few short weeks. What would the kids' reaction be? Had Valorie poisoned them against him? Would any of them even want to see or talk to him? The world around Lloyd became a blur as he drove through the city. There was nothingness all around him. He was empty inside. A stupor overcame him as he cruised along, oblivious to his surroundings, until the blaring of a car horn jerked him back to reality and a red light stared him in the face. He stomped on his breaks barely avoiding a broad-side collision as a big SUV whizzed by in front of him.

"That's all I need," he thought, a major accident on top of everything else. He sat there in his shiny beamer, hands gripping the wheel, staring straight ahead. "Maybe that was a way out," he mused. Maybe pulling out in front of a semi would solve a lot of problems.

Finally, he arrived. There it was — his house, his beautiful, spacious house in the suburbs. It seemed surreal that he was actually there, sitting in front of his home again. He noticed the professionally manicured lawn and shrubbery. He looked up and down the street. Nothing had changed. All the neighbor's homes looked the same. On the outside everything looked perfect. "It was late afternoon, so the kids should be home from school," Lloyd thought. He could hardly move. He hadn't felt so unsure of himself since . . . he couldn't remember when. He pulled his keys out of the ignition and looked at them to make sure he still had a key to the house. Of course he did, but he couldn't remember until he actually looked at the wad of keys in his hand. Slowly he got out of the car and walked up to the front door. He felt like he should knock first, even though it was his own home. He reached out hesitatingly and tried the door. It opened easily which surprised Lloyd since Valorie always made sure the doors were locked after that fateful night.

Once inside, Lloyd could hear familiar sounds coming from the kitchen and family room. He walked quietly through the house toward the kitchen, suddenly appearing before his wife and children — to the surprise of all of them including Lloyd himself. The instant Valorie and the kids saw him enter the room everything came to an immediate halt. They all just stared at each other without saying a word. Lloyd felt paralyzed. His heart pounded. It suddenly seemed hot in the room. Valorie stood on the other side of the kitchen in front of the stove, motionless, holding a paring knife in her hand. The kids then suddenly jumped up and ran over to their dad whom they hadn't seen for weeks.

"Daddy," yelled Emily, as she hugged Lloyd, followed by her brother Gerald wrapping himself around Lloyd's waist.

"Hi guys," he said, reaching down to cuddle them in his arms. "How ya doing? I've missed you."

"We missed you too," said Emily. "Where have you been?"

"Just been working," reassured Lloyd, glancing at Valorie, who hadn't moved. "Okay if daddy eats dinner with you guys tonight?" asked Lloyd, more to his wife than the kids.

"Yeah, yeah," replied both Emily and Gerald excitedly.

"Do you think it would be okay with Mom?" prompted Lloyd.

"Yes, daddy," assured Emily, a little confused by her father's question and completely oblivious to the horrendous trauma both her parents had recently experienced.

Lloyd looked again at Valorie for some signal. A look of disgust covered her face as she turned her eyes aside and shook her head ever so slightly. Lloyd didn't know if that meant "no" or if it was just part of her expression of disgust.

"Why don't you ask Mom if it'd be okay if I ate with you guys tonight," prompted Lloyd, knowing how to manipulate the situation.

"Please, Mom, please," responded Emily taking her cue and willing to beg if necessary to have her dad home for a while.

Valorie hesitated for what seemed like a long time, her expression of disgust turning to sternness. Finally relenting, she said, "Okay, he can stay — for dinner," meaning dinner only.

Final preparations having been made and Valorie having put down the knife, the family sat down to eat together for the first time since mom and dad had gone after each other in court. The conversation was dominated by the kids, who were non-stop chatter, leaving no opportunity for any communication between Lloyd and Valorie, not that there would be any real communication between them with the children present anyway. Lloyd hung around after dinner to help clean up and tuck the children in bed — a precious routine he sorely missed. He was glad Valorie had reluctantly agreed to let him stay long enough to do that. But he was hoping for more — an opportunity to talk to his wife before she consulted a divorce lawyer. At the same time, he'd already thought about it himself, so he couldn't fault her for doing so. "At least they should try to talk before getting a divorce," he thought.

He waited downstairs in the living room for Valorie to come down. Eventually she did appear in the spacious, elegantly decorated room, wearing her robe, ready to go to bed.

"Can we talk?" Lloyd asked cautiously.

"About what?" snapped Valorie. "You got what you wanted — dinner with the kids. Now get out, I want to go to bed."

"Do you want a divorce?" asked Lloyd, getting right to the heart of the matter.

"Yes, I do," declared Valorie.

Lloyd didn't respond. The D word. He didn't think he'd ever hear it in reference to his own marriage. "How could this have happened," he wondered. He leaves town for one night and his wife does a one-eighty on him. It still seemed incredible. Was she really capable of such a thing? Her admission in open court still echoed in his head.

"Alright," he finally conceded. "Do you want to try to work through it cooperatively, or do you want to get your own lawyer?"

"Cooperatively?" Valorie mocked. "Do you think I

would trust you for one minute after what you did to me in court?"

"After what I did to you? What about what you did to me? You want to talk about trust?! I leave town for one night and you turn into some sort of dog in heat! What happened to you?!" yelled Lloyd.

"Nothing happened to me!" mocked Valorie. "I'm the same person! I've just been brutalized — twice! Once by that scum client of yours and once by you, my own husband!" shouted Valorie, becoming red in the face. "So don't talk to me about trust!"

"What was I supposed to do?!" demanded Lloyd.

"You could've trusted me — that I was telling you the truth! But you didn't, did you. You went into lawyer mode and believed your client over your own wife! So you bet — trust in this marriage is gone!"

"You're damn right it's gone! You weren't brutalized — you agreed to it! You admitted it in open court!"

"There you go again sounding like a stinkin' lawyer! What happened to you?! You used to be compassionate and understanding. I used to be married to a human being. Now I'm married to some kind of law dog, a robot who filters everything through some legal matrix!"

"And it's a good thing — you probably never would've admitted it otherwise."

"That's right! Because there was nothing to admit!" yelled Valorie with absolute conviction.

Valorie just stood there glaring at Lloyd and he right back at her, both having ripped into each other all over again. Inwardly, they were both shaking their heads at the tragic situation in which they found themselves. Was divorce the only solution? It looked like there were indeed "irreconcilable differences" in their marriage — the legal standard for obtaining a divorce. Yet strangely, neither of them really wanted to quit. At that moment, they were angry and despised each other. But they both knew there was something that still needed to be excised before they could honestly say they'd done all they could to save their marriage and family.

It was several minutes but Valorie's expression eventually began to soften, and then looking down at the floor, tears gradually began to fall from her eyes and drip on the carpet. She appeared mortally wounded and defenseless. The person who just moments before came across as a furious, even ferocious fighter, now appeared to be little more than an exhausted, vulnerable casualty of war.

Lloyd didn't know how to react to the sudden change in Valorie's demeanor. He knew she was capable of physical assault as well as verbal abuse — albeit justified when it happened. He thought he better be cautious. He carefully reached out and began to catch her tears in the palm of his hand. Neither of them moved. The tears continued to fall. Finally, Lloyd moved closer to his wife. She didn't recoil, but didn't accept his advance either.

Finally, Valorie spoke — ever so softly. "What I did to you, I did in the court room, not in the bedroom."

Lloyd didn't say anything.

Valorie continued, "I lied. You probably don't believe me, but I lied to hurt you, to get back at you."

Lloyd pulled back and looked at Valorie with a confused expression on his face. "What are you talking about?" he finally asked.

"You didn't believe me, and dragged me through the gutter, so I said we 'kept at it until I was done'. I said it was consensual just to get back at you for hurting me, for not believing me."

Lloyd was having a hard time processing what his wife was saying. Was she recanting her testimony in court? Had she deliberately committed perjury? Why would she admit to something that wasn't true? Had he badgered her so much that she finally just "confessed" to get him off her back? He suddenly caught himself — caught himself thinking like a lawyer, instead of a husband. Was it possible that he had done that much damage to their relationship? That he had hurt his wife so deeply that she would say almost anything to strike back? Had he cut her so deeply that she was willing to bleed all over herself as long as some of it got on him? And a lot of it did get on him. There's nothing worse for a man than to know that his wife has been unfaithful. And that was what she had "admitted" — in open court under oath. Infidelity. Now she was saying it was a lie — a fabricated "admission" calculated to hurt him for not trusting and believing in her. Lloyd was beginning to understand her thought process — if he doesn't believe me anyway, I might as well admit it, and in the process stick it to him for abandoning me. Is that really what happened? Lloyd gently guided Valorie over to the couch and sat down with her.

"So it wasn't consensual?" he finally asked.

"No," Valorie said firmly.

"Why did you say otherwise?"

"To hurt you. I couldn't believe that you didn't believe me. That our marriage wasn't stronger than that. That you would actually cross-examine me in court. That you seemed to feel nothing but contempt for me at a time when I needed you more than ever."

The magnitude of what Lloyd had done to his wife was finally sinking in. He had let his own doubts so undermine his relationship with his wife that he had nearly destroyed it altogether. Somehow, apart from the overwhelming intensity of the courtroom, he was able to sort it out now. And he believed his wife. Believed what she was telling him in the quiet privacy and security of their home, as husband and wife, clinging to what was left of their marriage. Lloyd sat there next to Valorie for a long time. He felt so ashamed of himself and at the same time so indebted to Valorie. How could he ever make it up to her? Somehow, all the doubts he previously harbored just melted away.

"I am so sorry," he finally said. "I thought I was going to explode in court. I didn't know what to think, or what to say, or what to do. I couldn't bear the thought that what had happened may have been consensual. But that thought grew and became cancerous. I just hope it's not terminal."

Valorie finally looked up at Lloyd. "I hope not too," she said with the slightest glint of a smile.

Lloyd gently took her hand and raised it to his lips, caressing it tenderly. Finally, he felt safe again — for the first time since he watched his wife walk into court as the prosecutor's prime witness. The confusion and darkness seemed to literally drain out of him as he basked in the light of his wife's willingness to forgive and try again. At peace once again, though he knew he would spend the rest of his life making it up to her.

"I'm really tired," Valorie finally said. "And I'm sorry too. Sorry that I let my anger provoke me into saying something I knew would wound you deeply." The two of them sat there looking at each other, realizing how close they had come to destroying their marriage, or more accurately, allowing a traumatic event to destroy their marriage. They then stood up and slowly made their way up the stairs where they slept, wrapped in one another's arms for the first time in months. How quickly things had changed, once the truth was allowed to work its purifying magic.

CHAPTER 15

Reconciliation

The next several days saw the McCallum's readjusting to life as they had once known it. Lloyd relished his role as doting husband and devoted father. He wasn't working, so the family had time to play. No stress. No demands. No deadlines. No worries. It was time to take a real vacation, so off they went to where everybody goes — Disneyland. A week in southern California, away from western Washington's rainy weather, was just what the doctor ordered.

It seemed like it'd been a long time since they'd all just played and laughed together. They always made it a point to stay at a motel with a swimming pool so the kids could have something to do even when they weren't out and about sightseeing. And once the kids were safely tucked in bed watching a video, Lloyd and Valorie could enjoy a relaxing evening dip in the pool themselves. He marveled at how exquisite his wife looked in a swim suit. If Sports Illustrated needed a model to include in their next swim suit issue, she would definitely qualify. But of course, neither of them would ever even consider it. She was his and his alone, and they both appreciated that now more than ever.

The next morning the family was up early and headed to the theme park. The place didn't look as big as it did when Lloyd was a kid himself. But it was still just as fun, especially now with kids of his own. He and Valorie relished this time together, riding the rides with their children, eating the food, watching other people enjoy themselves. It was all so surreal after what they'd been through. As they both sat on a bench watching their children, alternately laughing and screaming on Splash Mountain, Lloyd gazed at his wife like a newlywed. He couldn't seem to get enough of her. She looked so beautiful, so together, so calm. He marveled at how she could do it. Maybe she felt the same way he did — finally at peace again. Reconciled and whole again. The entire ordeal of the rape and carnage in court seemed like a long time ago already.

The next few days were just more of the same — playing and relaxing in the sunny warmth of southern California. They all decided they wanted to go the beach before going home so off to Malibu they went. What an experience that was with the sites and sounds of golden scantily-clad bodies frolicking everywhere. Palm trees swaying in the breeze. The surf lapping the shore with its white foam. Valorie seemed to genuinely enjoy the escape from all the psychological dirt and grime of the last few months. Lloyd was glad he could help her through the recovery process.
Finally, it was time to head for home.

"I wish we could stay here forever," announced little Gerald longingly.

"Me too," his sister chimed in.

"Me three," added Valorie playfully.

"Well, that's three against one," declared Gerald, looking at his dad.

"Who says I'm against it?" replied Lloyd.

"So it's unanimous, we stay forever," concluded Gerald.

All four of them laughed, realizing, albeit reluctantly, that their fantasy life was over and it was time to go back to real life.

"I'm afraid spring break's over and it's time to get back to school," reminded Lloyd.

"Ah, man! I don't want to go back to school," complained Gerald.

"Me either," added Emily.

"Yes you do," encouraged Lloyd and Valorie almost simultaneously.

"You know you enjoy it when you're there," reassured Lloyd. "It's going to be time to try out for baseball before long." Lloyd was resorting to a tried and true parental trick — divert their attention and get them thinking about something fun. "It's so easy to manipulate kids," he thought. Too bad it doesn't work so well with adults. There'd be a lot less problems in the world if adults could so easily be persuaded to do the right thing. But as history bears out, people tend to abuse the power of influence for their own ends, which are nothing remotely akin to the right thing.

"Alright, load 'em up, head 'em out," announced Lloyd, as the family all grabbed their suitcases and made their way to the hotel lobby for the shuttle ride to the airport. The flight back to Washington was uneventful and upon arriving home, it appeared that nothing had been disturbed in their absence — always a concern, especially since the break-in and Valorie's assault.

The first of the week found the family up and happily engaged getting Emily and Gerald ready and off to school. This was different though. Lloyd was home. He enjoyed the change of pace. It had been a long time since he'd been able to have breakfast with Valorie and the kids. They both found it very therapeutic and one of the many little things they did together to facilitate the delicate process of reconciliation.

"Hey, don't forget to finish your cereal there pal," reminded Lloyd, always the taskmaster.

"I don't have time, dad," protested Gerald.

"Yes you do. You've got plenty of time. It doesn't take that long to walk four blocks," insisted Lloyd.

"Come on, Gerald," called Emily, already standing by the front door anxious to be on her way.

"It's dad's fault," complained Gerald.

Lloyd glanced at his son with a disbelieving but resigned look on his face, realizing that parents usually get blamed for everything. Gerald gulped down the last of his cereal and dashed toward the door.

"Whoa, get back here," ordered Lloyd. "And you too, missy," referring to Emily. "I want my hugs and kisses before you guys take off."

"Dad!" protested Emily. "Get over here," insisted Lloyd smiling. Whereupon both children dutifully ran back to the kitchen table to give their dad a hug and kiss before leaving. Then it was Valorie's turn, though she was used to the morning routine, having been through it thousands of times.

"Okay, love you. Have a good day," called Lloyd as his precious little ones ran out the door. Lloyd looked at Valorie sitting on the other side of the table. This was indeed unique — home in the morning, just the two of them, with nowhere to rush off to. It was like an extension of their vacation. He could get used to this.

So the days passed uneventfully, Lloyd and Valorie adjusting to life after the trial. The wounds they had inflicted on one another were deep and it would take time, but at least they were making progress. Trust in a marriage, once damaged, is difficult to regain. But they kept at it. Lloyd had trouble though, not working. He'd always been so busy reaching for the brass ring that this forced sabbatical was tough. He had to find other ways to fill his time, so he was gone more and more from home. He joined a health club and worked out. He rekindled his interest in old cars and went to car shows. He even contacted some of his old army buddies to reconnect with his past and relive old memories. Nevertheless, he was adrift. He missed the excitement of his life as a trial lawyer. He'd always been on the cutting edge as it were. Little did he realize what lay ahead.

CHAPTER 16

Re-enter the Beast

"So how was your day?" queried Lloyd, as the family sat down for dinner on a pleasant evening in late spring.

"It was...okay," replied Valorie, not wanting to disclose everything. She was obviously holding back something.

"What?" Lloyd almost demanded.

"Let's talk about it later, okay," suggested Valorie. Later couldn't come soon enough for Lloyd. He felt like they'd been making such good progress, he didn't want anything to undermine that. So when the kids were safely tucked in bed for the night and all the doors checked, Lloyd sat down with his wife to hear the rest of the story.

"Well," she started slowly, "I went and picked up the kids at school today, and as I was leaving I noticed this guy standing on the corner across from the school. I could've sworn it was that client of yours."

"What client?" questioned Lloyd intensely.

"Roundtree," responded Valorie, looking directly at Lloyd with a hint of terror in her eyes.

Lloyd was speechless. He stared at Valorie, but saw

Willie Roundtree in his mind's eye. Slowly he began to tense up — every muscle in his body reacting to the thought of Willie Roundtree hanging around their neighborhood. Even worse, hanging around their children's school.

"What did he do?" questioned Lloyd.

"Nothing that I could see, just stood there, watching us as we drove away."

Lloyd lapsed into silence. "Are you sure it was him?" he finally ventured.

"No, I'm not sure. The guy just gave me an eerie feeling when I looked at him."

"If it was him, I'm going to kill him."

"Don't even talk like that," cautioned Valorie. "We have it good. Let's don't let something like this mess things up."

Lloyd just sat there, shaking his head. Everything they'd worked so hard to restore was being threatened by the re-appearance of the one person in their lives who had nearly destroyed it all. How could this be? Lloyd felt the whole gamut of emotions sweep over him.

"You really think it was him?" asked Lloyd again.

"I don't know," replied Valorie. "I don't really think so. He'd be crazy to come back here."

"Well, let's don't take any chances. Let's make sure we don't let the kids go back and forth to school alone. One of us has to be with them all the time."

"Isn't that over-reacting a little?" questioned Valorie. "Roundtree's never bothered children has he?"

"He's a rapist," snapped Lloyd. "That means he's capable of anything, including pedophilia."

Valorie buried her face in her hands at the mere thought of something like that happening to her precious innocent children. That would be an even worse nightmare than her own ordeal.

"Well, we'll just have to be very careful," cautioned

Lloyd. "I knew it was too good to be true. I knew things were going too well."

"Look, let's don't let something that's probably nothing get to us and ruin everything we've gained the last couple of months," said Valorie.

"You're right. We just need to be vigilant, that's all." And with that, the emotionally drained couple retired to bed, hoping against hope that the person Valorie had seen was not the monster that had torn their lives apart.

The days passed uneventfully, happiness seemingly surrounding the McCallum family. Lloyd was getting more used to being at home and Valorie was basking in the daily attention her husband lavished upon her. Their relationship seemed better than ever, though it required constant vigilance to maintain the progress they'd made.

*   *   *

"Hey, I'm going to run to the store, be back shortly," announced Lloyd one day about mid-afternoon. "You got the kids, right?" he reminded as he went out the door.

"Yeah, yeah, got it covered," replied Valorie, feeling glad the school year was almost over. It had become routine for one of them to pick up the kids at school and drive them home, rather than let them walk the distance alone. Weeks had gone by with no sign of any suspicious characters around the school. Then the phone rang.

"Hi, Valorie," a voice said on the other end. Valorie immediately recognized her mother's voice calling long distance.

"Hey, how are you?" Valorie happily inquired. Mother and daughter didn't have that much contact, but they felt a closeness between them nevertheless. When one of them did call the other, it tended to be a lengthy conversation, catching up on all the latest happenings.

"So how are the kids and every little thing?" questioned Mom, a retired real estate broker with money to

171

travel the world.

"Everything's just great. The kids are enjoying school and things are . . . good."

"Humm, from 'great' to just 'good' in the two sentences," replied Valorie's mother. "So which is it?"
"Well, things are much better than they were, let's put it that way. Where are you, anyway?" asked Valorie, trying to shift the focus.

"I'm actually in England now. London is unbelievable, and expensive, but so interesting."

"Glad to hear you're having a good time, Mom."

"So, I could detect a hint of resignation in your voice a minute ago. How are things, really?" pressed Valorie's mother.

Valorie then recited the whole story for her mother. The rape. The hospitalization. The investigation. The trial. The near collapse of her marriage. Everything.
Before long a whole hour had passed. It was therapeutic for Valorie though, and a relief to be able to share her trauma with someone safe. Her Mom was a good listener and unparalleled in her ability to reassure her children. But suddenly the sound of the door bell ringing interrupted their conversation.

"Mom, somebody's at the door. I can't believe we've been talking for over an hour. So good to hear from you. I better see about the kids. Take care over there in Europe. Bye," concluded Valorie as she hurried to hang up the phone and answer the door.

As Valorie opened the front door of their suburban home, there stood none other than Willie Roundtree, holding the hands of both her children standing on either side of him. She gasped and covered her mouth as she absorbed the image before her.

"Hello, Ms. McCallum," drawled Roundtree with a sick little smile on his face. "I'm baaack," he laughed.

"What do you want?" Valorie demanded as she instinctively reached for her children.

"Whoa, not so fast," replied Roundtree as he pulled the children back from her.

"Mr. Willie gave us some candy," volunteered Emily.

"He's nice to us," she added.

Valorie glanced at Emily with a look of anger mixed with terror. How many times had she told her children not to accept anything from strangers?

Her eyes became enflamed as they shifted back to Roundtree. "Let them go," she demanded, as she reached for them again, stepping outside the door to do so. Valorie stood practically nose to nose with her nemesis, staring into the abyss of his dark eyes. The two stood there, face to face, for what seemed like a long time, neither willing to back off.

"Sure," smiled Roundtree finally, releasing his grip on the children.

"Get in the house, now!" ordered Valorie, pulling them past her through the door and placing herself between them and Roundtree.

"If you ever . . . " started Valorie.

"Shut your mouth, you wench," snarled Roundtree as he reached out and grabbed her by the face and pulled her toward him, his large hand wrapping around her mouth and chin, his fingers and thumb digging into her cheeks. "I can have you whenever I want and don't you forget it," he hissed in her face. "And if you feel anything for those kids of yours, you'll do what I want, when I want." Roundtree snickered as he considered how he once again had subdued his victim.

Valorie slowly reached up and pried Roundtree's hand off her face, but didn't otherwise move from in front of him. Leaning her head forward slightly, she almost whispered,

"If you ever touch my children again, I'll kill you myself." And with that she planted both hands on his chest and shoved him off the steps, literally screaming, "Now get

B. L. McCoy

off our property!"

Roundtree went reeling backwards down the steps, but without watching where he landed, Valorie turned and practically leaped into the house and slammed the door, gasping for breath. She could hardly process what had happened in the preceding two minutes. That monster, Willie Roungtree, had come back to torment her all over again. How could this be? How could she tell Lloyd? What would he think? What would he do? How would it affect their relationship now that things were practically back to normal? Valorie began to cry uncontrollably.

As she did, she sank to the floor with her back against the wall — literally and figuratively. Several minutes passed as Valorie sat there on the floor in the fetal position.

"What's wrong, Mom?" questioned Emily, eventually noticing her mom sitting on the floor in the hall way.

"Oh, nothing," replied Valorie. "Don't you like Mr. Willie?" asked Emily.

"No, I don't," answered Valorie, almost shouting. "You are to have nothing to do with that man. How many times have I told you not to talk to strangers or take anything from people you don't know?"

Emily put her hands up to her mouth and started to tear up. "I'm sorry, mommy," she offered.

"Listen to me when I tell you things," Valorie continued, despite her daughter's tearful reaction.

"I'm sorry," Emily said again. There was silence for a moment as Valorie tried to compose herself.

"I'm sorry too, sweetheart," Valorie finally said, reaching out and pulling her daughter into her embrace. "Some day I'll explain why I don't want you to see Mr. Willie any more, but for now you'll just have to trust me, okay?" Emily nodded her child-like agreement, looking to Valorie for some reassurance that she was back in her mother's good graces.

174

"Where's Gerald?" asked Valorie.

"In the family room," replied Emily.

"I need to talk to him, so why don't you go upstairs and change out of your school clothes, okay."

"Okay, Mom," said Emily obediently.

"Gerald," called Valorie.

"In here," came the reply from the family room. As Valorie walked into the room she questioned, "Are you supposed to be watching TV right after school, young man?" Gerald looked at his mom for some clue about her state of mind. That would determine how he answered. He perceived that Valorie was very serious, so he just picked up the remote and turned the TV off.

"Sorry, Mom," he offered.

"You know better, don't you." Gerald just pursed his lips and looked down. "I need to talk to you about something very serious," Valorie began. "Why were you hanging around that Mr. Willie character?"

"We weren't hanging around him, Mom. When you didn't come pick us up, he just came up to us and offered Emily some candy, and before I could say anything she took it. He said he knew you and Dad, and so it was okay."

"How many times have I told you kids not to talk to strangers or take anything from people you don't know? You know better than that, don't you," demanded Valorie, taking her son by the shoulders and looking him directly in the eyes. "He was a nice guy, Mom," suggested Gerald.

"No, he isn't a nice guy," shouted Valorie. "You have no idea who he is."

"Well," Gerald reminded his mother in his own defense, "when you didn't come pick us up, we just started walking home and that's when Mr. Willie came up to us."

Valorie just shook her head, realizing it was her fault that her children had been exposed to such terrible danger. Lloyd reminded her before he left about the kids, and she had gotten on the phone with her mother and forgotten all about them. Inexcusable, she thought. No telling what a guy like Willie Roundtree is capable of. Actually, Valorie knew better than anyone what a guy like him is capable of.

Her mind turned to visualizing Roundtree alone with her children, talking to them, giving them food, touching them, holding their hands, controlling them. She suddenly jumped up, ran to the front door and looked out the window to see if he was gone. He was, thank goodness. But he wasn't gone, not really. He was back in her life — again! He was mocking her. She could feel his presence, even though he wasn't physically there. How could she protect her children from him? How could she protect herself? When would he show up again? What might he do? Despite everything she'd been through and the strength she'd developed from it all, she felt extremely vulnerable, even helpless.

She looked around her house and thought of everything she and Lloyd had worked so hard to acquire, to build together. But the tangible things were just the tip of the iceberg. All the progress they had made to preserve their marriage and protect their family, all the heartache, the tears, the joy, the struggles, the financial success — all of it, was now at risk. Valorie couldn't stand the thought of losing it all, having come so close to losing it before. She'd been on the brink before and it was a very scary place. She would have to talk to Lloyd, though she loathed the thought. How would he react? What would he think? Would he be suspicious? Would he blame her for not being more attentive to the safety of their children? Valorie knew she couldn't face the likes of Willie Roundtree alone, no matter how Lloyd reacted.

That night after dinner, Valorie mechanically went through the motions of putting the kids to bed, trying to act normal but not doing too well. Lloyd, being the consummate judge of character from years of practice as a trial lawyer, finally decided to ask his wife what was troubling her.

"Nothing," she said. Lloyd didn't pursue it — at least not immediately. He could read his wife like a book and knew with a little time and space she would disclose what was on her mind. He waited. They both went into the family room and sat down — ostensibly to watch a little TV. Valorie picked up the remote but then put it down on the couch beside her. Lloyd could sense that she was about ready to talk. Finally, after several minutes of silence Valorie turned off the TV and began to recount what had happened earlier that day. She described how she unexpectedly opened the door to find, to her horror, Willie Roundtree standing on their front steps with their children in hand. She told Lloyd how she had let herself get distracted on the phone with her mother and forgotten to go pick up the kids. She blamed herself. Finally, she reluctantly told her husband how Roundtree had grabbed her face and threatened her and the children. Valorie was crying as she finished describing the sordid encounter, her tears streaming down her flawless face.

Lloyd just listened, without saying a word, his eyes fixed on his wife. He then tilted his head back and shut his eyes, mentally trying to assimilate what he'd just heard. Finally, he gently reached out and pulled Volorie in close to him and wrapped his arms around her.

"It wasn't your fault," he began. "Don't beat yourself up over it. At least we know for sure who's been hanging around the school. We have a predator circling our family."

"What are we going to do?" probed Valorie.

"We could get a restraining order against him," Lloyd replied.

"Do you think that would work?"

"I don't know, but it's worth a try. I don't think those things are very effective, but it might help."

"How long does that take and how's it enforced?"

"We could go down to the courthouse and probably get one in a day. But the cops are the ones who enforce restraining orders and usually by the time they show up, the damage is done."

"That's not very comforting," confessed Valorie.

"I know," agreed Lloyd, "but at least it's a start."

CHAPTER 17

Restraining Order

The next day found Lloyd and Valorie at the courthouse filling out papers for a restraining order against Mr. William Roundtree. The process wasn't complicated, but actually writing out the affidavit and rehearsing the sordid details again was complicated, at least emotionally. Valorie struggled to capture the facts on paper as she re-lived the terrifying scene of her innocent children standing on the front steps of her home — in the clutches of her rapist! Was there no limit to his depravity? What might he do next? How could she and her husband protect them? Too many thoughts swirling around in her head to concentrate. Too many people bustling around in the hallway outside the courtroom. Too many bad memories in this very courthouse where her husband mercilessly shredded her on the witness stand. All of it. All of it was too much. But she had to do this.

Finally, Valorie finished her affidavit and other papers and was ready to submit them to the judge. She was glad Lloyd was there. He could do that part. After all, he was a lawyer and certainly had a stake in this case — like no other. They went into the courtroom together and waited for their matter to be called. It was a light docket that day so the McCallums didn't have to wait long. Within a few minutes the judge spoke directly to them as they sat in the gallery.

"Good morning, Mr. McCallum, what brings you here today?" questioned Judge Weston, a trim middle-aged man, known for his no-nonsense approach to handling legal disputes.

Lloyd instinctively stood up to respond to the judge's invitation to come forward and present the business that brought him there.

"I'm here representing myself and my wife, your Honor. May I approach the bench and lay the matter before the court?"

The judge nodded his permission as he asked, "Are you sure that's wise? — to represent yourself and your wife? You must have a personal stake in this matter."

"Yes, your Honor, I definitely do have a personal stake in this matter," whereupon Lloyd rehearsed for the judge the recent events involving Willie Roundtree and their children. Upon hearing the factual basis for the McCallum's request for an immediate restraining order, the judge asked, "Who is this Willie Roundtree?"

Lloyd paused for what seemed like an eternity, his mind racing through all the events of the last couple of years, starting with the first time he represented Willie Roundtree on a rape charge — for which he was acquitted. Then the second time he represented him on a rape charge — his own wife's rape — for which he was acquitted again! Who is this Willie Roundtree? Lloyd repeated to himself.

He began, "I first met William Roundtree a couple of years ago as a client, and then again when our firm represented him in another criminal matter. He has, as my wife's affidavit states, become a thorn in our side and now poses a threat to me and my family." Lloyd was careful to omit the fact that he had defended Roundtree in his wife's rape case.

"Was he dissatisfied with your representation?" queried Judge Weston.

"No, he was acquitted both times on all charges."

"And now for no apparent reason, he wants to menace you and your family?"

"We're afraid he wants to do more than that, your Honor, and based on this latest confrontation my wife had with him, I think he's capable of anything. He has it in for us for some reason and so we just want to keep him away from us."

"Well okay, Mr. McCallum. Based on the history and your wife's sworn affidavit, I'll sign and issue this restraining order effective immediately. Please keep a certified copy on your person at all times and instruct your wife to do likewise, otherwise, as you know, the police will not enforce it."

"Thank you, Judge Weston, I hope this does some good and provides a modicum of protection."

"I hope so too, Mr. McCallum," said the judge as he looked intently at Lloyd, a respected member of the Bar, now embroiled in a threatening situation with a former client, who as it turns out, is a confirmed sociopath.

*   *   *

The ride home was a somber one — Lloyd and Valorie both realizing that a restraining order was thin protection against the likes of Willie Roundtree. Lloyd couldn't help but remember the many times he had made the trip home from the courthouse in years past. How he relished the quiet escape from the grimy world of criminal law — he could just cruise along in his yuppie-mobile, flashing his successful suburban image for all to see. His perfect little all-American family safely tucked away in an upper-middle class community, unsoiled by the world he worked in. What he wouldn't give

181

to have it all back again. It was so easy to compartmentalize his life, to separate himself from what he did down town. His court room prowess was like a narcotic — it made him feel powerful, even invincible, never mind that he spent his energy protecting the scum of the earth. He was Lloyd McCallum, criminal defense lawyer par excellance! Somehow he imagined that made him invincible everywhere, even at home. But now, he was painfully aware that he was extremely vulnerable — he and his family both. All his lawyer skills had little applicability in this arena. He was now dealing with forces which operated completely outside the law.

Nevertheless, he and Valorie had a restraining order which they could show any law enforcement officer who would then enforce it on the spot. Lloyd hoped beyond hope that he and his wife would never be put in a position to have to rely on it. Maybe if they could put Roundtree on notice that they had a restraining order, he would get the message and leave well enough alone. Lloyd decided he would try and contact him somehow. But how? How would he make contact with the likes of Willie Roundtree? Years of association with the criminal element in the city had provided Lloyd with a long list of unsavory characters. His rolodex of clients read like a who's who of criminals. One of them would likely know where Willie Roundtree hung out, since the firm's lawyers had always met Roundtree down at the county jail and had no idea where he actually lived.

First thing the next morning, Lloyd was on the phone with his former secretary.

"Sally, hi, this is Lloyd."

"Hi," she said enthusiastically. "How've you been? How's the sabbatical?"

"Well, it feels more like forced retirement, but it's okay for now," Lloyd replied. "How've you been?"

"Honestly, I've missed you. We all have. It's just not

the same around here without you."

"Well, that's nice of you to say. Tell everybody hello for me. But I need a favor. Could you get into the storage room and dig out my rolodex and look up some people for me? I need to contact a couple of them to do a little detective work."

"Sure," replied Sally, "but do you really want to arouse any of those people?"

"Yeah, I know, but not all of them are losers. I need to track down a couple guys who hopefully can help me find who I'm really looking for. They're Duane Jackson and Lamar Franklin." Lloyd struggled to recall their names.

"Well, if you give me two minutes, I'll go get your rolodex right now and look them up. I think I know right where it is."

"Thanks so much. Could you give me a call back when you've got it?"

"You bet. Good to hear from you, Lloyd. I'll call ya right back."

Five minutes later Lloyd's phone rang — it was his secretary with the names and numbers of two of Lloyd's former clients — real gang bangers who know the streets and what's happening in the city. As he contemplated calling them, he began to breathe a little harder — this time he would be calling them for help instead of the other way around. And these guys don't do anything for free — there's always the expectation of some sort of return favor. Did he really want to get involved with them? Could he trust them not to take advantage of him somehow if given the chance? Lloyd figured he had to take that chance — it would be worth it if he could find Willie Roundtree and convince him to leave his family alone.

That afternoon, while Valorie and the kids were out running errands, Lloyd called the first name on his list — Duane Jackson — a guy Lloyd had defended on an aggravated assault charge after he'd tried to kill his girlfriend for going out with another guy. Jackson was a big black man in his mid-thirties who traveled in all the wrong circles and claimed to know everybody in the city — at least all the unsavory types. He prided himself on his "contacts."

Lloyd punched in the phone number he had for Duane, not knowing what he might encounter on the other end.

"Yeah, what up?" answered a voice.

"Is this Duane Jackson?"

"Yeah, who's this?" Jackson demanded.

"This is Lloyd McCallum."

"Who?"

"Lloyd McCallum, your lawyer, remember?"

"Oh, yeah. What you up to, man?"

"I need a favor, Duane."

"From me? What you want?"

"I know we haven't exactly stayed in touch, but you still got your contacts, right?"

"Yeah, course I do, man."

"So you stayin' out of trouble?"

"Who wants to know?"

"Just making conversation, that's all. I need some information. I need to know where I can find somebody. His name's Willie Roundtree. I know he's in the city, but I have no idea where."

"Yeah, no problem, man. I'll see what I can do and let you know. How do I get hold a you?"

"Just call me back on this number."

"What you want with him, anyway?"

"Who wants to know?" Lloyd said, reversing the tables on his former client.

"Yeah, okay. I'll get back to you. I guess I can do that much for you — you saved my butt once upon a time."

Lloyd went about his business trying to live a normal

life, but his "normal life" had long since vanished. He was just existing again. But things were at least better now with Valorie.

Eventually Jackson got back to Lloyd with the information he needed — the whereabouts of Willie Roundtree. He stewed over what he should do, how he should handle the situation. Could he reason with the man? Would it turn into a confrontation? What might be the ramifications for his family? Would the Restraining Order become null and void if Lloyd himself initiated contact with Willie? All these things and more ran through Lloyd's mind. But he had to do something — he couldn't just wait for Willie to make the next move. He couldn't just wait for him to invade his family's life and threaten them again, or actually do something ugly. Lloyd knew he had to act.

That evening Lloyd told Valorie he was going out.

"Where?" questioned his wife.

"I've got to try and do something."

"What are you going to do?"

"I've got to try and reason with Willie."

"How are you going to do that? You know that guy — he's creepy. What if he gets violent?"

"I don't think it'll come to that. He knows I'm a lawyer, so that should tame him down a little."

"Right. Guy's like him aren't intimidated by the law or anything akin to it."

"Well, I'm going anyway."

"Lloyd, you can't do that. We have a Restraining Order — let's let the system do its job."

"I can't believe what I just heard. You know the system breaks down — you were a victim of that sort of thing just recently — remember?"

"I know, but I don't want you going out into that sleazy world trying to talk to somebody like Willie Roundtree. The guy's got no scruples."

B. L. McCoy

Valorie got up and approached Lloyd, wrapping herself around him as if she could physically restrain him. She embraced him hoping to persuade him to stay home. Notwithstanding, he left the house about 6:00 pm and drove toward the city. Valorie didn't know when, or if, she would see her husband again.

*   *   *

It was a little unnerving to Lloyd to be driving down town again — especially late in the day. It seemed like it had been a long time since he'd been down town, and he'd always done his business in the city during regular business hours. This was very different. He wasn't going to the marble halls of the courthouse to showcase his talent as a lawyer. He was going to a sleazy part of town as just a regular guy — afraid for the safety of his family. And afraid for his own safety. But he was driven, driven by the need to protect what was his. At least it wasn't dark yet. Hopefully, he would find Willie where Jackson told him he hung out, and he could talk to him face to face during the day with people around. Once night falls in places like where Lloyd was going, things usually got a lot more tense.

As he drove into the predominantly black neighborhood, things quickly deteriorated. There was more graffiti on the walls of buildings, more broken windows, more trash in the street, more broken people wandering the sidewalks, more loud rap music, more tenements, more stench, more of all things undesirable. Lloyd drove slowly with all the doors securely locked. He hadn't seen such depressed conditions since his days in the Army in Latin-America.

Finally, Lloyd pulled his car over to the curb in front of an old run-down diner indentified by a neon sign that read "Louie's." It looked as though he might be the only white man in the whole neighborhood. As he got out of his car, some of the local thugs looked at him like he must be crazy to have invaded their turf. Lloyd silently agreed with them. He couldn't look afraid however, or they'd be on him like a hunk of meat. He walked into Louie's like he owned the place, hoping his car would still be there when he came out. The front door opened into a bay area with a serving counter directly across from the door and booths to the right and left of the door. Lloyd quickly looked around the place for Willie but didn't see anyone that even resembled him. Then he heard the sound of pool balls banging together in another room toward the back of the dining area. He decided to investigate and walked toward the sound.

As he entered the separate room, there were several pool tables with a half a dozen black guys standing around playing the game. Lloyd looked through the smoke filled room and there he was — Willie Roundtree standing next to a table with a pool cue in his hand. Lloyd froze, not knowing quite what to do now that he actually had Willie in his sights. He walked by a couple of dark figures toward Willie who still hadn't seen him. As he got closer, Willie finally noticed a white man in their pool hall and turned to squarely face Lloyd, who walked up to within a few inches of his nemesis.

"You remember me?" Lloyd asked pointedly.

"Sure, you're the lawyer. What brings you out to the hood? You lost?"

"No, I'm not lost. Is there somewhere we can talk?"

"We can talk right here, with my homies."

"Alright. I have something for you."

Lloyd reached into his jacket pocket whereupon Willie and almost everyone else in the room flinched and started to reach for their weapons — whatever they might be carrying. Lloyd pulled out a copy of the Restraining Order, showing he only had a piece of paper.

"This is a Restraining Order. I want you to stay away from my family."

Willie looked at Lloyd with that familiar smirk, as if

to say, "This guy's really gutsy." He took the paper, glanced at it, and then crumpled it up and stuffed it back in Lloyd's jacket pocket.

"That's what I think of your Restraining Order, Mr. Lawyer. I ain't had nothin' to do with your family. Now get your little white hynie outta here before I sic my homies on you."

"Leave 'em alone, Willie. I mean it," insisted Lloyd.

"What you sayin', boy?" Willie demanded, and with a glance of his eye, motioned to two men standing by who quickly grabbed Lloyd by his arms and held him. Lloyd knew it was useless to struggle. Willie stepped toward Lloyd, and nose to nose said, "You better watch your mouth. You outta your league here, boy."

The two men were so close they were practically breathing each other's air. Willie then suddenly grabbed Lloyd by the face, with his fingers and thumb digging into his cheeks — like he'd done to Valorie — and practically hissing at Lloyd said, "That little wench of yours is mine whenever I want, and don't you forget it." And then to rub salt in the wound, Willie reminded Lloyd that "The last time was her doin' — you even proved it in court!"

Willie paused to let the irony of that whole experience sink in. He relished the fact that he'd raped the wife of the man he had standing in front of him, and that man did nothing then and could do nothing now. Indeed, not only had he done nothing, he had protected him and kept him out of prison. He still couldn't believe Lloyd had done it — defended his own wife's rapist. And won!

Willie continued his verbal abuse, "Next time it'll be my doin'. How'd you like to take my case again, counselor? Third time's a charm they say."

And with that, Willie shoved Lloyd's head back and smiled. He nodded at the two men who released Lloyd to leave under his own power. Lloyd just stood there for what seemed like a long time, staring at Willie, the two men realizing that this was just the beginning of all out war between them. Lloyd turned around and walked out feeling an odd combination of relief and intense rage. His car was still there, but it had been keyed down the driver's side — a clear message not to come back. As he got in, he realized that he had indeed ventured into hell — the underbelly of society. All the way home he wondered how he was going to protect his wife and children from this despicable predator — a man who, but for him, would be locked up in prison.

CHAPTER 18

Home Invasion

The days turned into weeks with the McCallum's trying to live life as normal as possible, not knowing when their world might be rocked by the intrusion of Willie Roundtree. Summer ended and it was time for school to start again. The kids were excited and so were Lloyd and Valorie — they were starting middle school this year which meant no more walking to and from school. There was a neighborhood car pool with parents taking turns driving the kids to and from school every day. It was perfect — there were five families so each took a turn once a week. Friday was Valorie's day which was nice because she had four consecutive days to do what she needed to do without having to stop in the middle of the afternoon to go pick up the kids. Valorie made sure that each of the other parents knew about her concern for her children and even gave them a copy of the Restraining Order in case Willie happened to show up. There was neighborhood solidarity when it came to protecting what was theirs, especially the children. Valorie felt like she could relax a little with everyone in the neighborhood on alert.

Lloyd, on the other hand, knew better, although he tried not to undermine Valorie's relative peace of mind. He knew it was just a matter of time before his old client would get bored and try something just for the thrill of it. Of course, the maddening part of it all was not knowing what or when. That's the thing about predators, at least the human type — they take pleasure in antagonizing their prey. It's about power and control. They're like terrorists — terrorizing their victims before an act of violence is as important as actually inflicting harm. They get an exhilarating sense of omnipotence. No one can stop them. They are like silent slithering snakes that crawl around and all of a sudden pop up and bite you with no warning whatsoever. You have to be on the lookout all the time. You can never relax, never live a normal life free of worry. They like it that way — always keeping their target off balance. For the victim, it becomes almost like a kind of mental illness — always wondering when the snake is going to strike. It destroys peace of mind like no other form of torture. This is what Lloyd lived with day in and day out. How could he protect them? The frightening part of it all was that he knew he really couldn't. Skilled predators are almost impossible to stop.

*   *   *

It was a nice fall day in western Washington so the McCallum's decided to pick up Gerald and Emily after school and take them to Point Defiance Park for a picnic and tour of the aquarium — something they hadn't done together for a long time. It was so nice to just get away from the daily routine and go do something different. Point Defiance Park was a large drive through state park with a zoo, aquarium, restaurant, hiking paths, salt water beach and lots of picnic sites — the perfect family recreation area.

As they entered the park, Gerald yelled, "Hey, there's a good place, Dad."

"Looks good to me," replied Lloyd.

The family pulled into the parking area, piled out of the car and hauled their picnic stuff to the nearest table. The day was perfect — hardly a cloud in the sky — a rarity in western Washington that time of year. There were a lot of other people who apparently had the same idea — the park was full but not over-crowded.

"So who wants bar-b-cue chicken?" announced Valorie.

"I do," came the kids' combined chorus — practiced over many years.

It was good eating and good times. The McCallum's hadn't had a lot of time to just relax in years past. Lloyd was building his law practice and reputation and Valorie was gliding through life as the attractive wife of a successful attorney, doing what suburban soccer moms do. It was nice to just chill for a while and act like everything was back to normal.

After downing the chicken and other goodies, the whole family headed to the aquarium for a look at the shark tank, among other things. Those creatures are veritable shredders, Lloyd thought. They search out and consume anything they can. They're like heartless psychopaths of the ocean — kind of like some of the people Lloyd had dealt with as a lawyer. And they call lawyers sharks! But it's not the lawyers you have to watch out for — it's the Willie Roundtree's of the world. Those ravenous creatures that consume anybody that gets in their way. Lloyd found himself wishing he could just throw Willie in the shark tank during feeding time and watch him disappear. Once again, thoughts of Willie Roundtree invaded his consciousness and interfered with what little time he had with his family.

Soon, play time was over and it was time to go home. They'd seen all there was to see at the aquarium and oohed and aahed over enough strange sea creatures to last them a while. The kids were tired and fell asleep on the way home, giving Lloyd and Valorie a chance to talk.

"So how you doing?" ventured Valorie.

"Oh, I'm fine," replied Lloyd.

"I noticed you spacing out at the aquarium. What were you thinking?"

"I think you know what I was thinking."

"Why don't you tell me."

"I was thinking about what's going to happen."

Valorie knew what that meant. "Maybe's he's forgotten about us or gone somewhere else, or maybe he's dead by now." "I wouldn't count on it. I think he's just waiting for us to become complacent."

"It's been a couple of months since you confronted him. Maybe he got the message."

"No, guys like that don't get the message. They just keep coming at you until they destroy you, or you destroy them."

"How can you be so sure?"

"Because I knew people like that in the Army. Not our guys, but the other guys. Guerrilla types. It's just a matter of time."

"I hope you're wrong."

"So do I, but I'm not too optimistic."

About then the McCallum's arrived home, hit the garage door opener and drove straight into their spacious garage.

"Okay, wake up you two. We're home and it's bed time."

"Ah, Dad, can you give us a ride on your back?"

"Okay, hop on Emily and I'll come back for you, Gerald."

Having delivered the first little person to her bedroom, Lloyd came back and got Gerald while Valorie carried picnic stuff in to the kitchen. He was just coming down stairs from Gerald's bedroom when he turned toward the rear of the house and saw Valorie standing outside the kitchen —

looking absolutely horrified. Lloyd rushed over to her. As he looked in the kitchen he saw what Valorie saw — sprayed graffiti on the kitchen wall. One word — WENCH. Lloyd instinctively grabbed Valorie and turned her away from it, shielding her eyes as if he could erase the image from her mind. Both her hands were clasped tightly over her mouth in utter terror. She could hardly breathe. Her knees became weak and she began to sink to the floor despite Lloyd holding her. As she sank down she began to groan — an agonizing, helpless groan — the kind of sound a doomed prey makes just before being torn apart by a ravenous predator. Lloyd tried to hold her up, but couldn't. They both sat in a heap on the floor with Valorie's face buried in Lloyd's chest. She sobbed while he stared at the wall. He could hardly console his wife because of his own feelings of anger and frustration. Who does he think he is? Lloyd could not believe the man would actually come in his house and leave his "calling card" on their kitchen wall. Thank goodness the children didn't see it. How did he get in? How did he get in without anybody seeing him? Where were the neighbors? Was there nothing he could do to protect his family? His mind raced. Another traumatic assault on an already weakened family. How much more could they endure? There was nowhere to hide. Nowhere to feel safe and secure from the likes of Willie Roundtree.

Lloyd finally carried Valorie upstairs and put her to bed, with plenty of sleep-aids to knock her out for the night. He sat in the chair across the bedroom and stared into the darkness. The words on the wall kept echoing in his head — WENCH. WENCH. WENCH. It was like Roundtree was staking his claim — invading the sanctity of their home to spit in their face and send a message — that Valorie belonged to him now. She was his to do with as he pleased — whenever he pleased. He now ruled their lives. Lloyd could hardly comprehend what was happening. He eventually fell asleep envisioning his hands around Willie's throat.

The next morning found Lloyd still asleep in the chair and Valorie still in bed out cold. That was good — at least she got a good night's sleep. Lloyd could hear the kids rustling around down stairs so he went down to help them get ready to catch their ride to school. He went out with them to tell the neighbor that they'd had an intruder in their home the day before so please keep a close eye on Gerald and Emily during drop-off and pick-up. Lloyd didn't want to get too specific and have to explain too much of the history, but he wondered aloud how Roundtree got in their house without anyone seeing or hearing anything. The neighbor, a middle-age investment broker with young children of his own, said they were gone nearly all day too, so he had no clue. He was a good guy as neighbors go, and offered moral support, but Lloyd knew this was a situation that called for a lot more than moral support and he was going to have to handle it himself.

He contacted the police who filed a report that the Restraining Order had been violated. That prompted the court to issue an arrest warrant for Willie Roundtree. Of course, the police wouldn't try to track him down and arrest him, they'd just wait for him to get pulled over for a traffic violation or something and upon checking for outstanding warrants, arrest him then. There were just too many reported violations of restraining orders for the police to go looking for those types all the time. Lloyd knew that, but at least now there was a report on file with law enforcement authorities.

He then contacted a security company and arranged for the installation of a new highly sophisticated home security system. They agreed to put a rush on the order and had it done in a couple of days. Lloyd and Valorie agreed never to turn it off for any reason. Finally, he decided to obtain a concealed weapons permit and carry his gun — a 357 magnum revolver. He also got a small handgun for Valorie and took her to the firing range and taught her how to use it.

She wasn't too excited about that — she didn't like guns, but knew it might save her life some day, or more importantly, save her children. She also got a concealed weapons permit so she would never be without armed protection. This was all very unnerving for Valorie — she did not like confrontation. But when she reflected back on the night Willie Roundtree raped her and threatened her children, she knew she was capable of killing him if she had to. His coming into the house and violating the sanctity of her home a second time was enough to bring out the fight in her — only this time it wouldn't be in a courtroom.

*   *   *

The days faded into weeks which passed uneventfully, though there was clearly an uneasy feeling in the McCallum home. The children were entirely oblivious to any threat to them or their family, which Lloyd and Valorie intentionally fostered, but the constant strain took its toll on them. They could never really relax or let their guard down. They could never enjoy time together without wondering when Willie Roundtree would strike again. They were hyper-protective of their children, who could not be left alone. Lloyd and Valorie couldn't remember the last time they'd been able to just enjoy some wholesome recreation together as a married couple. Their visit to the Point Defiance aquarium with the kids seemed like a long time ago. Life was becoming a serious burden. Something had to happen to ease the strain on them. Finally, after dinner one night, Lloyd broached the idea of a "vacation."

"Let's go somewhere," he blurted out.

Valorie looked at her husband like he'd just suggested a trip to Mars or something.

"We have to do something," he continued. "We have to get out of here."

"And just what did you have in mind?" queried Valorie.

"I don't know, but we need a break. I'm about to go crazy."

"What do we do with the kids?"

"The Larsons would keep them for a couple of days."

"The neighbors next door?"

"Yes, they're good people. They know our kids, and their kids are about the same age. It'd be okay for just a couple of days."

Lloyd was desperate, and he sounded desperate. Valorie felt the stress of it all too, but she worried about the children. She still had visions of them standing on the front steps in the grip of that creep. But she knew that if she didn't allow Lloyd some kind of respite, he would go crazy and possibly do something stupid. Maybe it would be okay to go for just two days, she reasoned. She sat for a long time just looking at her husband — a man who once ruled his world. But no longer. He was suffering. He was losing his self-respect. He was no longer the provider and protector of his family. He felt powerless and vulnerable. He felt manipulated by a career criminal who had enticed him to misuse his skills.

Valorie could feel the pressure building inside him. She knew that he had a fierce temper deep down inside and was capable of violence, though he had always kept it under control. After all, he had served in the Army and been meticulously trained in the art of war. But all that happened before she knew him — all she really knew was that he had been involved in some pretty intense things before he became a lawyer — things that he preferred not to talk about. She realized that her husband was on the edge and she needed to listen to him.

"Alright, where do you want to go?" she finally asked. Lloyd immediately looked at Valorie to make sure she was taking him seriously. He paused for a moment and then relief washed over his face.

"How 'bout if we go over to the coast. We could rent a condo and just chill."

"Alright," Valorie replied simply.

"You mean it?" asked Lloyd excitedly. "You're okay with being gone for a while?"

"I'm okay with being gone for a while," she echoed.

Lloyd seemed to be instantly transformed. He jumped up and went right in to the computer and began searching for a place to stay. Within minutes he was back with reservations at a place in Ocean Shores on the Washington coast. He even printed off an information brochure to show Valorie all the amenities. He was ready to go — right then.

"Do you want to talk to the Larsons or do you want me to?" asked Valorie.

"I'll talk to them — first thing tomorrow, and make all the arrangements," replied Lloyd.

Tomorrow couldn't come fast enough for Lloyd. He was up early and over at the neighbors before breakfast. Fortunately, they were available and happy to take Gerald and Emily for a couple of days. The only thing Lloyd and Valorie were concerned about was the kids getting back and forth to school. While they were actually in school or at the Larson's, they were safe. It was the drop-off and pick-up that was the weak link. Lloyd made sure the neighbors understood the importance of vigilance during those times. Without going into too much detail, he explained that the recent intruder in their home had probably been stalking them, so not only was their home at risk, but they, the McCallums, were at risk personally as well. The Larson's assured Lloyd that they would take good care of their children.

The next day, Lloyd and Valorie were off to Ocean Shores for a much needed respite from the stress and strain of living in constant fear. As they drove away from the city, they literally felt the weight lift off their shoulders. It was like they had been released from prison. They were free to live again. To feel joy again. To love again.

The route to Ocean Shores, Washington was a beautiful one — lined with evergreen trees and rich blue skies overhead. The air was fresh and the livin' easy. Lloyd felt like he was back in his old life — cruising along in his yuppie-mobile with the world on a string. He even put on his Foster-Grant shades and cranked up the stereo to the classic rock sounds of Credence Clearwater Revival. He tapped out the rhythm with his fingers on the steering wheel and nodded his head to the beat. He looked over at Valorie, and for the first time in a long time, felt pure joy. It felt so good to feel normal again and leave all the ugliness of the past year behind them.

The condo Lloyd had reserved was everything the brochure said it was. It was right on the beach with all the amenities of a high-end hotel, complete with balcony, fully stocked kitchen, king size bed, and Jacuzzi in the bath. There was still plenty of time for an afternoon stroll on the beach, which Lloyd and Valorie couldn't wait to do.

As soon as they walked in they dropped their bags on the floor, jumped in their shorts and headed for the sand. They frolicked in the surf and threw a Nerf football around. It did weird things in the ocean breeze and made them laugh. Before long, the sun began to fade and the McCallums sat down on the beach to watch the big orange ball gradually disappear into the watery horizon. It was unbelievable. There they were — alive again. Actually feeling human again. The evening only got better as Lloyd and Valorie enjoyed a refreshing dip in the Jacuzzi, dinner together, and some serious love-making, eventually falling asleep in one another's arms — something that had definitely been missing from their relationship.

The next morning brought another beautiful day with the sun shining and the surf adding its touch of continuous white noise. They finally got up around 9:00, had a leisure

B. L. McCoy

breakfast which Lloyd took pleasure in making, and headed off to browse the antique shops in town. Ocean Shores is a quaint sea-side town with plenty of history. One antique store was particularly interesting — it had all kinds of native-American artifacts and crafts. Valorie reveled in the shear relaxation of pawing through hand-made jewelry and trying on whatever struck her fancy. Lloyd simply enjoyed watching his wife enjoy herself. They felt together again, after so much turmoil and commotion in their lives.

That evening featured a street concert with local bands providing the entertainment. The evening was absolutely beautiful. A cool ocean breeze caressed performers and spectators alike. Hundreds of people from all walks of life strolling around enjoying the free entertainment, meeting and greeting with no other motive than to just relax and share a pleasant experience. It was ecstasy for Lloyd and Valorie. Two days of pure escapism. They finally got back to the condo around 9:00 pm — only to hear the phone ringing as they came in the door. Everything was about to change — dramatically.

———— ✹ ————

CHAPTER 19

Shattered Calm

Lloyd answered the phone with a cheerful "Hello."
"Lloyd, this is Skip Larson. We've been trying to get hold of you all afternoon. I don't know how to say this, but Emily is missing. We went to pick her up at school this afternoon and she didn't come out. I went back in with Gerald and we couldn't find her anywhere."

"What? Back up. Did you say you don't have Emily? What do you mean she's missing?" demanded Lloyd in an instantly agitated voice.

"When she didn't come out, we went in the school and straight to her classroom. Her teacher was still there and I asked her where Emily went. She said the last time she saw her she was headed out the door of the classroom toward the building exit."

"So what happened? Why didn't she come out with Gerald?"

"Gerald thought she was right behind him, but when he came out to get in the car she wasn't there."

"Oh my God," groaned Lloyd.

"What's going on?" asked Valorie.

"Emily's missing and the Larson's don't know where she is."

"How can that be? She knows she's not supposed to go anywhere by herself, especially while we're gone." Valorie put her hands over her mouth as pure fear swept over her.

"I know, but they've been looking for her since school got out and nothing, no sign of her."

"What do we do?" questioned Valorie.

Lloyd again spoke into the phone, "Did you go to the office and ask around for her? Look everywhere?"

"Yes. We even looked in the gym thinking she might have had some after-school thing or whatever, but nothing," said Larson.

"Did any other kids see anything?"

"No, not that was reported."

"How could she have gotten out of that building without anybody seeing where she went?"

"There is one possibility according to the principal. There's an auxiliary fire exit right across the hall from Emily's class room that can only be opened from the inside. Maybe she went out there for some reason."

"Why would she do that?" questioned Lloyd.

"I'd never noticed that door before the principal mentioned it, but that's about the only possibility," Larson reasoned.

"Where's that door go?"

"Nowhere really, there's just a fire lane back there next to that vacant green-belt area."

"Anybody could access that area and no one would know," said Lloyd, thinking out loud. "Has anybody contacted the police?"

"Not yet, we wanted to talk to you and Valorie first."

"We're coming home. We'll be there in two hours."

"We're really sorry, Lloyd. We just don't know how

Emily could've disappeared in a matter of seconds. It's not like she's a toddler or something."

"Alright, we'll be home in two hours," repeated Lloyd. Lloyd hung up the phone literally shaking. His worst fears had been realized. Valorie looked at him incredulously. How could this happen? Where was their little girl? What happened to her? Was she abducted? What horrible things might their innocent Emily experience at the hands of wicked people? How would they get her back? Would she be emotionally scarred forever?

Lloyd and Valorie hurriedly threw their belongings in their bags and flew out the door, not taking time to check out or talk to anybody. The drive home was not like the trip out to the coast. Lloyd raced down the same evergreen-lined highway, not noticing anything, not listening to anything, not enjoying anything. He drove through the night, staring straight ahead, thinking about one thing and one thing only. His concern for Emily became overwhelming. He hoped against hope that she had not been abducted. Yet, he couldn't help but think that Willie Roundtree may have had something to do with it. He didn't dare even mention that possibility to Valorie, yet he knew that she had already thought of it herself. They both just sat in the car racing through the night in complete silence and utter disbelief.

Shortly after 11:00 pm Lloyd and Valorie were banging on their neighbor's front door. The Larson's quickly opened the door and invited them in. Their staccato conversation retraced the same information they had exchanged during their phone conversation. Did the Larson's know anything more? Had anyone contacted them? Had they heard from Emily? Did Gerald remember anything he hadn't told them earlier? Did the school people have any more information? There were lots of questions but no answers. The Larson's were extremely apologetic, but it really wasn't their fault. Something had happened to Emily in the moments between when she walked out of her classroom and when she should've walked out of the building with her brother. Everybody agreed it was time to contact the police.

Lloyd and Valorie took Gerald, rather curtly said good night to the Larson's, and went home. A full report was called into the police, identifying Emily and identifying Willie Roundtree as the prime suspect in her disappearance. The police informed Lloyd that they wouldn't classify it as a kidnapping and call in the FBI until tomorrow. Too many kids just "take off" they said, and then turn up the next day having spent the night at a friend's. It was department policy to hold it for twenty-four hours before involving the feds. Lloyd and Valorie were not pacified and got very little sleep that night, knowing full well that Emily was not spending the night at a friend's.

The next morning Gerald was up as usual getting ready to leave for school when his mother came down and informed him that he would not be going to school that day. Valorie looked like she'd been through the mill. Her hair was a mess, her eyes were blood-shot, and she was wearing the same jogging suit she wore home from the coast the night before. She rummaged around the refrigerator for something to drink. Gerald had never seen his mother quite like this before.

"Is Emily gone?" he finally ventured.

"We hope not," replied Valorie in a barely audible voice.

"Are we going to look for her?" asked Gerald.

"Yes, we're going to look for her and we're going to find her," said Valorie, her voice rising.

"Where is she?"

"We don't know. But Dad thinks he might know where to start looking for her."

"Is he going to go look for her today?"

"Yes, today."

"Are we all going?"

"No, just Dad."

"How come I can't go to school? I'm not sick or anything."

"Because."

"Because why?"

"Because I say so, that's why!" Valorie said tersely. "Emily's gone and we don't want to lose you too."

Valorie tried to focus her blood-shot eyes on her son as tears welled up and ran down her cheeks. About that time Lloyd heard the commotion downstairs and came down himself. He too looked like he'd been through the ringer. He could hardly function. Gerald had two zombies for parents. Then a sound penetrated their consciousness — it was the phone ringing. Lloyd hesitated to pick it up, not knowing what he might hear on the other end.

"Mr. McCallum?"

"Yes."

"This is Mr. Hernandez, the principal at your children's school. Your daughter, Emily, is here. She says she was dropped off this morning by a friend of her mom and dad's. I know your neighbor, Mr. Larson, was looking for her yesterday after school and couldn't find her. He seemed pretty worried, but she's here this morning wanting to go to class."

"Is she okay?" stammered Lloyd.

"Yes, she looks fine."

"Keep her there in your office. I'm on my way right now."

"Alright, see you in a few minutes."

Lloyd hung up the phone and looked incredulously at Valorie who seemed to simultaneously melt with anticipation. Could it be that easy? Could their little girl just reappear without a scratch? Lloyd grabbed his car keys and rushed out the door.

The five minute drive to the kids' school took way too long as far as Lloyd was concerned. He pulled up and stopped in a no-parking zone right in front of the main entrance, barely taking time to throw the car in park before jumping out and running for the door. He burst into the main office and saw Emily sitting calmly with Mr. Hernandez. He hurriedly approached and crouching down face to face with his daughter, abruptly scooped her up in a tearful embrace. Lloyd couldn't believe his good fortune — he was actually holding his little girl in his arms. He couldn't wait to get back home to Valorie and quickly walked out of the office, repeatedly thanking Mr. Hernandez as he went. He carefully placed her in the back seat in a seat belt and drove home, constantly looking at her in the rear-view mirror.

Once home, Lloyd carefully removed his daughter from the back seat of the car and carried her in the house to Valorie's waiting arms. Mother and daughter hugged like it had been ages since they had seen each other — at least Valorie acted like it'd been that long. Finally, the hugging and kissing were over and Lloyd and Valorie began to ask their daughter questions.

"Mr. Larson called and told us he couldn't find you after school yesterday, so we came home, but when we got here he still didn't know where you were. We worried about you all night. Where were you?" asked Lloyd in his best non-lawyer manner.

"I went to your friend's house. He told me he was supposed to pick me up yesterday — that it was a surprise, instead of going home with Mr. Larson."

"What friend?" asked Lloyd tersely. "He was outside the fire door across the hall from my room and when I came out he pointed at me to come over to the door. When I got close, he told me to open the door, so I did."

"Where was your teacher?"

"She was in the room."

"Did she see him?"

"I don't think so."

"Did he ever tell you his name?"

"He knew my name was Emily and he said he was supposed to pick me up — that it was a surprise."

"Yes, I know it was supposed to be a surprise. Did he ever tell you his name?"

"He was nice, Daddy. Are you mad at me?"

Lloyd ignored his daughter's tender question. He was now in fact-finding mode.

"How did you get out of the school?"

"I went out the fire door."

"Where'd you go from there?"

"We walked through the woods out to the road and got in your friend's car."

"What friend? Does he have a name?" pressed Lloyd, becoming agitated.

"Lloyd," cautioned Valorie.

Lloyd and Valorie exchanged glances.

"He's Mr. Willie," announced Emily like she was introducing a neighborhood hero.

"Mr. Willie?" asked Lloyd incredulously, looking at Valorie again. "What's he look like?"

"He's nice, daddy. He's a nice black man. He gave me some candy on the way to his house."

"Where did he take you, Emily?"

"He took me to his house and we had a sleep-over."

"Where's his house?"

"A long ways from here — in the city."

"Did anything happen to you? Did anybody touch you or hurt you?"

"No, we just had some dinner and watched TV at his house."

"Was anybody else there?"

"No, just us."

"Where'd you sleep?"

"Mr. Willie said I could sleep on the couch, so he got a blanket and we had a sleep-over."

"Where'd Mr. Willie sleep?" asked Lloyd in a forced tone.

"Oh, he slept in his bedroom. And then this morning Mr. Willie gave me some cereal for breakfast and said he was going to take me back to school, so he dropped me off instead of Mr. Larson. Is that okay, Daddy?"

"No, it's not okay. Mom's told you before, many times, not to go anywhere with anybody, remember? We went over this the last time that guy gave you candy." Father and daughter looked intently into one another's eyes.

"But we're glad you're home safe now."

"Mr. Willie said to give you this," Emily finally said cautiously, reaching into her backpack.

Lloyd took a crumpled piece of paper from his daughter and slowly opened it. Carefully he read the few words scrawled on the paper.

"Have a nice day, counselor."

Lloyd could not believe what he was reading. The shear audacity of that scum. Lloyd's mind went into overdrive.

"He comes into my family and takes my child! Who the hell does he think he is?! He thinks he can just toy with us and humiliate us whenever he gets the urge. He thinks he's untouchable. Like there's nothing I can do about it. Well, he's in for a rude awakening," Lloyd said to himself with teeth clenched.

"Why don't you go upstairs with Mom and take a bath and put on some clean clothes," Lloyd finally said to his daughter.

"What are you going to do?" questioned Valorie.

"I'm going to find that SOB, that's what I'm going to do."

Valorie knew there was no use trying to reason with her husband right then, so she just quietly took Emily by the hand and went upstairs to clean up – they both needed to wash away the previous night.

CHAPTER 20

Operation Confrontation

Lloyd knew from his days in the Army that any assault operation had to be planned out carefully. He'd tried to talk to Roundtree and get him to respect the Restraining Order — without success. Since then, the man had violated their home and left threatening graffiti on the kitchen wall and now had gone so far as to actually kidnap their daughter. Lloyd knew there was no stopping him without a violent confrontation. Willie delighted in terrorizing people. He loved to see people squirm under pressure. Lloyd would have to be thoroughly prepared.

He began to go through the planning process, harkening back to his experience in Special Forces. An operations order is comprised of five parts — mission, men, equipment, weather, and terrain — each of which must be analyzed and evaluated. First, what's the mission? What is it that needs to be accomplished? Next, the personnel — who's going to do it? What expertise is required to carry out the mission? Then, what equipment is required? What weaponry may be needed? Next, what's the weather going to be like? Is it going to be a night operation? If so, what will the moon be that night? And finally, what's the terrain like? Is it hilly, flat, urban or rural? All of these things had to be considered and planned for, with back-up or contingency plans in case things changed in the middle of the operation. Lloyd knew the routine well — as both an Army officer and a trial lawyer. He knew to plan on the unexpected.

So, what was the mission? Lloyd had to think about that. It wasn't as obvious as he once thought. Ultimately, he knew he had to convince Willie to leave his family alone — for good. But how could he do that? Willie had already demonstrated that he was not going to be deterred. He delighted in antagonizing them. Lloyd figured that if he really put Willie on his back and threatened him to within an inch of his life, he might get the message and leave them alone. Lloyd would have to catch him alone somewhere by surprise and mess him up good. Lloyd knew how to handle himself — he'd been trained in martial arts to some extent, but Willie would probably be armed. How would Lloyd deal with that? He would have to take a weapon with him and be prepared to use it.

Suddenly, Lloyd realized what he was doing. He was planning a vigilante operation, relying in all probability, on the use of deadly force. But he was a lawyer — an officer of the court, who could not only be arrested but disbarred for violating the law. He stood to lose everything — even his ability to practice law and support his family. But why worry about supporting his family if he didn't have a family — if Willie Roundtree took his family away from him? First, his wife and now his daughter. They weren't safe. He had to protect them. He had no choice.

To pull off the operation would require some surveillance. Lloyd knew better than to walk into a situation without good intelligence. He decided to use Duane Jackson to collect some intel. He would need to know Willie's daily routine, if he had one. When did he come and go? Where exactly did he live — what was the neighborhood like, what streets provided ingress and egress, was there an alley behind the house, did anyone else live in the house besides Willie? Emily said she didn't see anybody else the night she was there, but Lloyd couldn't count on that. Hopefully he lived alone. In any event, he would eventually have to decide the best time and place to confront the man — one on one.

Lloyd contacted Duane the next morning and gave him his to-do list — all the things Lloyd needed to know to get in and out in one piece. Days went by and nothing. Lloyd grew impatient. He hoped Duane hadn't gotten a better offer elsewhere and sold him out. Finally, Duane called back with most of the needed information including the most important information of all — where Willie lived.

He related that Willie followed the same basic routine almost every day. He gets up late, drives down town for lunch at Louie's and spends most of the day shooting pool and hanging out with his homies. Except every Friday afternoon, he goes over to the welfare office, picks up his unemployment check and promptly cashes it at the nearest bank. Then he heads to one of the neighborhood bars where he eventually gets wasted. He gets home around 1:00 o'clock — usually alone, but sometimes with a woman. That was the best Duane could do but it was probably enough for what Lloyd planned to do. One more thing Duane added — there is an alley behind Willie's house. Lloyd decided that would be his avenue of approach.

As Lloyd processed the information he'd gotten from Duane, he decided the best time to initiate contact would be on a Friday night — as Willie was getting home from his evening's entertainment. Lloyd figured he'd be a lot easier to handle under the influence, and probably less likely to remember what happened. At this point Lloyd didn't care if Willie remembered what happened to him, he just wanted to make a strong impression on his long-time nemesis — an unmistakable impression!

Lloyd became preoccupied with the prospect of confronting his antagonist one on one. He could hardly think about anything else. He went through the scenario over and over his head, trying to nail down every detail of the operation. And that's what it was — a military operation — an ambush. Lloyd had planned and carried out other ambushes in the Army, but this one was different. This one involved initiating a violent assault, not in a war zone, but in a residential neighborhood.

Lloyd struggled with the legality of what he was planning. He couldn't shake his training in the law and his respect for the rule of law. But he'd tried that. He'd tried using a Restraining Order to keep Willie away from him and his family and Willie just mocked it — he not only mocked it, but committed other crimes against his family in the meantime. He burglarized and defaced their home. He even kidnapped Emily. There was only one way to stop it.

As the appointed day arrived, Lloyd was obviously on edge. He hadn't shared his plans with Valorie, but she knew something was up. The kids were finally asleep and Lloyd and Valorie were alone getting ready for bed themselves when Valorie decided to find out what was brewing.

"What are you doing?" she finally asked him.

"What do you mean?" responded Lloyd.

"You're getting ready to do something, aren't you."

"Yeah, I'm getting ready to do something."

"What?"

"I'm going to stop this garbage once and for all."

"And just how do you plan to do that?"

"I'm going to pay our friend a visit."

"By yourself?"

"Yes, by myself."

"Don't you think that's a little risky?"

"I know it's risky, but I'm going to do what I have to to protect my family."

"You know Willie Roundtree is an animal. He'll kill you, Lloyd, and then what? What happens to us — me and the kids?"

"I'll make sure that doesn't happen."

"Sure! And how are you going to do that? Are you going to kill him first? Then what? They come and haul you off to prison and we're still left alone!"

"I'm just going to deliver a message — one that will convince him to leave us alone."

"Do you really think that's going to work? It'll just make him all the more psycho!"

"We have no choice, Valorie. We already know he's not going to leave us alone. I've got to get to him and put him on his back. That's the only thing he understands."

"What if something goes wrong?"

"Nothing's going to go wrong. I've thought through this thing so many times I could do it in my sleep."

"You can't control Willie Roundtree. Nobody can. That's the problem. How can you be so sure something won't go wrong?"

"Because I'm prepared to kill him."

The words just hung in the air like a foul odor as Lloyd and Valorie stood there staring at each other. Neither one of them could believe it had come to this — that they were actually talking about killing someone. And yet they both knew it may well come to that. They were totally exposed to the ravages of a wild animal and the only way they could protect themselves was to use deadly force if necessary.

"When are you going to do this?" Valorie finally ventured.

"Tomorrow night. I'm going to Willie's house and wait for him. I've got some intel so I'm not going in blind."

"Reliable intel?" questioned Valorie, harkening back to his

days in the Army.

"I think so. I trust the source."

"Well, you better make sure."

"I'm sure."

That night was a restless night for both the McCallums. The next day was even worse. There was little conversation throughout the day with both of them just trying to busy themselves around the house and yard. The kids' going and coming from school was uneventful, but they were extremely cautious after what had happened to Emily. Finally, evening came and the kids were in bed for the night. It was Friday night — time to take care of business.

Lloyd slipped upstairs and began by changing his clothes. He put on all black — black cargo pants, long sleeve pull-over shirt, socks, shoes and cap. He then went to his bedroom closet and retrieved his 357 magnum revolver and holstered it on his left side, handle to the front — he preferred to reach across his body for his hand gun — it took less elbow room. He then slipped on a black nylon wind breaker to cover the gun. Finally, he put on black leather gloves. He looked menacing, even criminal. He came downstairs and approached Valorie who gasped when she saw him. She had never seen her husband dressed in such garb. Nor had she ever seen that look in his eyes. Her husband was going hunting, and she knew he — they — had everything to lose. But she also knew that they had tried everything to protect themselves — to no avail.

Lloyd said nothing as he kissed his beloved wife good-bye. They just stood there looking into one another's eyes for what seemed like a long time, then Lloyd turned, made his way to the garage, got in his car and drove into the night.

Valorie was sick inside. How could it have come to this? No matter what, their lives were never going to be the same. Indeed, their lives had not been the same since that fateful night Willie Roundtree first broke into their house and raped her. All the ugliness that had ensued from that one act of despicable depravity was incomprehensible. Their peace and security in every respect was nonexistent. They were reduced to the law of the jungle — mere survival — kill or be killed.

*   *   *

As Lloyd drove toward the city, he felt his stomach get tighter and tighter. This was not a courtroom appearance he was going to. He would not be exchanging pleasantries with court personnel and opposing counsel. He would not be doing verbal battle this time. He would be engaging in hand-to-hand combat with a man who could actually kill him. Lloyd carefully weaved his way through the inner city toward Willie's neighborhood. It was midnight already and very dark. A light mist settled on the streets which glistened from the occasional corner street light.

Lloyd arrived at the staging area, a side street a block from Willie's house, and parked his car, still sporting scratches down the side from his visit to Louie's. He sat there, hands gripping the steering wheel, staring into the darkness. His mind raced. He didn't know what to expect. All he knew was that he had to face Willie and put him on his back. He had to knock him down. He had to scare him to within an inch of his life. He had to make him leave his family alone. Lloyd finally slipped out of the car, careful to trip the lock before closing the door so as not to make any noise. The alley to Willie's house lay to the right just in front of where Lloyd had parked. He quickly moved into the darkness and silently crept toward Willie's back yard.

Lloyd was surprised at how quiet the neighborhood was on a Friday night. The alley stunk of old half-filled garbage cans lining the sides of the narrow roadway. As he got closer, he recognized the layout from Duane's description. There was a broken down six foot wooden fence surrounding the back

216

yard with a sagging gate which Lloyd found unlocked. He slowly opened the gate and slipped into the backyard which was relatively small and unkempt. There were no lights or sounds. The fence went up both sides of the house toward the front, separating Willie's house from the houses on either side in the old crowded neighborhood. There was no garage, but a small dirt drive-way allowed off-street parking in front of the house. Lloyd would wait for Willie in the shadows by the driveway. He pictured Willie coming home, getting out of his car and starting for the front door. Lloyd planned to jump him before he got there. Everything was in place.

Lloyd waited. He waited longer. He waited into the night — trying to stay focused. Lloyd went back to his days in the Army — waiting in ambush. It was boring. It was agonizing. It was scary. But when the enemy showed up, all hell broke loose — in an instant the whole area exploded into a deafening roar of gunfire and a light show of muzzle flashes. Bodies and body parts flew everywhere. There's no way to describe it but pure carnage. It would be so easy to just ambush and execute Willie, but Lloyd couldn't bring himself to do that. He wasn't a murderer.

Suddenly, Lloyd heard a car approaching. He peeked out of the shadows as it slowly meandered toward the house. It had to be Willie. Lloyd's body immediately tensed up and he began to breathe faster. Sure enough, the car jockeyed its way into the driveway and stopped — not ten feet from where Lloyd was hiding. Nothing happened. The driver just sat there in the car. Had he seen something? Did he suspect something? Had he been tipped off? Lloyd waited. He couldn't risk jumping Willie in the car and possibly getting shot at point blank range. He had to wait for Willie to get out where he could see him and catch him before he got in the house.

Finally, the car door opened and Willie emerged — slowly, a little under the influence, just like Duane had said.

217

He threw the car door shut and turned toward the front door of the house. Just as he cleared the front left fender of his car, Lloyd grabbed him by the shoulders from behind and spun him around. Before Willie could react, Lloyd grabbed him by the face, squeezing his cheeks between his fingers and thumb and driving him back against the front of the house, holding him there like he'd been nailed against the wall. Practically nose to nose, Lloyd began his lesson on peaceful co-existence.

"Do you know who I am? This is Lloyd McCallum talking to you."

Willie's eyes widened.

"It's just you and me, Willie. You're going to leave me and my family alone — forever."

Willie heard that as a death threat and immediately reacted. With his right hand he knocked Lloyd's grip off his face and with his left fist he drilled Lloyd in the ribs. The surprise blow to the body stunned Lloyd who hadn't absorbed a punch like that in a long time. Lloyd lurched back.

"You're right, counselor, it's just you and me. I been waitin' for this for a long time," whereupon Willie threw a hard right cross catching Lloyd just below the left eye. Lloyd immediately countered with a powerful right fist to Willie's mid-section. He could hear the air belching out of his lungs as Willie gasped for breath. Lloyd moved in with a left elbow smash to Willie's face. Willie swung wildly at Lloyd who was too close to suffer any damage.

Suddenly, Willie head butted Lloyd sending him reeling back. Willie could see that Lloyd was dazed and came in for the kill. Lloyd bent over inviting the advance, but as Willie closed in Lloyd responded with a fierce upper-cut to the groin. Willie groaned with nauseating pain as his knees buckled and he slumped back against the house. Both men tried to recover from the other's debilitating assault. Lloyd was seeing double from Willie's head butt, though he was aware that Willie was trying to make his way to the backyard and into the house. Lloyd gave chase. Both men stumbled along the side of the house into the backyard where Lloyd caught up to Willie and tackled him. Willie rolled over on his back and tried to kick Lloyd off him. Lloyd managed to get to his feet and viciously kicked Willie, who somehow managed to roll over and get to his feet himself. Willie then suddenly upped the ante and pulled a knife. He lunged at Lloyd and barely missed with the shiny blade. He smiled fiendishly as he stood there with his four inch long switch-blade.

"I'm going to cut you up and feed your lily white flesh to that pretty little wench of yours."

Lloyd backed up a step and got ready. He remembered the filthy graffiti Willie left on their kitchen wall.

Willie then came at Lloyd, thrusting his knife at his chest. Lloyd had practiced reacting to such an assault many times and knew how to defend against it. In an instant he grabbed Willie's wrist with his right hand and with his open left hand, swung cross-ways striking Willie's extended elbow with tremendous force breaking his arm at the joint. Willie screamed in agony, dropped the knife and ran for the back door of the house.

Lloyd started to give chase but Willie got to the door just in time to release his dog which came roaring out of house at Lloyd. The dog was a huge black Doberman and it came at Lloyd with a vengeance. It bounded toward Lloyd and leaped up at his face with its foaming mouth gaping wide open. Lloyd could do nothing but put his arm up to protect his face. The dog bit down on Lloyd's left arm with tremendous force and began to tear away the flesh.

The searing pain felt like his whole arm had caught on fire. Instantly blood began to gush out. The attack seemed to go on in slow motion forever — the dog's huge teeth tearing at Lloyd's arm like a killer shark in the midst of a feeding frenzy.

Finally, he had presence of mind to strike a horrendous blow to the dog's ribs with his right fist. It yelped in pain and let go, but not for long as the big Doberman crouched down, snarling, preparing to attack again. Willie stood at the back door yelling at the dog to "kill!" The huge animal obeyed and lunged at Lloyd's left thigh but only caught his pant leg, ripping a hole in his trousers.

Lloyd was quickly running out of options, he couldn't let the dog get hold of him again, and if he fell or was knocked down, he'd be shredded. He suddenly reached across his body, pulled out his gun and BOOM! — fired one shot into the dog's head. It instantly fell dead at his feet. He then pointed the gun at Willie and just stared at him. It would be so easy to just pull the trigger and end it. Willie stood there on his back porch, his useless right arm dangling at his side, almost daring Lloyd to shoot him.

"You shot my dog!" Willie finally yelled.

"Next time it'll be you," replied Lloyd. "Stay away from me and my family."

"You better end it now, white boy," Willey taunted.

"You come near me or my family again and I'll kill you," Lloyd said with absolute conviction.

The two men just glared at each other in silence as Lloyd slowly backed out of the yard, keeping his eye — and gun — trained on Willie. He then hurriedly made his way down the alley back to his car. By the time he got there, Lloyd couldn't even feel his left arm. Blood was streaming down and running off his hand, leaving a trail on the ground. His face was a mess too. His left eye was bruised and swollen and his forehead and nose were bleeding. He could hardly manage to get in his car and drive to the nearest emergency room.

Lloyd could only hope that he'd gotten his message across. At least he'd confronted the man and demonstrated his willingness to meet him on his terms. And there was no going back. No appealing to the law. No negotiating. The next time these two men met, if they ever did, one of them was going to die.

CHAPTER 21

Back in the Saddle

Lloyd's face healed pretty quickly, but his left arm was another matter. The dog had nearly crushed the arm causing serious damage to the muscles and nerves and permanently weakening his grip. Fortunately, Lloyd was right-handed, but the healing process was slow and agonizing. He even had a hard time doing routine tasks like mowing the lawn, working around the house, or carrying groceries. He was reminded daily of his encounter with Willie Roundtree. At least, he thought, Willie had some long-term issues as well. His right arm would never be the same after being fractured at the elbow. And Lloyd was pretty sure he'd never forget that shot to the groin.

Otherwise, life had basically returned to semi-normal. It had been several weeks since the fight at Willie's and Lloyd began to feel more and more like Willie was a just a bad memory. He also began to feel restless and wanted to get back to work. Lloyd had been off for nearly a year and needed to get back in the saddle. Valorie also seemed ready to return to life as they'd known it. There was, however, that constant nagging feeling that the McCallum's were not entirely safe.

Lloyd and Valorie were still extremely cautious when it came to their two children. Realizing how easy it was for Willie to abduct Emily from school made them shudder. If that were to somehow happen a second time, they would probably never see their little girl again. The way Willie's mind worked, he could rationalize killing Emily in retaliation for Lloyd killing his dog. So the McCallum's never left their children unattended. They even accompanied them to and from their classroom inside the school building.

It was a good time of year, though. The holiday season was upon them and spirits were high. Thanksgiving had come and gone and the whole neighborhood was preparing for Christmas. It was a delight to see how everybody decorated their homes in Briarwood. There was no shortage of lights silhouetting the homes and outlining Christmas figures on the lawns and even some roofs. The McCallum's were no exception. They went all out stringing lights around the outside of their home and the perennial trees in their front yard. It all was a welcome relief from the horrific events of the past year.

But Lloyd longed to be back at work. It was all he could do to keep busy, although Willie Roundtree had kept him plenty occupied — in fact totally pre-occupied. But Lloyd needed the rush of courtroom battle. He had become very good at it and thoroughly enjoyed the verbal combat. Indeed, his encounter with Willie had made him appreciate the legal system all the more. Disputes should be resolved in a civil non-violent manner, not by a fight to the death where it's simply survival of the fittest. At least that's how things are supposed to work. So Lloyd decided to go talk to his mentor and friend, Gerald Everett, and tell him he wanted his job back — his "sabbatical" was over.

Lloyd figured that just before Christmas would be

a good time to go talk to his old boss — hopefully he'd be in good spirits and willing to bring Lloyd back starting the first of the year. Lloyd knew he could always appeal to his former boss' business interests since Lloyd had always been able to generate substantial revenue for the firm. So, come the middle of December, Lloyd made an appointment to go in and see Mr. Everett.

It was strange going back after a year away. It was surreal to walk into his old firm and not feel totally comfortable. Before being "laid off" he felt like he owned the place. He had developed such a reputation for winning that everybody kind of stooped and bowed around him. But that all changed very quickly when he began to unravel and lose his touch. Lloyd could still vividly remember his last conversation with Gerald, who at the end of the day was the consummate lawyer, capable of making the hard choices — including sending Lloyd on "sabbatical."

The offices of LANCASTER, VERNON and EVERETT were swank, exuding success in every respect. Nearly all the walls and room dividers were made of thick glass with decorative floor to ceiling blinds and colorful visual barriers. Even the receptionist's counter directly in front of the entrance was glass enclosed revealing her short skirt and shapely legs. To the left was the hall leading to the lawyers' and legal secretaries' offices. To the right were several conference rooms, all ornately furnished.

"Well, hello stranger," sang Loralee, the firm's attractive 20-something receptionist, as Lloyd walked in.

"Hey, how you doing?" responded Lloyd with a smile.

"I'm fine. Good to see you again."

"You are fine, indeed," said Lloyd with a wink, always the charmer.

Loralee, reacting with appropriate modesty replied, "Mr. McCallum, we've all missed you. Are you back with us now?"

"Well, I think it's time. Let's hope Gerald Everett thinks so too."

"I'm sure he does. I don't think he's been quite the same since you've been gone," assured Loralee as she buzzed Gerald on the intercom to let him know Lloyd was waiting. A moment later the receptionist informed Lloyd that he could go in. It seemed weird that he had to check in with the receptionist before proceeding to the inner sanctum of his old law firm. The meeting with his highly respected mentor was a much anticipated event, but not one Lloyd ever thought he'd have to endure. It felt like he was going hat-in-hand to ask if he could please have his job back. It almost felt like he was reduced to begging. Gerald had been relatively kind when he laid Lloyd off, calling it a "sabbatical" but he'd been laid-off nevertheless. As Lloyd walked into the spacious nicely furnished office, Gerald got up and walked toward him with hand outstretched and a warm greeting. He drew Lloyd into an embrace and invited him to sit down in one of the plush chairs in front of the large desk.

"So you're back! Good to see you. How have you been?" began Mr. Everett.

"I'm good. It's been good," replied Lloyd, nodding his head, while making sure his left arm was covered with a long sleeve shirt.

"It's hard to believe it's been a year already," said Everett.

"Yeah, it's gone by fast. It was nice to have the time off, but I'm definitely ready to get back at it. How's the case load these days?"

"Well, there's plenty of work, but we've been a little thin in the criminal law department. We could sure use you, Lloyd, if you're rested and ready."

"I was hoping you felt that way. I'm rested and ready — more than ready to have life return to normal."

"So what ever happened to that former client that was

giving you so much grief?"

"Well, he really had us stirred up there for a while, but I think he's finally faded into the past."

"Alright, good. How 'bout starting the first of next week. That'll give us time to get your office back in shape. By the way, how's Valorie and the kids?"

"They're good. We've had some quality time together the last several months and things are a lot better."

Gerald just sat there looking at Lloyd for several seconds. "I can't imagine what it must have been like to cross examine your wife on the stand," he finally said.

Lloyd too, just sat there for a while without answering, his mind reviewing all the events of the last year and a half. How he wished he could go back and change things, starting with the assault on his beloved Valorie. But somehow they had survived it all and remained in tact — or so they hoped. The last step was for Lloyd to go back to work and things would finally be back to normal again.

"Yeah, I'd rather not do that again," he said simply.

"Alright then. We'll see you first thing next week. Good to have you back, Lloyd."

"It's really good to be back. I'm looking forward to diving right in."

The two men stood up, shook hands, and Lloyd strode out of Gerald's office feeling like he finally had his life back. What a great feeling to be back on track after the unbelievable nightmare he and his family had been through.

———— ✖ ————

CHAPTER 22

"I Got 'Em"

Monday morning invoked the old familiar hustle-and-bustle routine the McCallum's had become accustomed to before the rape. Lloyd and Valorie were up early with the kids getting ready for the day. It was a new beginning and it felt like it. Everybody could sense a return to normal in the McCallum household.

They all gathered in the kitchen for breakfast before going their separate ways, and then it was Valorie off to school with the kids and Lloyd off to work. Yes, work — what a welcome blessing to once again to be anxiously engaged. He couldn't wait to immerse himself in it again. The thrill of victory and the agony of defeat — the old World-wide Sports intro made famous by sportscaster Jim McKay. Only the practice of law, especially criminal law, was a lot more serious than any sporting event. Yet the lawyers often viewed it as just that — sport. May the best man win. Not necessarily the best case, or truth and justice, or even the most worthy litigant. The best man, i.e., the best lawyer. Lloyd still loved it.

As he drove downtown a flood of memories washed over him. He was back in the saddle — on his way to the office — his office, his own think tank, where his mind controlled his environment and served as his weapon of choice. LANCASTER, VERNON and EVERETT was a good place to work. The firm enjoyed a solid reputation in the legal community and its location in the middle of the business district put it at the center of all the action. The firm's principals traveled in all the right circles and Lloyd was now back in the middle of all that upward-mobility maneuvering. He didn't have to consciously pursue upward-mobility however, it had come to him simply by virtue of his prowess in the courtroom.

As Lloyd pulled into the underground parking garage below the high-rise building containing his law firm, he took his time wending his way toward the old familiar parking stall. The sound of the tires' subdued screeching as he turned the sharp corners, the echo of car doors shutting, the tapping of foot steps as people hurried to the elevators was a welcome reminder of his former life. Everything seemed so much more acute now, so much more vivid, even exciting. The ride up the elevator to the 20th floor was exhilarating. Finally, he swung open the big glass doors to the firm's reception area. He was home at last. It was like he'd never left.

On his desk was a stack of files and his ever loyal secretary, Sally, was johnny-on-the-spot, ready to bring Lloyd up to date on every one of them. The first order of business — an armed robbery of a small local bank — by a woman, no less. "A female bank robber — that ought to be interesting," Lloyd thought.

"Alright, what-a-ya got?" Lloyd asked.

"You'll like her," said Sally, referring to their client.

"Heck yeah, I like all bank robbers, especially girl bank robbers."

"Well, this one is definitely a go-getter. She's former

military — served in the middle-east and everything."

"So how'd it go down?"

"She planned it out pretty well — knew when the armored car was going to be there to deliver the week's cash, and what the procedure was between delivery and securing the money in the vault. So after the armored car guys left and before it was stuck in the vault, she walked in and grabbed it."

"So how'd she get caught?"

"Pure happen-stance — the armored car guys came back because they'd overlooked a bag of cash they were supposed to drop off there instead of somewhere else. So just as our gal was exiting the bank the armored car folks showed up and jumped her. It's a good thing there was more than one of them too — guess she was a real handfull."

"Alright, so what's our defense?" probed Lloyd.

"Plead guilty," replied Sally with a perplexed smile.

"That's no defense," Lloyd retorted. "We have to come up with something. How long was she in the middle-east?"

"Two tours, a year each time. And she's only been back a few months."

"What's her job situation?"

"No job. Apparently the Army just discharged her with no follow-up whatsoever."

"Well, that's our defense — the government uses and abuses these people and when they're done with them, they just toss them aside like so much trash. It's called PTSD — post-traumatic stress disorder and it can make people act in very strange ways."

"I don't know, Lloyd, that could be stretching it — go rob a bank because you were traumatized in the military?"

"If she wasn't thinking rationally, and I'm sure we can get an expert to say that, then she doesn't have the mens rea. And if she doesn't have criminal intent, she hasn't committed a crime. The prosecution has to prove every element of the crime — including criminal intent — beyond a reasonable doubt. Put that together with the sympathy factor — poor vet with no job and suffering in this tough economy, we might just be able to raise a little doubt."

"Alright, I'll get on it," sighed Sally.

Lloyd was lovin' it. He was back in the saddle again — taking pot shots at the prosecution's case long before he ever set foot in the courtroom.

The days passed uneventfully. Lloyd hadn't missed a beat. His office once again felt like home away from home. He was back in the groove. Life was good. He threw himself into his bank robbery case just like the old days — building the case piece by piece, looking in every nook and cranny for the "reasonable doubt" that would free his client and win the case. Winning was what it was all about. The competition was exhilarating, even intoxicating. Seeing the expression on the prosecution's face when the verdict "not guilty" was read out loud by the jury was worth as much as the cold hard cash Lloyd got for his work. Yes!! To win in that arena was an adrenaline rush beyond comparison.

The robbery case and several others worked their way through the system, but Lloyd became fascinated with his female bank robbery suspect. It was time for Sally to set up an appointment with her. She had managed to post bail, so the appointment could take place in his office rather than at the jail. When the appointed time came, Lloyd was ready — he thought.

"Lloyd, Ms. Jefferson, your 10:00 o'clock appointment, is here," a voice announced through the intercom.

"Bring her on back," instructed Lloyd.

A couple minutes later Sally appeared at Lloyd's door with a young woman in tow.

"This is Mr. McCallum," she said politely, pointing her open hand toward Lloyd.

"Come in, come in," instructed Lloyd. "Have a seat." Lloyd was immediately impressed with his client. Ms.

Jefferson was an attractive Caucasian woman in her early thirties, auburn shoulder length hair, dark eyes, and nicely dressed in a navy blue pants suit. She sat down like she was ready to begin a military briefing — stiff and formal, no nonsense.

"So tell me about yourself," began Lloyd.

"What do ya want to know?" came the rather curt response.

"Let's start with why you're charged with holding up a bank," replied Lloyd, sensing that he needed to take control of the conversation right from the get-go and let his client know who was in charge.

"I was at my wits-end, that's why."

"What's that mean?"

"It means I was out of money, out of time, and out of my mind."

"Okay, it's the out-of-your-mind part that I'm interested in."

"It was like I went into some sort of trance or something. It felt like I was back in Iraq. 'Course it didn't help that I was flat broke and staring at all kinds of bills."

"Bills for what?"

"Medical bills."

"For what?"

"You name it — seems like I have it. But mostly prescription medications."

"For what? I'm starting to sound like a broken record here."

"For PTSD I guess they call it. They had me on all kinds of stuff, expensive stuff."

"Who had you on all kinds of stuff?"

"The VA, but they wouldn't pay for it. I had to pay for it out of my own pocket."

"And what were you paying for it with?"

"Now you're gettin' it — I didn't have the money, so

no medication. And then the dreams started again and all the frustration and the whole thing all over again."

"The whole what thing?"

"The war," she said softly, looking down at the floor.

Lloyd paused for a moment, realizing that he had broken her down in just a few short minutes. She was an honorably discharged veteran who was basically kicked to curb and left on her own — with some serious problems.

"What was your job in the military?" Lloyd finally asked.

"I was a psy-ops specialist attached to an SF team."

"Psychological warfare operations with Special Forces."

"That's right. Out there with the bad boys — way out there."

Lloyd could identify. He'd spent his share of time out in the bush with "the bad boys." Memories of his own days in SF came flooding back.

"Two tours?"

"Yes, two long years."

Lloyd just sat there looking at Andrea Jefferson — the all American girl, turned warrior. "Too bad they don't show the end from the beginning in all those Army commercials," he thought. Too bad they don't show people what happens to their bright-eyed, bushy-tailed young men and women after they've spent a year or two in combat. Even if they don't get shot up or blown apart, they come back with horrific images of killing and dying in their heads — images that would cripple the psyche of any normal person. But Andrea Jefferson knew how to survive — she knew how to survive under the most life-threatening circumstances. Survival — that's what it's about. You do what you have to to survive — and using any available means is permissible. That's what the Army had taught her. You couple that with a chemical imbalance in the brain and there goes criminal intent right out the window. Lloyd was already mentally preparing his opening statement for trial.

What a rush this trial was going to be, he thought. A war vet caught red-handed robbing a bank. How was he going to get her off? He'd put the war and the VA on trial. We send these kids half way around the world and expose them to horrific scenes of carnage and bloodshed and then dump them back on society — left to fend for themselves, after having been emotionally dismembered. What jury wouldn't feel sorry for someone like that? — especially if they suffered from a recognized mental disorder that impaired their ability to formulate criminal intent. What an opportunity for Lloyd to practice his skills as an advocate. The challenge was on and he threw himself into preparing his case.

Meanwhile, back at the McCallum home, life was good. Lloyd and Valorie were enjoying life like it was meant to be. Their relationship was back on track and the kids were growing like weeds. They were a family again. They hardly gave Willie Roundtree a thought any more.

But Willie Roundtree thought a lot about the McCallum's. He'd had two surgeries on his elbow just to be able to shave and button his shirt. But what really bothered him the most was that he couldn't shoot pool like he used to. He couldn't manipulate the pool cue with any accuracy at all. And it hurt all the time no matter what he did — a constant reminder that Lloyd McCallum had broken his arm — literally snapped it right at the elbow. He brooded over it. For Willie Roundtree, life was not good. He needed revenge. Contemplating his vengeance became his drug of choice. It felt good to think about how he would inflict pain on Lloyd McCallum. His mind relished the thought of destroying him. He became obsessed with it. Next time there would be no mercy. There would be no walking the kids home from school, no harmless graffiti on the kitchen wall, no pleasant little over-nighter with Emily, no fisticuffs in the back yard. No, next time Lloyd McCallum would feel pain — pain like he'd never felt it before. Willie was going to hurt Lloyd and hurt him bad. It was just a matter of how and when.

It never occurred to Willie to question why he felt such contempt for the man who had kept him out of prison twice. Willie was walking the streets a free man because of Lloyd McCallum. Why the intense dislike and obsessive need to get at him? Why couldn't he just enjoy his freedom and count his lucky stars that he wasn't in jail somewhere? Willie didn't understand why he was so jealous. But that was it. Jealousy. He hated other men who had everything. Not because he couldn't have it, but because he wouldn't have it — wouldn't do what it takes to earn it. Not only did he despise men who had it all, but what made it worse was they had enough largess to give it away — to lend their power and influence to rescue men like Willie Roundtree. So they must feel superior. They must be egotistical. They must think they're privileged. They must be brought down! All those condescending fat cats! And Willie figured he was just the one to do it. And if he got caught, he'd just plunk down a get-out-of-jail-free card, i.e., hire another lawyer like McCallum. After all, he'd managed to dodge the bullet twice already.

*   *   *

Before Lloyd knew it, the bank robbery trial was upon him. He'd prepared well and knew his strategy. And who was the prosecutor on the other side? — Frank Cartwright, of course. These two men had met many times before and Lloyd usually came out on top, so Cartwright had something to prove this time. He knew Lloyd's strategy of portraying the accused as some sort of poor war veteran who'd lost her way because of combat fatigue — popularly known as PTSD. But he didn't buy it. He couldn't wait to take Lloyd and his client to task. His argument: we take these young people off the street and make them into something. We make them into patriots, defenders of freedom. We give them the best training in the world and provide the best equipment, the best leadership, the best of everything. We instill confidence and a sense of purpose. We give them an opportunity to excel in a demanding environment and nearly all of them do. And then they come home to all kinds of government programs to help them succeed in civilian life. So what does Andrea Jefferson do? She decides to toss it all aside and rob a bank, justifying her actions by claiming some sort of mental detachment brought on by her military service — which she volunteered for! Nonsense! Cartwright couldn't wait to take Lloyd's case apart.

The trial went on for days with both sides duking it out. First, the prosecution's case with their experts and then the defense case with their experts — both sides saying that Lloyd's client was either perfectly sane and rational or severely traumatized and irrational. Either she had the capacity to formulate criminal intent or she was suffering from such extreme distress and delusional ideation that thinking clearly was beyond her mental capacity. In the end, the jury would have to decide whether she was guilty of the crime charged. After a full day of deliberation the judge was finally able to ask the all important question. "Has the jury reached a verdict?"

"Yes we have," replied the jury foreman.

"Please pass the verdict form to the Bailiff."

The Bailiff stiffly marched over to the jury box, retrieved the verdict form and handed it to the judge who read it and handed it back to the Bailiff to return it to the foreman.

"We the jury, in the case of the State of Washington vs. Andrea Jefferson, find the defendant Not Guilty on the charge of robbery in the first degree, Not Guilty on the charge of assault with a deadly weapon, Guilty on the charges of fleeing the scene of a crime and resisting arrest."

Lloyd was elated. He'd won again! He'd won a case that seemed like a slam-dunk for the prosecution. Fleeing the scene of a crime and resisting arrest was nothing compared to what Ms. Jefferson could've been nailed for.

He spontaneously embraced his client and she reciprocated, planting a big kiss on his cheek. They were both all smiles. Cartwright, on the other hand, could only sit there and shake his head in disbelief.

"Mr. McCallum," announced the judge, "the sentencing hearing for your client will be three weeks from today. Her bail bond is still in effect until that time, so for now she's free to go. Thank you, ladies and gentlemen of the jury, you too are free to go. Court is adjourned."

Lloyd looked at his client again and smiled. Andrea Jefferson was basically home free. What a feeling! This was Lloyd's first trial since coming back and he still had the touch. He wanted to celebrate. He wanted to do something personal for his client as well.

"I'd like you to meet my wife. How'd you like to come to dinner at our house tonight?"

Andrea hesitated for a moment and then said, "That would be very nice. Thank you."

Lloyd promptly pulled out his cell phone and called Valorie.

"Well, she's not answering, but I'm sure it'll be fine. It's late afternoon already, why don't you just follow me home and we'll surprise her. I'm sure she'd like to meet you too."

"Alright, if you're sure that's okay."

"Yeah, let's get out of here."

On the way home, Lloyd tried Valorie again but still no answer. Twenty minutes later Lloyd and Ms. Jefferson pulled into the McCallum's driveway. As they both got out of their cars Andrea remarked, "Wow, what a nice home," as she surveyed the big house and nicely landscaped yard.
"Yeah, we've worked pretty hard to try and make it our own little oasis," replied Lloyd.

By that time, Lloyd was on the front steps unlocking the front door. "Come in, make yourself at home," invited Lloyd. The house was totally quiet.

"Hey, Val?" Lloyd called out. "Anybody home?" Maybe everybody was out back. Lloyd walked through the house to the back sliding glass door but found nothing. He called up stairs but no answer. Valorie hadn't told him she had anything going that day. Where was she? And where were the kids? Lloyd then noticed a folded piece of paper on the kitchen counter. He walked over and opened it up. What he read literally made him sick to his stomach.

"I got 'em. You want 'em? Come get 'em. You call the cops and they're dead."

Lloyd recognized the handwritten scrawl. It was Roundtree's. He couldn't believe what he was reading. All the horror of the last couple of years came rushing back. This couldn't be happening. A deranged monster had his family. How did he get them? How did he get in the house again without tripping the alarm? Where were they? How would Lloyd get them back? What would Willie do to them? Lloyd knew there was no chance of negotiating with Willie. He knew the man hated him and just wanted to hurt him. But take his family?! Take his wife and children?! Lloyd could feel the pressure and rage mounting inside him. He just stared vacantly straight ahead, holding Willie's note in his hands.

"Is everything okay?" Andrea finally asked.

Lloyd didn't even attempt to answer, but slowly began to crumple the note up in his hands.

"Maybe we should do this some other time," Andrea ventured.

Lloyd just stood there in the kitchen, frozen. Finally he said,

"They have my family."

"Who has your family?"

"Willie Roundtree and his crew."

"Who's Willie Rountree?"

"A former client."

"Why would he take your family?"

"To hurt me."

"Why?"

"Because he hates me. He raped my wife and I got him off."

That made no sense to Andrea, but she knew that she had just stumbled into something way bigger than she'd bargained for.

"Maybe I just better go," she offered.

"Please don't go yet," replied Lloyd. "I need to talk to somebody."

"Alright, the least I can do is listen," Andrea conceded. Lloyd then led her into the family room and laid the whole story out for her — how he'd first represented Willie Roundtree on a rape charge and gotten him off — only to have him come back and rape his wife. How he had, through a bureaucratic fluke, ended up representing Roundtree at his wife's rape trial, unable to decide whether the rape was an assault or consensual. How he had cross-examined his wife on the stand — and managed to get Roundtree acquitted again. How Willie had somehow interpreted that to mean he was entitled to anything he wanted. And how he had systematically terrorized Lloyd's family ever since.

Andrea Jefferson could hardly believe the tale of horror she heard. How could such a thing happen to a guy like Lloyd McCallum? Her heart went out to him and his family.

"I know some people who could take care of this situation for you," she finally offered, referring to some of her former SF buddies.

Lloyd just looked at her and said simply, "I'm former SF. And I know how to take care of this situation."

There was a long pause. Neither Lloyd nor Andrea said anything.

"Let me help you," she finally said. "I know about SF

ops and you shouldn't try to do this alone. I don't have the money to pay you for your services, so let me pay you with my services."

"You don't know these guys," cautioned Lloyd.

"Believe me," said Andrea, "I know them. I've come face to face with the worst there is."

"Have you ever dealt with a hostage situation?"

"Not exactly, but I have done a snatch operation."

"Abducting someone isn't quite like extracting someone. It's a lot easier to kidnap an unsuspecting person than go in and break someone out — rescue a hostage."

"All the more reason you need my help," insisted Andrea.

"It'll take some careful planning and execution. We'll need to know exactly what we're doing. No margin for error. My family's lives are at stake."

"What choice do you have, Lloyd? You call the cops, they go in with guns blazing and your family's slaughtered. We can do this ourselves," assured Andrea, anxious to put her military skills to use again.

"We need intel," Lloyd said, thinking out loud.

"That's where I may be able to help," replied Andrea.

"I'm still in occasional contact with some pretty inquisitive people, people who know how to find out things. They should be able to find out where your family's being held. Then we can plan the tactical operation."

Lloyd then looked at Andrea for a long time, really trying to get a read on her. Was she someone he could trust to help pull off this kind of tactical extraction? He realized that he didn't really know her. And he'd just gotten her off a bank robbery charge by arguing that she suffered from PTSD and was mentally unstable.

"We can't screw this up," he said to her in no uncertain terms.

She knew what he was saying, and looking directly

into Lloyd's eyes, said simply, "We won't screw it up."

"Alright then," he said, abruptly standing up. "See what your buddies can find out and let's get to it. This can't wait."

Andrea then went her way and Lloyd went up stairs to an empty bedroom and tried to get some sleep. They never did get any dinner.

———— ✿ ————

CHAPTER 23

The Rescue Mission

First thing the next morning, the phone rang and woke Lloyd up. He'd finally fallen asleep around 3:00 a.m. and was sleeping hard at 6:30.

"I know where you're family's at," said the voice on the other end of the phone.

"What?" demanded Lloyd.

"This is Andrea. I know where they're holding your wife and kids."

"How'd you find out so fast?"

"I told you I know some pretty inquisitive people. How 'bout if I come over and we get started."
"Fine. I'll be here."

Lloyd then got on the phone and called his office to tell them that he wasn't going to be in for a few days. It occurred to him that he might never be in again if things didn't go well with this operation. He had to dismiss those thoughts. If things didn't go well, he could lose his family. The mere thought of such a horrific tragedy was more than he could imagine. He had to focus. Thirty minutes later

Andrea Jefferson was at his door.

"Come in," said Lloyd, as he walked back toward the kitchen/family room area of the house. "What have ya got?"

"They're being held in an old abandoned storage facility out toward Mt Rainier National Park."

"How can we be sure?"

"The guys I put on it don't make mistakes. They're professionals who know how to get intel — without alerting people."

"I sure hope so," Lloyd retorted.

Andrea immediately went to work, pulling out her lap top and doing a virtual recon of the storage facility. She set up on the kitchen table and spread out, converting the place into a regular TOC — tactical operations center. Lloyd liked what he saw. Here was a gal who had been there before and knew how to go about preparing an op order — a tactical plan of action.

"Show me," demanded Lloyd, looking over Andrea's shoulder at her computer.

She turned the computer slightly toward Lloyd, "Here's what it looks like from the outside. It's just an old wooden structure set up kind of like one of those old motels with a small office building in front and two wings of storage units out behind perpendicular to the office. From the aerial it looks like a big horse shoe."

The small complex was just outside Mt. Rainier National Park off the main highway maybe a couple hundred yards, with a two lane dirt road leading in to it.

"What's our best avenue of approach?" queried Lloyd.

"Well, that depends on where exactly they're holding your family. We should probably approach at the rear of the complex through the trees. They're for sure watching the road."

"How many storage units?" asked Lloyd.

"Looks like about a dozen, six in each wing, about 10

feet by 10 feet in size. They could theoretically be in any one of them," said Andrea.

"We'll start at the foot of each wing and work our way toward the office. We ought to be able to tell if there's been any traffic in and out of any of the storage units. If not, we'll know they're in the office building and we'll penetrate there."

"How many people do you think the guy'll have with him?" asked Andrea.

"What'd your intel people tell you?"

"They weren't sure but they thought maybe three."

"That's probably accurate. At the pool hall it looked like he had three flunkies in his little posse." Lloyd looked at Andrea and said simply, "Two each."

She responded with a slight nod and look of determination. They both knew they would be going into a situation where either or both of them could be killed, to say nothing of the risk to Lloyd's family.

It had been a long time since Lloyd had gone into a combat situation. But this was exactly that — a combat situation, where the stakes couldn't be higher. This was not going to be a war of words, but a war of fire power. The element of surprise was still available since Willie didn't know exactly when Lloyd would show up, but he knew he'd come. In fact, Willie relished the thought. He was finally going to be able to put the hurt on Lloyd McCallum.

The rest of the day was spent preparing every detail — they needed headsets for communication, night vision devices, plenty of weaponry, all black clothing, good weather conditions, woods to conceal their approach, and intel on where and when to strike for maximum effect. This last item was crucial but probably impossible to get until the last minute, depending on how things unfolded. Lloyd and Andrea divided up the tasks — he got the weapons, ammo and his clothing; she got the headsets, night vision devices and her clothing. Back at Lloyd's house they tested the equipment, reviewed hand signals, laid out their approach to the target and decided how they would search the storage units. They were as ready as they were going to get and determined to go that night. It had already been two days since Lloyd found Willie's note and he couldn't wait any longer. No telling what Willie might do to his family. He was especially afraid for Valorie. He knew what Willie was capable of. After all, he'd done it before.

At 9:00 pm Lloyd issued the order to "get ready" — a familiar jump command. Andrea responded quickly — she was jump qualified, among other things. They both made their way to separate rooms in the house and put on their tactical clothing including skin tight hoods. It was almost ceremonial. They carefully made sure everything fit snugly and nothing shone that could reflect light or hung loose that could catch on something, not even their boot laces. Finally, they applied the facial camouflage so thoroughly that their faces were completely black. Lloyd looked at himself in the full-length mirror. He could hardly absorb what he saw. Standing there, completely black from head to toe, his own eyes peering back at him from the black figure in the mirror. He felt a strange sense of detachment. He felt like the man in the mirror had been commissioned to kill. The lawyer in Lloyd had been laid aside and the soldier in him had been called to duty.

He walked over close to the mirror and looking directly into his own eyes, searched for something. He searched his own soul. Was he losing touch with reality? "Maybe so," he thought. He felt himself mentally disengaging from his surroundings. Only one thing mattered now — the mission. He was no longer in western Washington but back in Central America. He was in combat mode. He was going out on a Special Forces operation. Nothing mattered but the objective. Only this time they would be a team of two instead of six or more. And his partner was a female client. What was he getting himself into? But he had to see it through. What choice did he have?

About an hour later they met back in the staging area — the kitchen of Lloyd's home, where Lloyd handed Andrea her weapons of choice — a nine millimeter semi-automatic pistol and an AR-15 semi-automatic rifle modified to fire automatic. Lloyd decided on his 357 magnum and a pistol-grip pump-action 12 gauge shotgun. They both stood at the counter and loaded their weapons and filled their ammo pouches. Almost as an after-thought, Lloyd decided to take his hunting knife with him which he strapped to his leg. They then put on the headsets and night vision devices, turned out the lights and tested the equipment one more time. Everything worked like it was supposed to. Off came the night vision devices and Lloyd and his new-found combat buddy stood in the dim light just looking at each other. This was it. They took each other by the hand in an arm-wrestling grip, nodded, and headed out the door.

The drive out to the storage facility took about an hour, so by now it was approaching midnight. There was surprisingly little cloud cover, so snatches of moon light shone through the night air — perfect conditions for a night operation. No need for the night vision devices after all — a good thing since they can be a little cumbersome at times, but they would take them with them anyway. Andrea knew the land marks as they approached the dirt road that led in to the abandoned storage complex.

"We're getting close," she cautioned. "Only about a quarter of mile ahead. There's an old narrow logging road just before we get to the road into the facility, where we can leave the car. We can circle around through the woods on foot to the far end of the storage units and work our way up from there, like we talked about."

Lloyd listened intently even though Andrea was just reiterating what they'd already planned. Upon arriving, Lloyd turned onto the logging road and pulled in far enough so the car wasn't visible from the highway and turned off the lights. It was thick forest on both sides of the logging road. Indeed, the whole area was a forest reserve — perfect for infiltrating an old storage facility in the dark of night. The night air was crisp and the only sound was a slight breeze through the trees and an occasional car on the highway. Lloyd and Andrea got out and removed their weapons, locked and loaded, checked their headsets and started toward their objective.

Traversing forested terrain at night is usually slow and deliberate and this was no exception. Lloyd followed his wrist compass through the darkness, having plotted out on the map the direction he needed to go. It was slow going for several reasons — the underbrush was fairly thick, it was important to be extremely quiet, and Lloyd didn't know what kind of security might have been set up around the storage facility. Then he stopped.

"We should be getting close," he whispered into his mouthpiece.

"Roger that," replied Andrea.

"If I figured right, we're about 25 meters from the end of the storage units, but I don't see anything yet."

"I'll follow you," reassured Andrea.

Lloyd continued to make his way through the brush toward the target, carefully, step by step. Suddenly, there it was through the trees — just like it appeared in the aerials — two wings of storage units with all the doors facing in toward each other.

Lloyd instinctively crouched down and motioned for Andrea to come up beside him. "We're right where we want to be — at the far end of the horseshoe," whispered Lloyd.

"Good job," replied Andrea.

"No lights," observed Lloyd.

"Yeah, the only lights are up by the office," said Andrea.

"Do you hear anything?" questioned Lloyd.

"Not a sound," replied Andrea.

"Alright, I'll take the far wing and you take the near one. One unit at a time, alternating back and forth like we planned," instructed Lloyd.

"You got it," Andrea replied. "Piece a cake," she added. They both silently moved to their positions at the end of the two wings of storage units. Lloyd went first. He crept up by the door of the first unit and knelt down, looking for any sign of recent traffic into or out of the storage unit. Nothing. He then slowly stood up and looked through the small window in the garage-type door. Completely dark and no sound. He quickly looked through the window with his flashlight in a final effort to clear the unit. Nothing inside. He nodded to Andrea who was keeping a lookout while Lloyd searched the first unit. She then repeated the same procedure for the first unit on her side. No sign of recent traffic into or out of the unit and nothing visible inside. So far so good.

As the two former soldiers worked their way up toward the office, they became more vulnerable as there was little cover if Willie or one of his cronies happened to discover them. They had no choice, they had to make sure Lloyd's family weren't being held at gun point in one of the storage units before they approached the office.

Lloyd and Andrea had each searched three units alternating back and forth when the back door of the office building suddenly flew open. They instantly plastered themselves against the door of the fourth unit in their respective wings. The storage unit door was recessed in just enough to allow a body to snug up against the framework around the door, hopefully out of sight of the office. If not, a fire fight would explode and Lloyd's family would likely be murdered. Lloyd and Andrea stood perfectly motionless, barely breathing, their weapons held down at their side. It was one of Willie's homies with a little mutt, taking him out for a potty break. "What are the chances?" Lloyd mused.

"Hold your position," he whispered into his mouthpiece.

"Roger," came the almost inaudible reply.

Lloyd and his partner stood there stiff as a board for what seemed like an eternity, trying to become part of the woodwork. As the dog was doing its thing the large black man lit up a cigarette and just wandered back and forth oblivious to the presence of death dressed in black.

In a moment, the dog was at Lloyd's feet sniffing out the human scent. Fortunately, the man was more into his cigarette than his dog. Lloyd stooped down and snatched up the little dog wrapping his hand firmly around its muzzle to keep it quiet.

Within a couple of minutes the guy was done with his cigarette and started looking for the dog. First he whistled, then, "Here pooch." Nothing.

"Where'd ya go, ya little mutt?" the guy demanded, displaying instant irritation over the dog's disappearance. He walked to one side of the office building, then the other, looking around each corner, calling for the dog. Nothing. Lloyd and Andrea watched like predators waiting to strike. Finally the guy noticed that the door to the storage unit next to Andrea was ajar, leaving about a 12 inch opening at the bottom. He figured the dog must've run in there, so off he went toward the unit.

"Don't move," whispered Lloyd into his mouthpiece. As the guy got closer to Andrea's position, Lloyd crept around behind him. Within seconds the black man was at the storage unit next to Andrea's concealed position. He hadn't noticed a thing and was completely unaware of Lloyd approaching from behind. By the time he bent over and lifted open the door, Lloyd was right behind him and threw the dog to Andrea who caught it in mid-air and instantly muzzled it while Lloyd grabbed the man and shoved him into the storage unit. Before the guy could react Lloyd kicked both legs out from under him and he went down face first. Lloyd was on top of him in an instant — with his knife at his throat.

"You make a sound and I'll kill you," Lloyd growled in the man's ear.

"Who are you?" the man gasped.

"Where's my wife and kids?" demanded Lloyd, ignoring the question.

"I don't know what you're talkin' about."

Lloyd pushed his knife point about a half inch into the guy's neck. He groaned and squirmed under Lloyd's grip. "I said, where's my wife and kids?"

"I don't know. I swear."

"Last time — where's my wife and kids?" insisted Lloyd, as he pushed the knife in a little further.

"Okay okay, they're inside," as blood began streaming down the man's neck.

"Where inside?"

"They're all in the bedroom."

"Which bedroom?"

"There's only one."

"Where is it?"

"The other side of the living room."

"Describe the place — the floor plan."

"The back of the house is the kitchen and bathroom, the front is the living room and bedroom. The back door opens into the kitchen."

"Is it locked?"

"No. I left it unlocked when I came out for a smoke."

"Who else is in there?" Lloyd continued.

"Theo, Jackson, and Willie."

"Where are they?"

"When I came out they were all in the living room half asleep."

"What are they packin'?" pressed Lloyd.

"Theo and Jackson both got nines and Willie's got an uzi."

Lloyd removed his knife, grabbed the guy's head and slammed it down on the concrete floor knocking him out cold. He taped his hands behind his back, his ankles, and his mouth. By that time Andrea already had the dog taped up — quiet and immobilized.

"We better hurry before they come lookin' for this guy," Lloyd instructed.

He and Andrea slipped out of the storage unit and crept toward the office building, weapons at the ready. Two figures in black moving quickly but silently toward their objective. Within seconds they were at the rear of the building. Lloyd led the way, carefully ascending the few wooden steps to the back door. He glanced through the dirty glass panes in the upper half of the door and saw no one. Nor did he hear anything. The place was totally quiet with only a dim night light in the living room. He reached for the door knob and turned it, opening the door slowly and deliberately. He quickly stepped inside, followed immediately by Andrea. They were inside, in the kitchen, only a few yards from three armed men and Lloyd's defenseless family in a nearby room.

They crept across the kitchen floor toward the living room of the small house, shot gun and AR-15 ready to open fire at the first sign of resistance. Suddenly there was the sound of someone stirring in the living-room. Lloyd and Andrea froze in place. Then the kitchen light flashed on. In the door way stood one of Willie's cronies, gun at his side. He was caught completely by surprise as his eyes met Lloyd's, with no more than ten feet separating them. The man hesitated momentarily as his brain processed what his eyes saw — two figures dressed in black holding lethal weapons pointed directly at him. He moved to raise his hand gun whereupon Lloyd let loose with a blast from his shot gun.

The explosion was deafening as smoke and shot

spewed out of the gun's muzzle, filling the room with the smell of burnt ammo. The man's large black body was violently hurled back against the kitchen wall, his chest instantly shredded and his own blood spraying his face. His involuntary muscle reaction squeezed off a round into the kitchen floor as his already lifeless body bounced off the blood spattered wall and crumpled to the floor in a heap. Several shots immediately rang out from the living room piercing the kitchen wall like it was cardboard. Another of Willie's homies then rushed into the kitchen firing his nine millimeter wildly. One round slammed into Andrea's torso sending her reeling backwards and crashing into the back door, breaking out the glass. Lloyd side-stepped to the right and let loose with another blast from his shot gun, catching the guy in the hip and spinning him sideways. He screamed in agony and turned toward Lloyd, firing his hand gun as fast as he could pull the trigger.

Andrea, trying to remain upright, cut loose with her automatic rifle, riddling the guy until he collapsed to his knees and fell face down on the floor. The scene seemed to go on and on in slow motion, the guy twisting and turning with every round that slammed into his body, until he fell lifeless on the floor.

There was no time to tend to Andrea. Willie was still somewhere in the house and so was Lloyd's family. He kept his eye on the door to the living room, not knowing where Willie was. Suddenly the uzi shattered the momentary silence, splintering the wooden cabinets on the kitchen side of the wall. Lloyd hit the floor and crawled toward the door to the living room. A shadowy figure started across the room toward the bedroom. If Willie got to that room before Lloyd could stop him, his family would be massacred.

"Willie!" shouted Lloyd.

Willie instinctively turned toward Lloyd and sprayed the doorway with machine gun fire. Wood and plaster flew everywhere. Lloyd fired his 12 gauge from the prone position, hitting Willie's left arm and spinning him around. Uzi bullets riddled through the wall separating the living room and kitchen, lodging in the exterior wall behind Andrea, who lay bleeding on the floor. Another blast from Lloyd's shot gun missed, but it was enough to send Willie in the opposite direction, away from the bedroom. He dove behind the couch in the dark living room.

Then there was silence. Both men lay on the floor, breathing heavily, only twenty feet from each other, but unseen behind their makeshift barriers.

Finally, a voice out of the darkness taunted, "I knew you'd come. In the end, the law means nothin' to you. You're no different than me."

Lloyd knew he should keep quiet but couldn't resist. "When it comes to protecting my family, I am the law," he said.

"All your fancy lawyerin' is just BS. You the law now! An eye for an eye, right? I take your wife, you kill my homies. You just a damn killer, Mr. lawyer man. I oughta finish what I started a long time ago and just kill her now."

"Go for it, you filthy slime ball, and I'll cut you in half."

"Hah. On second thought, I'll just kill you, and have my way with your wife. Maybe she'll enjoy it as much as she did the first time."

Lloyd was quiet. His mind went right back to the awful events of that whole ordeal. How he had believed, then doubted, then believed his wife — seesawing back and forth when she needed him the most. How it hurt his wife that he'd ever doubted her. How he hurt now for her, with all that she'd been through — the trauma of the rape itself, his withholding his support, his publicly attacking her in court. How had she survived? Reliving all that heartache in a matter of seconds, on top of what was happening right then, sent Lloyd even deeper into a state of pure rage — pure homicidal rage. Nothing mattered now but his revenge. He would have his revenge no matter what.

"It's over, Willie," Lloyd announced, as he got up and stepped through the door into the living room, simultaneously squeezing off a blast from his 12 gauge. The roar of the huge gun in the small room was overwhelming as the concussion fractured the air. Lloyd scanned the room but saw nothing. He surmised that Willie must be behind the only piece of furniture in the room — the big over-stuffed couch. He quickly trained his weapon toward the couch and cut loose with another blast directly at it. Fabric and stuffing flew everywhere as Willie audibly grimaced, then raised his machine gun above the couch and began to fire indiscriminately. Lloyd hit the floor face down as bullets flew in every direction. The sound was frightening as the walls of the small room were shredded and splintered by gun fire.

Suddenly Willie got up and raced for the front door of the small building, still firing wildly. Before Lloyd could react, Willie was out the door and running into the woods. Lloyd jumped up, ran to the bedroom and burst open the door. There sat Valorie across the room on the floor with the children seated beside her. All three were tied up with duck tape over their mouths — but alive! The important thing was that they were alive! Lloyd breathed a sigh of relief as he rushed over to his beloved wife and children. He carefully removed the tape from their faces and began untying them. There was no time to waste. Lloyd kissed each one of them, then quickly issued instructions.

"Valorie, here's my cell phone, call 911 and go tend to Andrea. I think she's bleeding to death."

"Who's Andrea?" queried Valorie.

"She's in the other room. Just go take care of her. Be careful in case Willie comes back here. You kids stay right next to mom."

Lloyd rushed into the kitchen as Valorie tried to collect herself and the children. He stooped down to Andrea who was slumped against the wall, still bleeding from her chest wound.

"How ya doin?" he asked.

"Not so hot," came the soft reply.

"My wife'll take care of you until the paramedics get here. I gotta go after Willie."

Andrea nodded her agreement. "Get him, Lloyd. He doesn't deserve to live another day."

Lloyd paused, looking into Andrea's eyes, communicating pure empathy, one combat veteran to another. Andrea nodded slightly, as if to say, "Leave me. Go and complete the mission."

Lloyd stood up, turned and rushed out of the room, just as Valorie was coming in. As she stooped over Andrea, she called to her husband, "Come back, Lloyd."

He stopped and turned around long enough to make eye-to-eye contact with his wife, knowing full well what she meant — come back . . . alive! Then he disappeared out the front door.

———— ✿ ————

CHAPTER 24

"Well, Let's Do This"

Once outside Lloyd promptly put on his night vision goggles, which he hadn't needed until then. He scanned the area from right to left searching for anything that resembled a living creature — particularly anything that remotely resembled a human form. He listened intently. Just the faint nondescript sounds of the night. He looked to see if he could detect any tracks on the road leading in. Sure enough, there were some faint fresh foot-prints in the soft ground heading down the road toward the highway. Willie had a few minutes head start on him, but he was wounded in the left arm. That would slow him down slightly and make him more vulnerable. But Lloyd realized Willie only needed one hand to fire that uzi.

He reloaded his shot gun to max capacity and started down the road following the tracks. As long as the tracks were visible, Willie was in front of him and he didn't have to worry about getting ambushed. Lloyd moved quickly but cautiously down the road, keeping his eye on the tracks on the ground while scanning the area ahead of him. The night vision goggles gave him a distinct advantage. With them he could see well into the woods on either side of the road. They gave everything an eerie green tint, but things were clearly visible, especially movement of any kind. Lloyd continued down the road toward the highway, scanning from side to side. Nothing. A few more minutes and he reached the highway — with no sign of Willie anywhere. Lloyd figured his best bet was probably the all-night gas station less than a quarter of a mile down the highway. Willie would likely go there and try and jack a car.

Lloyd quickly moved along the tree line in that direction, still scanning the woods as he went. Within minutes he was at the perimeter of the small lighted station and removed his night vision goggles. The light emanating from the small box-shaped white structure with two covered gas pumps out front seemed especially bright. Lloyd scanned the area around the station for any sign of foul play. Nothing seemed out of place. The lights were on inside but Lloyd couldn't see anybody. No sign of life anywhere. By now it was just beginning to get light and the rest of the world was waking up. Lloyd's mind darted back to the storage facility wondering what was happening with Valorie and Andrea. He waited for any sign of activity in or around the gas station.

About then, two things happened. Lloyd could barely hear the faint sound of an emergency vehicle approaching in the distance. Valorie must have gotten hold of the paramedics and they were already on their way. Second, a car coming from the other direction suddenly appeared and pulled into the gas station. What are the chances, Lloyd thought. If Willie was hiding in the station, this would provide a perfect opportunity for him to grab the car and run.

A young woman nicely dressed got out of the gray Chevy Malibu and began filling the car. Lloyd waited, not wanting to expose himself or her to mayhem if Willie was inside the station. The driver just stood there pumping gas, taking in the early morning freshness. Presently she was done and was just replacing the pump nozzle when the sound of the emergency vehicle became loud enough to be distinctly heard approaching. Willie must have heard it and thought it was the police coming for him, because he suddenly rushed out of the station, his left arm red with blood, running toward the unsuspecting woman. He dashed across the short distance separating the station from the pump island and reached her just as she was getting in her car. Still wielding the uzi in his one good hand, Willie cupped the gun around her neck and yanked her out of the car.

The surprised woman screamed as she sprawled on the pavement. He pointed the gun at her as she looked up in horror. Was this it for her? Had a very ordinary day suddenly turned into the last day of her life?

At that moment Lloyd had to reveal his presence. "Willie!" he yelled from just inside the trees surrounding the station. Willie immediately opened fire toward Lloyd, spaying the trees in his direction. Bark and branches splintered everywhere as the machine gun riddled the landscape. Lloyd dropped to the ground and pulled out his hand gun since the shot gun was unusable in close proximity to the innocent woman. Willie jumped in the Malibu and started the engine. Lloyd stepped out of the trees and took aim. He fired the powerful 357 magnum at the silhouette in the car. The round smashed through the rear window, went through the car and out the windshield, but the car didn't stop. Its wheels kept spinning, burning rubber and sending up smoke as it continued out of the station onto the highway. Lloyd fired again. The car kept going. He ran into the station. The attendant, standing against the rear wall of the small office with his wrists taped together, looked terrified.

"Give me your car keys," demanded Lloyd, holding the shot gun in his left hand and 357 magnum in his right hand.

"They're in the drawer," said the young twenty-something excitedly, pointing both hands toward the counter. Lloyd hurriedly reached over the counter, yanked open the drawer and grabbed the keys. "I'll return them," he said as he ran out the door and around the side of the station where a late model maroon Mustang sat. He jumped in, started the souped-up engine and roared out of the station in hot pursuit. Willie was already out of sight, but Lloyd knew the area and there was only one way in and one way out of Mt. Rainier National Park. He floored the accelerator and raced to catch his prey. He wanted him more than ever now.

The road to Mt. Rainier National Park is a two lane state route lined with evergreen trees on both sides. There's little population out there and even less traffic. Lloyd flew down the road at 90 miles an hour searching ahead for any sign of a gray Malibu. The trees whizzed by creating a dark green blur on either side of Lloyd's speeding Mustang. The loud whine of the engine overpowered all other sounds as Lloyd pushed the car to maximum performance. Still no sign of Willie.

Then just as he rounded a curve in the road Lloyd could see a car approaching in the early morning mist. As the distance between the two vehicles quickly narrowed, a gray Chevy Malibu suddenly raced past him in the opposite direction. Lloyd caught a glimpse of the driver — it was Willie Roundtree. Lloyd jammed on the brakes and cranked the steering wheel hard to the left nearly flipping the car over but successfully spinning it around 180 degrees. In the process the engine died. Lloyd hurriedly restarted the car and floored it. The rear wheels immediately broke loose and spun, sending up smoke from the burning rubber. Lloyd had no idea where Willie was going, but he couldn't let him get back to the storage facility before he did. If Valorie and the kids were still there, it would all be for naught.

Lloyd raced down the highway as fast as he could go

— with one thing on his mind. His family was still in danger. He had to stop Willie. Soon the gas station came into view up ahead. Just beyond that, Lloyd could see what looked like the gray Malibu. Suddenly a red emergency vehicle pulled out from the road leading in to the storage facility, lights flashing, on its way to the nearest hospital.

"Good," Lloyd thought. "Hopefully Andrea would survive and Valorie and the kids were safe."

The ambulance no sooner pulled out onto the highway when Willie's brake lights came on and he cranked a hard left turn, skidding onto the road leading in to the storage units.

Lloyd figured he had him for sure now. He raced toward the road and turned in, accelerating as he hit the dirt surface of the road, throwing dirt and rocks everywhere. The engine screamed as the wheels spun. The small office building immediately came into view — and so did Willie, who was just getting out of the Malibu and heading toward the office. Lloyd raced up behind the Malibu, slammed the Mustang in park and jumped out.

"Willie!" he yelled.

Willie turned and waved his arm, wildly spraying a volley of machine gun fire toward Lloyd who ducked behind the Mustang's open door. Willie repeated the motion, but this time the gun was silent. He pulled the trigger again and again as he waved the uzi back and forth. Nothing. Lloyd stood up and came out from behind the car door. He pulled off his black hood and stood there staring at Willie. Lloyd dropped his hand gun on the ground and slowly started walking toward his prey. Willie backed up closer and closer to the office building. Lloyd couldn't let him get inside. There may still be weapons lying around in there.

"Well, counselor, it's just you and me," taunted Willie. Lloyd didn't say a word. He just kept walking toward Willie.

"Why don't we talk this out," offered Willie, realizing the jig was up.

"We're done talking," replied Lloyd, as he continued to walk toward the man who had done everything he could to destroy his life.

Willie kept backing up, getting closer and closer to the office building. Lloyd kept coming and was now only 20 feet from Willie. He could already feel the satisfaction of killing the filthy animal that stood in front of him.

Suddenly, the office door flew open and out came Emily, running toward her father crying, "Daddy, daddy." The little girl was oblivious to the taut situation unfolding between her father and the family nemesis. Lloyd was shocked. Why were Valorie and the kids still here? How did Emily get away from Valorie? Where was she?

As Emily ran past Willie he reached out and grabbed her and yanked her over in front of him. A smile appeared on his face as he held onto Lloyd's only daughter. Lloyd stopped dead in his tracks.

"Well, counselor, you sure we're done talking?"

"Let her go, Willie."

Willie chuckled. "Hell, I think I'll take her home with me again."

"Let her go" said Lloyd softly, looking out from under his eyebrows.

"Step aside," growled Willie. "If you don't, I'll twist little missy's head off right here in front of you."

"You do anything to her and I'll gut you like a fish." Then without warning the front door of the office flew open again and out came Valorie like a banshee, screaming and charging at Willie. In an instant she was on him, yelling, punching, and scratching, obsessed with rescuing her daughter even at the peril of her own life. Willie shoved Emily to the ground and turned his attention to Valorie. He tried to fend off her blows — unsuccessfully. Valorie kept coming, swinging wildly at him with both hands.

Suddenly Willie cocked his right arm back and hit

her — full force in the face with a closed fist. The blow sent Valorie reeling backwards, landing flat on her back on the ground. She struggled to get up. Lloyd sprang to his wife's aid, positioning himself between her and Willie, who just stood there with an evil smirk on his face. Lloyd reached for Emily and gave her to the open arms of her mother still lying on the ground. He stood erect and turned toward Willie.

Only about 10 feet separated the two men now and Lloyd knew his family was finally out of harms way. There was nothing to prevent Willie's well-deserved execution. Lloyd relished the thought of finally delivering the fatal stroke that would bring death to this miserable dog. He stepped toward the creature he had come to hate. As he did so, Willie pulled out his last weapon — the switchblade he always kept tucked in his pants. He pushed the button and the shiny stainless steel blade instantly flipped open and locked in place. Lloyd stopped.

"Is this how you want to do it?" he asked.

"You're in my world now," replied Willie as he stepped toward Lloyd.

"No, you're in my world," said Lloyd as he pulled out his old SF field knife — a custom made hunting knife with a six inch razor-sharp blade.

Willie smiled. "Well, let's do this," he said.

Lloyd crouched in the ready position for hand to hand combat. Willie circled to his right. Lloyd moved to his left to cut off Willie's access to either the office or his wife and daughter who were still on the ground behind him. Willie twirled his switchblade in a circular fashion as he moved toward Lloyd. As the two men inched closer to each other, Willie lunged at Lloyd with a broad swipe from right to left. Then instantly turning his wrist, he swiped back the other way. He grinned. This was the way Willie had lived his whole life — on the edge.

Lloyd's knife blade glistened in the early morning sun

light as he carefully sized up his opponent. It had been a long time since Lloyd had participated in any hand to hand combat drills and he'd never actually engaged in hand to hand combat with a knife. This was "on the job training" of the most serious kind — life or death — no room for error.

Suddenly Willie lunged at Lloyd again, coming straight in at him. Lloyd jumped back and countered with a swipe of his knife, barely catching the under side of Willie's right arm — his only good arm. Again Willie lunged, waving his knife at Lloyd's face. Lloyd leaned back, but with his left hand slapped Willie's right arm to the inside and quickly punched him in his right side. The force of the blow to his ribs forced a groan out of Willie. He wildly swung back with his knife. Lloyd ducked and lunged low at Willie, raking his knife across Willie's left thigh. The cut opened up his leg like a slice of beef and blood spurted out. Willie screamed profanities in pain and staggered back. He transferred his knife to his weakened left hand, picked up a soft ball size rock with the other hand and hurled it at Lloyd with all he had. The stone found its mark and glanced off Lloyd's left temple as he tried to dodge the make-shift missile. The blow stunned him, and Willie, transferring his knife back to his right hand, came at him with a vengeance, swinging the knife wildly back and forth. Lloyd could barely defend himself but managed to counter at just the right moment. He lunged and sunk his knife deep into Willie's left shoulder. For a brief instant both men stood face to face — long enough for Willie to drive his knife into Lloyd's left arm pit. The two combatants stood there eyeball to eyeball — both impaled by the other's blade.

As his only available counter, Lloyd violently head-butted Willie. Both men staggered back but held on to their knives, which they pulled out of each other's battered bodies, covered with blood. Before Willie could regroup, Lloyd stepped forward and kicked him in the groin with everything he had. The blow incapacitated Willie and he fell on the ground in pure agony. Lloyd staggered over to Willie and kicked his knife away, then fell on his knees next to his antagonist.

Willie lay on his side holding his groin in pain. Lloyd somehow mustered the strength to roll him over on his face, crawled on top of him, cupped his left hand around his forehead and pulled his head back. With his right hand he placed his hunting knife under the man's neck. With one quick slice, Willie would practically be decapitated. He was about to do it when he thought he heard someone yelling. It was faint at first — human communication seemed so foreign under the circumstances. Lloyd could hardly decipher the sound. Then it got louder and louder.

"Lloyd! Lloyd!"

Lloyd looked up from his grizzly task and saw his wife running toward him. He looked down again, ready to finish what he had started.

"Lloyd! You can't! You can't do it!"

Lloyd began to slowly drag the blade across the man's throat.

"Stop!" yelled Valorie as she fell on her knees next to her husband and reached for his knife hand. "You're not a murderer," she reasoned.

Lloyd looked at her with a kind of vacant stare.

"Please, let me have the knife," urged Valorie.

Lloyd looked deep into his wife's eyes, searching for a connection to reality. Finally, he relaxed his grip on the knife and Valorie carefully removed it from his hand and tossed it on the ground.

"I've already called the police. They should be here any minute."

Meanwhile, Willie lay motionless, face down on the ground, bleeding from the neck and several other places.

"Come on, sit up. Let me stop that bleeding until

they get here," instructed Valorie, surveying the damage to her husband. Just then Emily and Gerald both came running up excitedly and threw their arms around their father. It was the sweetest reunion they could've ever hoped for.

Moments later the police arrived — two Pierce County Deputy Sheriffs. As they got out of their vehicles and surveyed the carnage, one of them asked, "What happened here?"

Lloyd looked at him with streaks of camouflage still on his face. "It's a very long story," he said.

At that point Valorie took over. "That guy abducted us," pointing at Willie "and this guy rescued us," patting her husband on the chest. "They both need immediate medical help," she continued.

"They're on their way," replied the Deputy. Just then Willie's unintelligible voice was heard. Everyone present shifted their attention to the apparently lifeless body lying nearby. Willie lifted his head and looking toward Lloyd said in a low raspy tone, "He's my lawyer. Anything he says is confidential."

All Lloyd could do was sit there on the ground and shake his head. "They're gonna get everything, and you're goin' away for a very long time," he replied, not even bothering to look at the filthy creature lying a few feet away. There was a long pause as Lloyd and Valorie contemplated the audacity of Willie's remark.

"Would you help me get him on his feet?" Valorie finally asked, looking toward one of the Deputies. Immediately he stepped forward, took Lloyd by the arm and with Valorie lifted him upright. With a human crutch on either side Lloyd hobbled toward the office building.

He had scarcely gone two steps when suddenly a wild commotion erupted behind him. Willie had somehow gotten to his feet and came charging at Lloyd with Lloyd's hunting knife raised over his head. He came rushing straight at

Lloyd, bent on killing the man who had twice kept him out of prison. In an instant the other Deputy drew his weapon and — BOOM BOOM BOOM — fired three slugs into Willie's chest at point blank range. The force of the rounds slamming into his torso stopped him cold and Willie just stood there for a second. His eyes rolled back in his head, and then he fell — stiff as a board flat on his back. The impact of his body hitting the ground sent up puffs of dust from around his already lifeless corpse.

Lloyd looked incredulously at his former client. Was it finally over? Could he and his family finally rest in peace? Lloyd staggered over and looked down into Willie's face. Was he really dead? He stooped over to take a closer look. William Roundtree was dead — at last.

Epilog

Lloyd McCallum recovered from his wounds and following a brief period of recuperation, returned to work at LANCASTER, VERNON and EVERETT. He continued to do criminal defense work, but was a lot more careful about what kind of cases he took on. He's now a named partner in the firm of LANCASTER, VERNON, EVERETT and McCALLUM.

Valorie McCallum also recovered from her wounds and while still a dedicated wife and mother, has become active in women's rights. She has also written a book about her experience, in support of victims of assault, entitled "Loss of Consortium" — a legal term meaning the loss of companionship, association and intimacy a couple suffers when one or the other of them is injured or killed.

The McCallum's children, Gerald and Emily, are both in college and planning to go to law school, but practice in an area other than criminal defense.

Andrea Jefferson recovered from her wounds and with the help of the VA enrolled in college. And William Roundtree was buried at government expense in an obscure cemetery outside Tacoma, WA.

ABOUT THE AUTHOR

    Brian L. McCoy is a retired attorney who practiced law for over 32 years primarily in the area of personal injury and civil litigation. He also served as a superior court judge pro tem and superior court arbitrator. He holds degrees from Brigham Young University (BA), University of Oklahoma (MA), and Seattle University (JD) and worked as an adjunct professor of law at Pacific Lutheran University. Before becoming an attorney he served as a military intelligence officer/A Team leader in the U.S. Special Forces 7th Group, Canal Zone, Panama. Brian is married to Janet L. McCoy and they reside in Riverton, Utah.

www.ingramcontent.com/pod-product-compliance
Lightning Source LLC
Chambersburg PA
CBHW030240200626
46816CB00002BA/452